The Big Three

CATHERINE SPECTER

920
BOOKS

Published by Nine Twenty Books
www.ninetwentybooks.com

Dedication

· · ·

For Marianna

Acknowledgements

• • •

First and foremost, thank you to my parents, Marianna and George Specter. From my heart to the written page, they are in every book I write. I regret beyond words that my mother did not live to see this book published. Special thanks to my brother, Jonathan Specter, for being a supportive tornado. His twenty years on Wall Street helped this book and others in the pipeline. An immeasurable amount of gratitude to readers of my advice column, *Cat's Call*, who tuned in every week for nearly a decade to read my column and suggested time and again that I write a book… Cat's Call: Here it is! Big thanks to author Martin J. Smith, whose friendship has helped me more than he knows. You deserve that amazing view, Marty. Many thanks to Robert Cotta, P.E., for his informative and engaging conversations about architecture, and for explaining how "an MIT education is like drinking from a fire hose." Thank you to Robert Paladino, AIA, who was kind enough to share his expertise in architecture and all things Harvard. Thank you to my friend, mastering engineer Drew Lavyne, for his music industry insight. Thank you to my friend, Melanie van Tiel. In 2001 she said, "You should write an advice column." It was one of countless crazy things she has said in the past eighteen years. If you don't like this book, let's blame her. Thank you to my aunt and friend, Linda Cohen. She rescued an injured, homeless, wolf-like dog from the side of the highway and brought him into my life.

She also brought three other dogs, a guinea pig, a furry turtle, a baby raccoon, and an alligator, but the wolfy dog eats my haute cuisine baked sticks. Last but not least, thank you to every editor—newspaper and otherwise—with whom I have worked. Each of you has inspired me in some way.

1

· · ·

It was a hot Saturday night in midsummer. I was camped out on my ninety-inch white living room sofa with the television turned to a home decorating show, a women's magazine in my lap, a cordless phone to my left, and two remote controls to my right. This was not an uncommon Saturday evening ritual, except usually there would be nail-painting supplies strewn about the coffee table and I'd be wearing a face mask. My fingers and toes were already done and I'd used a face mask the evening before, which means Friday night was just as riveting. My lack of exciting weekend plans was due to my insistence on working—at some point in the day—seven days a week.

I was dressed elegantly: pajama bottoms, tank top, no bra, and flip-flops. My light-brown hair was in a high ponytail, still damp from a shower and drying naturally, assisted by the intermittent cool breeze that gave me goose bumps every time the central air kicked on.

I half-watched the decorating show while half-reading an article about relationship no-noes versus yeses. In only ten minutes I had learned several invaluable lessons. One, men like it when women say suggestive things to them in nonsexual environments, such as offices. Two, men like it when women say suggestive things to them before heading out to nonsexual environments, such as office parties. Three, men like it when women say suggestive things to them during actual sex.

I filed those gems into my mental Rolodex. Every third article advised women to turn men on in any way possible. To bolster the advice, the articles quoted men who said things like: "My girlfriend, Jackie, got me really hot at last year's Christmas party when she whispered, within earshot of my boss, 'I'm not wearing any underwear.'"

Some articles exposed men's dirty little secrets, such as: men like it when women call out their name during sex. Oh, file that one. Or, men like it when women are naked. Really, they do? Every article about male-female relations had the same message: Get out there, girls, and sex up your man!

It might seem as though I could use those lessons since I was sitting alone on a Saturday night. But I didn't need them. I knew what to do to men. With them. For them. How to turn them on and off. I could write a "men" book, I knew so much.

What I didn't know was how to be brave. How to let yourself go. When it was safe to let your guard down. How to show you're not perfect. When to accept gifts, both tangible and emotional, without feeling indebted. I'd heard "I love you" many times, but saying "I love you too" always caused a sea change shortly thereafter, and the current would sweep me to a deserted island, and then I'd have to swim home.

The decorating show reached its conclusion and the "after" decor wasn't much better than the "before" decor. My eyes scanned my new living room for places to shove unpacked boxes. The bare, white walls comforted me, appearing a soft yellow in the lamplight. The high ceilings encouraged full, easy breathing. The central air chilled me comfortably, just enough to remind me of how stifling my last apartment had been.

Looking around my new space, I wondered if my unmarriedness would be permanent. I thought briefly about a few exes, what they were doing, and if I would find them attractive if I met them now. Eventually that road led me full circle and I remembered why they were exes. Then I sighed and smiled, thinking about my current guy, Mr. Always Positive & Happy, who had a ton of potential.

Another home decorating show was beginning and I couldn't bear it. I stood up and tried to slide my feet into my flip-flops, not realizing my left leg was asleep. As I placed my weight onto my left leg to shoe my right foot, I fell over. Actually, I fell backward, and suddenly I was back on the couch. I screamed out in pain, the way one does when pain first hits, whether or not the pain is cryworthy. I had badly scraped my right calf on the edge of the coffee table when I had tried to get my balance. As I brought up my leg to inspect the damage, I scraped my right foot on the underside of the coffee table.

I now understood why my mother had always hated my coffee table. On countless occasions she had offered to buy me a new one but I always refused, as a show of adulthood. To be fair, she hated it because it was cheap and ugly. Now I hated it because it crippled me. I was truly in pain, with my right calf and foot bleeding. The wounds hurt worse than brush burns I got as a kid. It had been so many years since I'd experienced this kind of discomfort, I was surprised how much it hurt. To top it off, my left leg was still asleep. One would expect it to wake up in the face of pain from its comrade.

I stood slowly, and then expertly finagled my left toes through the fabric straps of my flip-flops. Then I leaned forward, placed my weight on the damn, stupid, ugly coffee table, and did the same with my right foot. Then I placed both hands on the coffee table and shoved it hard, several feet away. Even though it was fairly light and wholly crappy, it didn't slide across the shiny wood floor with the *whoosh* I hoped for. It was an anticlimactic moment of revenge.

I limped to my kitchen and turned on the faucet. Once the water ran super-cold, I soaked a few paper towels and sat down on the floor. I rolled up the right leg of my pajama bottoms, tore the paper towel in half, pressed one piece against my calf, and laid the other on my foot. Droplets of water ran down my leg, onto the floor, which then crept to the seat of my pajama bottoms. Within moments I felt the wetness against my butt.

I was a sad sight. *Moderately attractive unmarried woman, crippled by hideous coffee table, dies tragically on kitchen floor covered in scraps of wet paper towel.* I was a newspaper columnist so I could already visualize the headline.

Then the doorbell rang. My first thought was, *Thank God, pizza*! My second thought was, *Shit, he's going to take off before I make it to the door.* Feeling the true fear of losing pizza when you really need it, I used all my strength to stand. I pressed the sopping paper towels hard against my skin so they would stick as I hobbled down the hallway. I couldn't worry about how beat-up I looked to the innocent delivery guy who had no idea he'd just stumbled onto a war scene. Nor could I worry about how pathetic I looked—single woman, home alone on a weekend night, who'd clearly walked through hell just to get a pizza. And I couldn't worry that I had incorrectly counted the bills in my wallet and I would only be able to give him a thirty-seven cent tip. *Stupid Amanda*, I thought— that's my name, Amanda Morgan—*this is a bad way to start off in a new neighborhood.* Everyone knows one of the cardinal rules of getting in with a new neighborhood was getting in good with the pizza guy.

I stumbled into the front door. My left leg was still partially asleep, enjoying a REM I envied, while my right leg was in scorching pain and covered in paper towel scraps. I looked constipated because I was walking slightly hunched over with bowed legs (hardly the posture to be in when you answer the door at night and you're not wearing a bra). In the second it took to turn the doorknob, I remembered I didn't have my wallet. I yelled, "One second!" and hobbled back to the kitchen. I didn't realize I had loosed the door just enough for it to open a few inches. I also didn't realize the person at the door could see me walking, apparently constipated and wounded, and fumbling through my wallet on the kitchen counter.

I turned back toward the door with a small wad of cash in hand. I assumed the pizza guy could hear me through the door, and I yelled with a laugh, "Sorry about the wait. I had a little accident." In hindsight, that statement, more than anything about my posture or gait, would convince anyone that I had a bowel problem.

I was still counting my cash, praying I had miscounted earlier and would be able to offer a proper tip, when I finally reached the front door and opened it fully. I heard the guy say "Hi" with a small laugh. When I looked up, I couldn't believe my eyes.

2

. . .

Standing in my doorway, under the porch light and with small bugs hovering around his head, was my ex-boyfriend, Paul. *The* ex-boyfriend.

In recent years I had spent countless nights wishing this moment would arrive, hoping Paul would make good on his promise to come back, and many nights getting over the realization that he never would. Yet there he was.

Paul just stood there, grinning in the warm way he always did when something about me made him smile. I tried to speak but as a knee-jerk reaction I cleared my throat, which produced a most unladylike sound. And then it all flooded back: One leg of my pajamas was rolled up, the other was down, blood-soaked paper towels were stuck to my right leg, I was hunched over, and my breasts were nearly hanging out of my tank top. My hair was in a messy, cheerleader-type ponytail atop my head. I had no makeup on and, worst of all, I was home. The only thing I could think was, *Thank God I used a face mask yesterday.*

Sensing that the powers of speech and movement were unavailable to me, Paul pulled open the screen door and leaned in without stepping inside. I found myself desperately wanting to hear his voice, a voice I used to love, knowing he was about to say something profound after all this time. I didn't want to speak but I was anxious for the awkward silence to be filled. He eyed my body up and down, and then rested his eyes on mine and said in his gentle voice, "Is this a bad time?"

I laughed, warmed by his familiar tone, and because of how ridiculous I looked. Then I remembered I was holding cash in my hand, the implications of which upped the ridiculous quotient tenfold.

• • •

I didn't invite Paul into my house. It was bad enough for him to see me in such a sad physical state; I didn't need him to see the raw excitement that comprised my Saturday night. *Oh God, what could he be thinking*?

After all that time apart, after all the letters and phone calls and e-mails and missing one another, he had finally made his way back to me and it was a disaster. There was only thing to do: Call my best friend, Anne. She must've seen my number on her caller ID because she answered and said, "You better have saved me some pizza."

"You're not going to believe this," I said.

"What?" I could tell Anne was in the midst of a chick flick marathon because her usual interested tone was clipped with a disinclination to know.

"Guess who just rang my doorbell," I said.

"Who? John?"

"No."

John Mayes was a reporter friend at work who used to ask me out fairly often. Eventually he stopped asking, but when he learned I'd moved to his neighborhood, he made numerous promises to help me "settle in."

"Who, then?" Anne asked between loud gulps of something.

"What are you drinking?" I asked.

"Who stopped by?"

"What are you drinking?"

"Beer," she said.

"Paul," I said.

"What?"

"Yep."

There was silence from Anne. No snarky comments. Not even a swallow.

Then she said, "Paul."

"Yes," I said.

"Oh...my..."

"I know."

"What did he want?" Anne asked with intense interest. My news was far juicier than whatever movie she was watching.

"I'm not sure," I said. My cavalier tone undid Anne.

"You're not sure? What did he say?"

"Not much. I didn't invite him in."

"What? You didn't even—"

"I couldn't! You can't imagine what I look like right now."

"So you look like hell, and you have bad manners," she said.

"Right," I said.

"Amanda, really, what happened?"

I told Anne about my crippling injury, about the wet paper towels affixed to my bloody leg, my braless-ness, my apparent constipation, and my unintended cheap tip, which wasn't an integral part of the story but it added to my overall pathetic image. After Anne's laughter subsided, I finally told her about my brief doorway visit with Paul.

"So," Anne said, waiting for me to conclude my story with a big bang. "Did you tell him about Timothy?"

"No."

"Okay, good," she said.

Anne then spoke in a very office-like tone of voice she reserved only for matters of men, slow restaurant service, and bad manicures that went outside the line. "Your ex-boyfriend shows up after how many friggin' years, and absolutely nothing happened."

"Pretty much," I said.

"Where did you leave it?"

"He's calling me tomorrow."

"That's something, I guess."

"Yeah. Something," I said.

"Call me crazy," Anne said, "but you don't sound excited."

"I'm in shock. To see him standing there, his face inches from mine, it's a lot to take in."

"It's amazing," Anne said. "I mean a-*ma*-zing."

"Know what the worst part is?"

"What?"

"I never got my pizza."

3

$\cdot\ \cdot\ \cdot$

After hanging up with Anne, I went upstairs to my office and started leafing through work mail, both e-mail and snail. As a newspaper columnist it never ceased to amaze me how open people were willing to be about intimate details of their life. I was the opposite—fiercely private, to the dismay of every man who entered my world.

In my experience, men weren't to be trusted. They wanted you to open up, but they didn't do anything with it, besides eventually leave you. I likened it to people asking to see the contents of your refrigerator. You oblige them, despite the possible embarrassment of what they might discover in there. Before you know it, they're running out the door with armfuls of food and you have nothing left to eat. (Which is why getting in good with the pizza guy is paramount.)

I read e-mail after e-mail but I couldn't stop thinking about Paul. I had tried to be casual on the phone with Anne but the magnitude of his visit was sinking in. My life was so different than when he last knew me! Back then I was just getting my feet wet. And I had so many plans. Plans to become a diplomat, plans to finish ten novels, plans to move here or there, plans out the wazoo.

Paul was the opposite. He had one plan: Finish graduate school, move to New York or stay in Los Angeles, become a big-time music producer, and marry me, pretty much in that order. Simple. A straight line. The simplicity of his life was the opposite of mine. Where I was flitting about, Paul was on solid ground. For all his creativity and big dreams, Paul was surprisingly calculating and practical. I was the big-picture thinker, but Paul knew exactly what he wanted, and he was dedicated to achieving it. He loved two things: music and me. I loved a thousand things. Back in the day, Paul was one of them.

I stopped reading work mail as my mind floated back to my early days with Paul. He and I met when we were in graduate school. I was taking more than a full course load to finish early while he took a light course load and worked on the side as a musician. We always knew I would finish my degree before he finished his, and it loomed over us that at some point in the near future, I would probably move away.

In terms of relationships, Paul was less mature. After we got serious—which didn't take long—he reaped the benefits of all my experiences, but he had no similar ones of his own. When we had problems my experience shined like a beacon and he couldn't keep up. Essentially, my knowledge of what not to do spurred his desire to measure up.

Most women would scream *hooray!* at the thought of a man trying to please them, but the adage is true: Be careful what you wish for. If a man is always trying to meet your expectations, he isn't meeting them. I wrote that in a column years later and it was a big hit. Too bad it didn't bode as well for my relationship with Paul.

Eventually I realized that staying with a man in the hope that one day he will meet your expectations means gambling with your life. I hadn't been willing to gamble mine away. Poor, lovely, romantic Paul, whose judgment was always clouded with insecurity and selfishness. His desire to please me allowed him the liberty of incessantly letting me down. In the end, the depth of our love simply prolonged the inevitable. He wanted us to get married but I wasn't ready. I loved him, but his constant striving to be the man I deserved (his words, not mine) made me fear I'd spend a lifetime waiting for that man to show up.

I looked at the clock and noticed it was quite late and my head was swimming and incapable of work. Too many articles in that stupid women's magazine. One too many exes at my front door. Too many pieces of dried, crusty paper towel on my leg.

There was only one thing to do: Go to bed. After scouring my cabinets in search of bandages and ultimately finding none, I MacGyver'd two—one each for my calf and foot—by slicing a Ziploc bag in half and Scotch-taping it to the pieces of paper towel stuck to my still-bleeding wounds. I heard and felt the crinkling of plastic against my skin as I slid into bed.

Of course, once I got myself comfortable enough to not move again, the phone rang. Unfortunately I had left the cordless phone downstairs on its charger. Until I bought a new set with several handsets, and decent battery life, I had to rely on a regular corded phone in my bedroom. Since Anne was the last person I talked to, and she knew I was going to crash, it had to be Paul. Very few people had my new telephone number, and Paul was now one of them. The phone's ring seemed unusually loud, like even if I tried to ignore it, it wouldn't let me. I slid my arm out from under the fluffy comforter and felt the bracing cold that only central AC can create. I stretched for the phone, trying to keep my legs still, and answered.

"What's shakin', girl?" the voice said. It took me a moment to register the voice, and once I did I became immediately annoyed.

"I'm sleeping," I said, and hung up.

It was John Mayes. *Was* being the key word. He was calling for a friendly chat and didn't deserve my level of irritation, but I was tired and my leg hurt. I felt immediately guilty, but not enough to call back and apologize. I stretched my body just enough to lift the phone, reach underneath it, and unplug it.

4

• • •

By the time Monday arrived, I felt like the weekend had lasted a week. Saturday night was only thirty-six hours ago but depending upon the moment, it felt like thirty-six minutes or thirty-six days. My Sunday had consisted of breakfast, thinking about Paul, doing the *New York Times* crossword puzzle, erasing incorrect letters in the puzzle because I was thinking about Paul, doing laundry but not folding and putting away the laundry, ending up with pink-but-should-be-white clothes because I was thinking about Paul, wondering when Paul was going to call and what I should say when he did, talking to Anne over lunch, practicing "pretend you're Paul" dialogue with her, reminiscing about past boyfriends, going for a run, trying to work on my next column, and thinking about Paul.

I was happy to be downtown at the newspaper. I was grateful for the distraction of ringing phones, news streaming on multiple monitors and TVs hanging from the ceiling on steel arms, keyboards clicking, and people milling around. Even the outdated utilitarian decor was a comfort.

As I walked to my desk, John Mayes yelled, "How goes the smoking ban?" from five desks away. I gave a big thumbs-up, which immediately made me want to smoke. I was quite proud of myself for smoking only one cigarette per day, although pissed I had shared my quitting plan with anyone else. John was my good friend, despite his annoying habit of calling me just as I got into bed. He deserved credit for being the one who gave me the idea of "mostly quitting." He was a marathoner who once smoked two packs a day and eventually quit by smoking less and less until, according to him, he "forgot about smoking most of the time." I was determined to get to that point. He mouthed the words *sorry for calling* and I waved it off.

I smiled countless "Hi's" as I slung my purse and workbag over the back of my chair and got situated at my desk. Most of the time I liked being in the office. I got along well with all the reporters, columnists, and editors, and they in turn enjoyed talking about my column, or subjects tangential to it. My column was unique as it was mainly about dating and relationships. The men in the office frequently inquired about my love life, though I knew they cared only about my sex life. If not mine, the sex lives of people who wrote letters to my column.

The best thing about my desk at the paper was its location— near a window, an enviable thing at a newspaper. I had space from my colleagues and I could instant-message on the computer without anyone being the wiser. I knew Anne would hit me up online, hungry to know how the Paul call had gone the night before. I also knew there would be an e-mail from Ravenna, another of my dear friends, who certainly knew the breaking Paul story by now, via Anne. I didn't see Ravenna as often as we both would have liked, because she lived out of town and was constantly busy. She was French and modern and well traveled, and her life was ten times more glamorous than mine. Still, we felt like we shared the same heart. We were connected by something stronger than geography.

And there in my inbox was Ravenna's e-mail letting me know she was in town for a couple days! I e-mailed her back immediately and we made plans to meet for lunch. Then I went downstairs to the cafeteria, got a cup of tepid tea, and stepped outside to call

Anne. As usual she didn't bother with "Hello."

"I can't stand it anymore," she said. "What happened?"

"He called," I said, placing a cigarette between my teeth.

"Are you smoking?" she asked, though not in a chastising way.

"No."

"I can hear it in your mouth."

"It's not lit." I was telling the truth.

"I don't care. I was just curious." Anne was a nonsmoker but she liked smokers.

"Paul called around nine," I began. "The first five minutes were awkward. I mean, how do you catch up on so many years?"

"I'm trying to remember. It's been…," Anne clicked her teeth, "ten years?"

"Somewhere around there, since we last saw each other." Again the magnitude of how long it had been washed over me.

"So is he different? What has he been doing? Is he successful? Where does he live? Are you going to see him?"

"Yes, he's different," I said. "But also the same. I had to get used to hearing his voice again."

"It's not like you haven't spoken in a decade." Anne was right. Though Paul and I hadn't seen each other, we had talked.

"I know, but it's totally different knowing he's here."

"True. Continue," Anne said.

"Well, he's extremely successful, no surprise there. I always knew he would be. I even reminded me that I used to tell him how successful he'd be one day, and he thanked me for all the support I gave him over the years."

"Remember when he got that Emmy or whatever and thanked you in his acceptance speech, and he totally forgot to thank all the people he should have thanked?"

"It wasn't an Emmy," I laughed.

"Oh right. Grammy Award, then."

"It wasn't a Grammy," I said. "But close enough."

I remembered it well. If I hadn't been in love with Paul before that moment, I would have been from then on.

I continued, "He works with huge stars now, even bigger than when we last spoke. He lives in New York. For now, he emphasized."

"Hmm," Anne said. I could sense a raised eyebrow in her inflection. "Did you tell him about Timothy?"

"No."

"Why not?"

"What should I tell him? I haven't even talked to Timothy in days. And of course I'm dying to talk to him again, and who shows up? Paul!"

"Paul wouldn't be Paul if his timing was good," Anne said.

"I'm seeing him tomorrow," I said.

"He's not wasting any time."

"He wanted to see me tonight but we both have to work," I said.

"A Tuesday date is good," Anne said.

"Why?"

"Don't ask me," she said. "You're the advice columnist. You wrote a column about weekday dates."

"Oh, yes. A long time ago." Anne remembered my columns better than I did. *That's right, I'm an advice giver!* Every once in a blue moon I forgot, or nearly forgot, because despite the "advice" aspect of my column, it was still work, which included paychecks, deadlines, coworkers, company expectations, bosses, working weekends, commuting, parking, and the constant threat of losing your job. Suddenly I felt a ton of pressure.

"You have to write about this! Your life is like a soap opera."

"Ugh, Anne, don't say that. I hate soap operas."

"Of course, because they're so unrealistic. Or maybe they're not," she added with an *aha!* tone.

We laughed. It felt good.

"Tomorrow night isn't a date," I said. "We're just going to catch up."

"Uh, yes, it is a date. Let's figure out what you're going to wear."

5

. . .

By the time I returned to my desk, my editor, Mia, had left a note stuck to the ancient computer monitor I never used because I insisted on using my own laptop. It said, *Daniel wants you in his office ASAP*. Great, just what I needed.

Daniel Perry was the editor-in-chief of the paper; a former *Wall Street Journal* reporter who'd made a name for himself years earlier in a very *All The President's Men* way by uncovering back-room deals and unsavory doings between the telecom industry, the SEC, and the FCC. Daniel had talked to more CEOs and industry insiders and lobbyists than anyone could count. It was widely considered an industry coup when he accepted the lofty position at our city's paper.

Despite being a big shot newsperson who commented regularly on major television news programs, Daniel was in his early fifties and still unmarried, probably because he didn't think any woman was good enough for him. To say Daniel Perry had an ego would be an understatement. To say Daniel Perry was a prick would be a compliment. To say Daniel Perry didn't like me was a truth as obvious as the earth's roundness and the sky's blueness.

It was common knowledge Daniel Perry had it in for me and took every opportunity to make me quit. Despite my column's large readership and fan base, I had received one raise in five years—an extra seventy-five dollars per month. My column's popularity was the only reason Daniel Perry kept me around. He hated when any kudos were thrown my way because subjects like relationships and dating and the foibles of regular life were beneath him and his haughty perspective.

Like Daniel Perry, I too had appeared on television and radio, though nothing big and splashy. I only wished our similarities ended there. Rumor had it Daniel Perry hated that my background was in politics. He would have no respect for someone who would ditch that life to be a lowly lifestyle columnist. Worse yet, an advice columnist. He never said so, but I knew it. Or maybe he just hated me. Yes, he just hated me.

When he first came on board at the paper I sent him a "welcome" e-mail. I had recently read a blandly written but factually interesting piece he wrote for a niche magazine. I thought it would be a nice gesture to say, "I read the article, it was fascinating, welcome aboard." I assumed he'd be happy to know he wasn't seen by his new colleagues only as a chief editor and administrator, but also still as a writer and investigative journalist. He never responded to my e-mail. He never even mentioned it after we met. He did, however, send me an obnoxious e-mail weeks later, criticizing one of my columns.

I thought about all of that every time I was summoned to his office, because I was the only person *summoned* to Daniel Perry's office. Mia and I got along famously and never once did she summon me. I had worked with many other editors, both at the newspaper and elsewhere, and none had ever summoned me. But Daniel Perry was all about summoning. It made me feel small and him feel big, I suppose, though I could tell from his build he probably wasn't. *Snap*!

Daniel's office was a glass-enclosed box in the center of the main newsroom, where he could survey his domain and make everyone feel watched and nervous and impressed. Likewise, everyone in the newsroom could see in, and I knew it lightened their days to watch my facial expressions for pain and suffering during every summoning.

I grabbed a notepad before heading to Daniel's glass cage because he liked people to take notes when he spoke. I never took notes. I doodled. I drew his initials with skulls and crossbones. I wrote limericks with his name. I wrote shopping and to-do lists. I jotted ideas for my next column. Never once did I write a single word uttered by Daniel Perry.

He saw me heading toward his office, but by the time I got there he was reading something, or pretending to, and didn't acknowledge me. I stood at the glass door and waited, feeling eyes upon me. Daniel continued to read, so of course I had to knock. Only after that small humiliation did he glance up and wave me inside.

"Morgan," he said with his head lowered but his eyes raised to me. If he wore bifocals, he'd be looking above them.

"Hi," I said with a smile. "You wanted to see me?"

"Sit down," he said.

Daniel's office was like an echo chamber. Once the glass door closed, Daniel's voice was all you heard. I tiptoed to one of the fake Barcelona leather chairs situated in front of his desk.

"Do you know what I'm reading?" he said without looking at me.

"Um, no, I don't."

"To Whom It May Concern," he began to read aloud. "This past weekend I co-hosted the annual *Go Green!* benefit at Percy Hall. It was a marvelous affair attended by many upstanding and charitable members of our city. We raised tens of thousands of dollars, a task that should have been covered with immense respect by the media. To that end, I was mortified to read Amanda Morgan's review in today's paper."

Uh-oh.

Daniel inhaled quickly, sniffed, then continued reading the printed-out e-mail, slowly, carefully articulating every syllable, and injecting his own venom for effect. Finally he finished read-ing the letter, which essentially called me a despicable hack who should be fired immediately. Daniel took a deep breath before he put down the e-mail and picked up that day's newspaper.

"Does this sound familiar?" he said, holding the paper. I knew the question was rhetorical. I also knew he was about to start read-ing aloud the review I'd written. "Though nobody can deny the importance of such charitable endeavors for raising environmen-tal awareness, the mountain of money spent on elaborate affairs would be better used on the environment itself."

I tapped my pen rhythmically against my notepad as my eyes circled his office. Diplomas, framed clippings with his byline, pho-tos of Daniel Perry with important people, a half-dead plant. Man, I felt for that plant.

After what seemed like an eternity, Daniel raised his eyes to me and slapped the newspaper on his desk. Then we sat in silence for a good ten seconds.

"One reporting assignment," he said, "That's all you had to do."

He was going to fire me. I knew it. I could feel it. I'd felt it before, but this time I knew.

Should I speak? Daniel continued to look at me above imaginary bifocals. His lusterless dark hair was barely styled and needed a trim. He probably instructed his barber to keep his cut "practical." Gray hair at his temples fanned out like whiskers.

"You want to be a reporter?" He snorted. "Fat chance."

"Well, actually, no," I said.

"Excuse me?"

"I'm a columnist, not a reporter. Mia asked me to cover the party—pardon me, the benefit—because Terry has the flu." I sat up straight and added some pep to my tone. "In my defense, Daniel, I thought I covered it well. Didn't miss a detail."

"That's where you're right!" He stood up abruptly, took a few steps, and stared out at the newsroom. "Who doesn't love to read about bling and dresses and lukewarm chicken Kiev? My personal favorite was your expert assessment of the vodka fountain." He reached to pick up the newspaper again and continued reading my review. "One got the distinct sense if a vodka waterfall existed in the natural environment, every Range Rover in a ten-mile radius would head straight for it." Again Daniel slapped the newspaper on his desk.

"That was supposed to be funny," I said.

"Yes," he boomed, "it's hilarious when some of the paper's biggest advertisers and the city's richest, most prominent people are called self-indulgent alkies who drive around in fancy cars looking for the next party."

"I'm sorry. But it's only one bad letter. You should see how many I get like that about my column!" I laughed. Daniel Perry didn't.

"Amanda, it doesn't matter if someone disagrees with your take on Buffy's boyfriend. Or that you don't know the first thing about dating or relationships."

Whoa, this was bad. Like being in front of the firing squad where the shooters were purposely missing my vital organs just to keep me alive a little longer.

He continued, "This paper can't afford to lose one cent in advertising revenue. These people," he pointed at the e-mail lying on his desk, "they operate on a different plane. They don't understand the Internet. They don't care about it. If they don't see their business name covering a half page in print, then it doesn't exist. You sit on your laurels and prattle off about life and love when this paper could be sinking. And let me tell you, the first people to get kicked to the curb will be the superfluous ones." By superfluous ones, he meant me. "This is beyond unacceptable. You will write a formal apology to Mrs...," he stepped back to his desk and picked up the printed e-mail,

"Richmond."

"Yes. Of course," I said as sternly as if I'd said *affirmative, sir.*

Daniel Perry stood behind his desk and stared at me. I could hear him breathing through his nose like a dragon.

"Is that all?" I said carefully.

"For now. And don't even think about writing anything for us again."

"Uh—"

"Besides your column," he said.

"Right. Yes. Thank you."

I slinked away and closed the glass cage door softly behind me. I felt about two inches tall. Even so, I got the distinct feeling Daniel checked me out as I walked away.

6

· · ·

Thank goodness for lunch is all I could think while I endured the next two hours at my desk. I finally escaped to meet Ravenna, and found her waiting outside our favorite downtown bistro. Her flowing black hair, huge red-lipped smile, and affectionate hug always reminded me of a still from a French movie.

Ravenna and I considered each other as alter egos. She was wild in relationships while I played it cautious. She was temperamental and fiery and colorful and said exactly what was on her mind, no matter what the scene, while I often veiled my emotions. On the surface she had no insecurities and treated men with abandon, though under the surface she sang a different tune.

Ravenna was raised in France and moved to the United States after she finished college. That is, she left before completing a degree. We met on a frigid Sunday morning in New York, at the corner of Sixtieth and Fifth. It was nine degrees with a wind chill of negative four hundred. I was in the city with Paul while he looked for work. Ravenna was living there with her mother. There were only a few people brave enough to be outside that morning. I had left Paul asleep in our hotel while I fetched coffee. The moment I stepped onto Sixtieth I was assaulted by the arctic wind. I made it half a block to Fifth Avenue, and then quickly turned the corner and ducked into a doorway for relief.

Ravenna was standing with her back to the street, her shoulders hunched over, cupping her hand, trying to light a cigarette. She was swearing in French because the flame kept going out. I gave her a light and said how crazy we must be. She laughed, and then noticed a scrunched-up pack of cigarettes in my shaking hand and said, "A woman after my own heart." Although it hadn't been my plan, I decided to have a cigarette too, and we were friends from that moment on.

Ravenna remained wholly European in her tastes and sublimely French in her lifestyle and perspective. Her accent was a lovely and often funny accompaniment to her deep voice, and no matter how much coffee or red wine she drank, or how many strong cigarettes she smoked, her teeth were always white. She still lived in New York but her soul was across the ocean.

We sat at our usual table and enjoyed immediate and doting service from the waiters. Ravenna was seated for all of five seconds before a glass of red wine was placed in front of her, then she took out a cigarette and lit up. It was a nonsmoking restaurant, of course, but the panting men weren't about to stop her.

"Want one? Oh zat's right, you quit." She rolled her eyes at the word *quit*.

"I'm just trying to be good," I said.

"For God's sake, for all your bad you're zee most good person I know." A signature Ravenna observation; awkward verbiage but a crystal-clear point.

I smiled at her and shook my head.

"Is true! You're bad, which is why I love you." She patted my hand. "But damn it, if you were any more good I'd feel bad about myself."

When Ravenna swore her accent always placed an emphasis on the bad words.

"Fine, give me one," I said, waving a finger toward her pack of smokes.

"Zis is my girl." She gave me a cigarette, lit it for me, then leaned in and whispered, "Tell me everysing."

Obviously Anne had gotten to Ravenna already. E-mail, IM, text, whichever. It's amazing Anne got any work done.

"How much do you know?" I said with a sigh. Strangely, I wasn't as excited to talk about Paul as I would have predicted. Probably because of my run-in with Daniel Perry.

"Paul. Saturday night. Bleeding leg. Constipated. Date tomorrow. Zat's it."

I inhaled, then exhaled slowly.

"That about covers it," I said.

Ravenna leaned back and looked at me like I just said the world is flat.

"Excuse me?" she said. "Do you know what I give up to come to zis lunch?"

"Another lunch date?" I said slyly.

"Tall, handsome, and hopefully not Italian," she said.

Ravenna loved men and romance but she did her best to avoid falling in love. She believed that having a man adore you made you need the adoration. And she believed almost religiously that love produced pain and that was that. I once wrote a column about her and it received rave reviews. From everyone but Daniel Perry.

To me, Ravenna was a fabulous made-for-TV movie. In her midtwenties she fell madly in love with an Italian painter and eloped with him after a several-months-long affair that found them traipsing around Italy when she should have been dutifully studying art. Their marriage ended a few months later after Ravenna came home to their Manhattan apartment to find her husband in bed with her former roommate. To this day, the name "Sarah" cannot be uttered by any of us. Since that time, Ravenna had not engaged in another serious relationship or attended any weddings.

I decided to talk a little bit, to satisfy her more than myself.

"Paul called last night and we talked for a long time. Mostly about what we've been doing with our lives since—"

"Since he propose and you say no?"

"I wouldn't describe it like that," I said.

"Of course you would not. You never do. *Mon amie*, I sink he's been waiting for you all zis time."

"You know Paul. He probably got into one of his reminiscent phases and finally acted on it."

"No," she said, exhaling. "You were zee one. He propose to you, what, ten times?"

"Never with a ring," I said.

"Zis doesn't matter." Ravenna smushed out her cigarette.

"It does matter," I said.

"I never see a guy want to marry a woman so much. He had no money. He was still in school."

"I never cared that he didn't have money."

Ravenna looked at me knowingly, something only a handful of people in the world could do.

"I know you didn't care about zat. If zee ring were zee only problem, he would go wissout food to save money and buy you one."

"Yeah, and he'd never let me forget it." I regretted my comment even as it exited my mouth. *The old guilt, back again.*

"Perhaps," Ravenna said thoughtfully. "Zis was his problem."

"I always worried that one day I'd be in the middle of twenty hours of labor and he'd remind me how hungry he was years before, saving up to buy me a ring."

Ravenna laughed a little.

"You know he called me once," she said.

"Paul did? When?"

"In New York. Maybe five years ago." Ravenna pulled out another cigarette and lit it. "He was there for work and looked me up." She shrugged and put down the lighter.

"And?"

"He beg me to see him, so I meet him at zee museum."

Ravenna's mother was a bigwig at MoMA and once curated an exhibit of up-and-coming artists, including Ravenna. That was back when Ravenna was a professional working artist, one of her many career endeavors. She was wonderful but gave it up to open a boutique, the one pursuit out of dozens that lasted. In addition to the little store's success, she still worked occasionally as a gallery consultant.

"At first I sink he is hitting on me," Ravenna said.

I gave her a skeptical look.

"What was I supposed to sink? But it was just Paul being Paul. Very sweet. Saying all zee right sings."

"Sounds like Paul," I said.

"He wanted to know how to get you back," she said.

I tried to picture the scene while digesting the fact that I never knew about it.

"I told him, 'contact her only if you are serious.' I told him you are seeing someone. William, remember zat guy?"

"Yeah. Nice guy," I said.

"Small dick," Ravenna said.

We cracked up. Because it was true, and because it didn't matter because I never loved him.

"Paul was always so romantic," I said. "He wanted to live with me and marry me, yes. But he wasn't ready."

"You weren't ready," Ravenna said.

"True, I wasn't ready. But it was more than that."

"I know," Ravenna said.

We looked at each other as only very close friends can do until plates of food were placed before us. I didn't have much of an appetite and suddenly I was feeling a little sad. Ravenna could sense the change in my mood.

"My friend, you are sinking of your big three." Her *three* sounded more like *sree*.

That snapped me out of my malaise. "Why would you mention that?"

"Because I know you. I know you believe in three great loves. We talk about zis since we meet for zee first time. You said, 'A man once told me everyone has three great loves in life.' I never forget zat."

We sipped wine, something I never did in the afternoon, certainly not when I was working, except when I was with Ravenna. I dropped a few ice cubes in my glass. That habit always made Ravenna laugh because could anything be more un-French?

"Paul was one of them," Ravenna said.

"Yes."

"Did you tell him about Timothy?" Her *Timothy* sounded more like *Timossy*.

"No."

"Good. Is not his business. But I want to hear all about zat too."

"Let's save that for dessert," I said.

"You're blushing," she said. "And smiling. Look at you!"

"Well, it's just…," I could feel my cheeks getting warm, "Timothy makes me smile."

Suddenly my appetite was back.

"Tell me one more sing about Paul," Ravenna said as she put down her glass and began to eat. "How does he look?"

"Gorgeous."

"Figures," she said.

7

. . .

When I returned to the office, my editor, Mia, was leaning over my desk.

"This is good," she said. She tilted the paper to show me the column I'd been trying to put together for a few weeks. It would have been finished if Paul hadn't appeared and stolen my brain.

"Thanks," I said. "Should be ready in a couple weeks." I hung my purse on the back of my chair.

"So...Daniel?"

"Don't mention his name," I said.

"What did he want?" she said with a laugh.

"One guess."

"He didn't like your coverage of the benefit."

"To say the least. Do I look shorter? I lost a few inches in his office."

"Don't worry about it," Mia said. "We got a lot of feedback about the review. People loved it. Daniel knows that, by the way. In fact—"

"No," I said.

"C'mon."

"Never again," I said.

"Terry loved it too. He thinks you should start covering some events. With your own twist, of course."

"No way," I said.

"You're the only writer I know who doesn't want bylines," Mia said.

"I'm an enigma," I said.

Mia smiled, tapped the column draft, with her pen, and then returned to her desk.

I scrolled through e-mails and thought about my next column. Paul's reemergence had my mind swimming with *what if's*. Hearing Anne and Ravenna mention Timothy in every conversation had me preoccupied too. Timothy himself had me completely preoccupied until Paul's appearance. But I hadn't seen or talked to Timothy in a week, so I didn't know where we stood.

I read through a handful of column e-mails containing various personal stories. I had always been curious as to exactly what possessed people to sit down and write out their private affairs to a stranger. I questioned what they saw in my column that made them feel like I wasn't a stranger at all, but rather a trusted confidant. They weren't wrong to assume that; my readers knew I valued their privacy above all else. If someone sent me a question, and then had second thoughts and didn't want it published, I didn't publish it.

Daniel Perry thought that was crazy. On the only occasion I'd ever asked Mia to push my deadline back—by three hours—Daniel was incensed when he learned it was because the question-writer had e-mailed me at the last minute to request her story not be published. "They know what they're doing when they write to you," he had said. "It's anonymous, why do they give a shit?" I explained to him that some questions contained details that could possibly identify the writer, and sometimes people got scared their husband or boss or friend or boyfriend or girlfriend or dry cleaner would see it. Daniel had rolled his eyes because, you know, *people*.

I sat at my desk and thought, not for the first time, if some of the column e-mails I received were secretly from people I knew. Then for the first time ever, I wondered what I would write to a columnist like myself.

Dear Ms. Morgan: About ten years ago I was in a several-year relationship with a wonderful guy. He was loving, smart, funny, and ambitious, and I loved him very much, but our relationship weighed on me during the formative years of my career-like when I finally got a real job, he saw my success as something that would keep us apart. He was still in school and I was in the real world. Our schedules and geographical distance were tough variables to contend with. He didn't think we saw each other often enough and he wanted us to get married. He proposed many times and wanted me to live out West with him. Fast-forward a few years… He recently knocked on my door out of the blue! He wants us to get back together. It took a long time for me to get over our relationship, and I've had serious relationships since him. In fact, right now I'm dating someone I like very much. Yet again we live in different cities, though not too far apart and we visit each other often. This burgeoning relationship has great possibilities. I'd love your opinion on what I should do. By the way, I read your column religiously and I think you are the most brilliant, insightful, witty columnist in the world. I hear the editor-in-chief is a mad ogre tyrant who hates you, so I wanted to send my letter now, in case you get fired in the next few days.

8

. . .

I woke up Tuesday morning thankful to work from home. I'd told Mia, as I left the office the day before, that there was zero chance I'd be in the next day. She didn't question it. Instead she just waved goodbye without looking up from her work. I was not required to come to the office at all; I was freelance and therefore not an "official employee," as Daniel Perry was always quick to remind me. But the newspaper gave me a desk and an old, crappy computer anyway. John Mayes often commented about how I had it so good.

"Good" is a relative term when you pay for your own health insurance and all other work expenses. Almost everyone at the newspaper was in a union, and seeing as the industry was in a constant struggle since the advent—and subsequent popularity—of the Internet, employee status and union negotiations were always touchy topics floating around the office. I didn't have to worry about things like annually offered buyouts, mostly because the paper got me on the cheap. It wasn't a huge stretch to say they could buy me out with a twenty-dollar bill and a thermos of coffee.

I rolled out of bed, thinking about my upcoming evening with Paul. I was alternately excited and nervous, imagining how it would play out. Yet by the time my tea was ready, I was thinking about Timothy. That morning marked a full week since we last spoke—standing outside his apartment building in Washington,

DC. I went to visit him for the weekend and we had a great time, despite his obvious preoccupation with an upcoming business trip to Edinburgh, Scotland. He was so busy all the time, and I wondered occasionally if he was *too* busy: for a relationship, for a real social life, for me. Whenever I mentioned his busyness, he always said, "People make time for the important things." Since we now hadn't spoken for a week, I worried how important I was to him.

On Saturday evening, right about the time when Paul showed up, I had been starting to feel a hint of sadness creep in, like things with Timothy might be over. A week is a long time to go without talking to someone whose bed you were recently in. We'd texted in the days following our last weekend together, but he hadn't called me. And I hadn't called him. Now he was in Scotland for a week, and I was free to focus on Paul.

Was that a sign? Was my current love interest supposed to be away when Paul came to town? Why am I calling Timothy a "love interest?" Hold on, you can call him that, it doesn't mean you love him. And why hadn't he called me? Wasn't it important to talk to me? He's such a gentleman, but would a true gentleman wait so long to call? We've been dating for a few months already; shouldn't we be talking more often? When we said goodbye, he whispered how much he was going to miss me and please don't forget him. Forget him? Is he crazy? But what if he'd forgotten me?

I carried my tea into my office and brought up my e-mail on the computer. It was mostly junk, as can be expected, but a few in the list caught my interest—one from Mia, one from John Mayes, one from Terry the society columnist, and two from Daniel Perry. Two from Daniel? *What could I have possibly done wrong in the last twenty-four hours?*

I opened John's e-mail first because it wouldn't be important or depressing. I was correct; it was merely an e-invite to one of his races. Terry's e-mail was a funny thank-you for covering the *Go Green!* benefit at Percy Hall. He had heard about the tongue-lashing I got from Daniel Perry and he apologized profusely, then mentioned it would have been a turn-on for him to get the lashing instead. Terry was gay and had a thing for "strong personalities." Unfortunately for Terry, Daniel Perry never summoned him to the glass cage. Daniel had no interest in society's happenings other than insisting we cover them with vigor because "society" paid for most of the locally based advertising. I decided to call Terry in a few minutes to give him the gory details. Not that I wanted to relive my recent summons to Daniel's office, but I knew it'd give Terry a thrill while he recuperated from the flu.

I assumed Mia's e-mail was a forwarded message to everyone in the department so I sucked it up and opened Daniel's e-mails instead. The first was brief, unpleasant, and included a pasted e-mail from yet another unhappy *Go Green!* attendee. "Next time," Daniel noted at the bottom, "perhaps you won't be so cavalier with your attitude." I sipped my sweet, rich tea as an antidote to Daniel's attitude and promptly hit Delete. In the millisecond it took to open his second e-mail I mentally tongue-lashed him back. *Next time? Fat chance, bucko. You can kiss my sweet little ass if you think I'm going to...oh no. No no no no no.* The second e-mail was a directive, not a request, to cover a major benefit later in the week. This time society's elite were benefitting worldwide famine, "or some such thing," he noted.

No, he couldn't do this to me! I wasn't a reporter! But yes, he could. I needed to keep Daniel Perry happy, or as happy as was possible for such a malcontent, because I needed my column. Damn Terry and his flu! I had a date with a major ex-boyfriend. I couldn't deal with Daniel Perry and high society and getting yelled at again, all while getting blown off by my current guy who was three thousand miles away, devoting all kinds of time to things like sleeping with UK supermodels and not calling me.

My heart was beating hard. It was one thing to write my column as a freelancer; I had near-total freedom to express myself. Truth was, even if the paper offered me a staff position, I wouldn't take it because then I'd be a cog in the wheel. But still I couldn't say no to Daniel's command because I knew he would threaten my column. He had done so before.

I had to call Terry. He answered in the midst of a coughing fit.

"Don't even cough, sniffle, or moan. Get up, get dressed, and get back to work," I said.

"Hey girl," he said with a phlegmy laugh. "Just read the e-mail. Daniel cc'd me."

"He must have blind cc'd you. I didn't see your name on there."

"You know how he is." Terry coughed again. He sounded awful.

"Terry, I can't do it. I want to help you, but I can't do it again."

"I'll owe you big. Dinner at Sasha big." Sasha was Terry's favorite people-watching restaurant. Decent food, deep purple walls, very hip. "Amanda, there's nobody else to do it, believe me. I asked around."

"Ask again," I said.

"Daniel knows people loved your *Go Green!* piece. He'd never admit it to you, but he could have gotten someone else to do this one. They're even talking about really promo-ing it."

"Oh God." My forehead fell into my hand.

"You have a fabulous closet, girl. Put on something fierce, drink wine, talk to people, no sweat."

Terry was inaccurate about the fabulousness of my wardrobe but I was too deflated to correct him.

"Yeah, right," I said with defeat. "I have a huge date tonight. I have to put this out of my mind until tomorrow."

"Can't wait to hear about it," Terry said, coughing again.

"You really sound terrible. Is there anything you need?"

"A huge date," he said.

"Call me if you need anything." Terry lived only a few neighborhoods away and it would be easy to bring him sustenance.

"Thanks, gorgeous. Hey, think of it this way, you have a big date tonight, tomorrow to think back on it, then the benefit on Thursday. That's a good week. Could be worse, you could be sick at home, not kissing anyone."

"I'll be out not kissing anyone," I said.

"That's not the Amanda I know."

"Please, if only I were half the slut you are."

"Girl, these days I'm not half the slut I am. But benefits are great for making out with strangers. The coatroom, I'm all over it."

"There won't be anyone at a fancy-shmancy charity benefit I'll want to make out with."

"You grew up with this kind of stuff, right? All those big political events. You probably kissed up congressmen before you graduated high school."

"Politicos can't kiss," I said, avoiding Terry's reference to my past.

"Tell me how you know that at Sasha next week," Terry said sleepily.

"You're a pain in my ass. Get some rest. I'll check on you tomorrow."

"You're a doll," he said.

So that was it. I was going to cover yet another big charity party, act the social butterfly, and then figure out a way to write it up with a twist, as Mia had said, without offending anyone. I already knew that no matter what I wrote, no matter how benign my assessment, I'd end up in the glass cage with Daniel Perry.

I didn't write back to Señor Editor to confirm I'd accepted my assignment. He knew I'd do it. I knew I'd do it. There was no reason to invite the opportunity for him to write back something like, "Watch your ass, you're on thin ice, Morgan." The self-important prick. Just the thought of Daniel Perry made me think about quitting my column, but the newspaper was my column's hub, and no writer in his or her right mind would forego that slot.

Just then my e-mail pinged. I turned to look at it, expecting bad news—perhaps Daniel on a tear or Mia alerting me to Daniel-mandated meeting changes that would screw up my schedule, or Terry saying he had bubonic plague, not the flu, and wouldn't be covering social news ever again.

When I saw Timothy's name in the "From" column, my entire mood changed in a flash. The e-mail was titled, "Hello from Scotland!" and the exclamation point mirrored my reaction. All the hurt and wondering from not talking to him for a week vanished at the sight of his name. Daniel Perry faded away. Terry's flu cured itself. Work was a breeze and all was right with the world.

Hi Amanda! How are you?! I hope everything is great. I just read your latest column and it's terrific! Things in Edinburgh are good but crazy! I meant to call you before my flight but I had to run my ass off to make it. Sorry we didn't talk after you left town last weekend. It's been crazy since we said goodbye outside my apartment. That morning I got to the office and the Scotland project was turned upside down. Guess who had to fix the problems? Yep, me. I slept in my office for two nights. I'd call you now but I'm in a huge meeting. I hope you haven't forgotten about me :). I'll be back in DC in a few days. - Tim

So there it was. Finally! Timothy was thousands of miles away thinking about me and reading my column and therefore probably not sleeping with gorgeous UK women and I couldn't stop smiling. Amazing how one little *ping* can change your whole mood.

I killed ten minutes reading Timothy's message several times, getting lost thinking about him and our amazing goodbye kiss the week before. I thought about how we'd been seeing each other for only a few months, all of them long-distance, and he'd already made a big impression on me, perhaps more than I'd realized or was willing to admit.

Still, there wasn't any proper excuse for not talking to me for a week, and by the time he returned from Edinburgh, it would be even longer. Why couldn't he call me *from* Scotland? We were still fairly casual as relationships go, but one little phone call, how hard is that? Even so, my happiness trumped my resentment as I noticed e-mails about my latest column piling up in my inbox.

I read every one. They made me feel professionally satisfied and appreciated, all those letters, notes, opinions, and intimate stories. Timothy may have been busy eating haggis and being an up-and-coming rock-star architect, and Paul was a big-time bicoastal music producer and...*oh my God, Paul!* Our date was in a matter of hours and I totally forgot about it. Paul, the longest relationship I ever had, the ex who trained in from Manhattan a few days ago just to get me back after all these years. The ex who'd been sitting in a downtown hotel room waiting for our date tonight, and he'd flown out of my head completely!

I quickly forgave myself for temporarily forgetting about Paul. Then I forgave myself for looking forward to our date while being happy about hearing from Timothy. I even forgave myself for not being 100 percent seduced by Timothy's e-mail. I also forgave Terry for having the flu. I didn't bother forgiving Daniel Perry for existing.

9

...

I was exhausted by the time Tuesday evening rolled around. I'd spent too much of the morning on a forgiveness bender and too much of the afternoon talking to Anne and Ravenna about what I was going to wear on my date with Paul, what I was going to say, and what I expected to happen. Naturally they assumed Paul and I would end up in bed. I had no intention of sleeping with him, and told them so. But I wore a fantastic bra-and-panty set, just in case.

We had agreed to meet in his hotel lobby. Paul had wanted to hire a car service and pick me up, but I liked the autonomy of driving myself, and escaping if necessary. I sat in my car, idling in the valet queue outside the landmark downtown hotel, and thought briefly about Timothy. It was one in the morning in Edinburgh, or maybe two in the morning—I could never remember—and he might still be awake. I pictured him working in his hotel room, preparing for tomorrow's meetings. My thoughts then jumped back to Paul, who was undoubtedly waiting inside for our big date to begin.

I knew exactly how it would start: I would saunter inside. The ornate, cavernous lobby would open up before me. I'd feel Paul there but not yet know where he was sitting. I'd sense him watching me, waiting for me to notice him. And that's exactly how it played out.

I hadn't reached the center of the grand lobby when my eyes fell on Paul. He was sitting on a burgundy velvet sofa, leaning forward, elbows on knees. When our eyes met, he smiled and stood. He tipped his head slightly to the side, a cute, nervous quirk he obviously hadn't lost, and adjusted his lapels. He was blushing, which made me blush. He was smiling like he couldn't help it. It was a scene from a movie, when the long-lost "one" reappears and no words are necessary. If the credits of our movie rolled at that moment, we'd remain locked, blushing and anticipatory, for all eternity.

This was the Paul I had long imagined. This Paul was handsome as ever, but now fully adult. Los Angeles and New York had brought out the man in him. The combination of working dreadfully long hours, making a name and a good living for himself, and surviving in a brutal business shined in his rich, twinkly blue eyes.

His light brown hair was still thick, but now cut short and lightened by West Coast sun. It was red carpet hair, purposely undone enough to look cool. His jeans fit perfectly, pooling perfectly over the tops of sharp, European loafers. His watch was visible beneath his cuff, of course, because the watch was meant to be seen. I couldn't even believe he was wearing a watch; Paul had always been self-scheduled and eschewed such obvious signs of materialism. He now looked like a model, polished and glossy, ripped from the pages of GQ.

"Hi," he almost whispered, as though his voice was muted by his smile. He took my hands and stepped in close and kissed my cheek. I hadn't felt his beautiful skin in forever, it seemed. I had forgotten how warm it was. How soft it was. His cheek lingered against mine for a moment and I felt a tingle in my knees. "You look beautiful," he said.

I tried to remain composed but I felt shaky. My hands were trembling slightly and my face was hot. I hoped it didn't show. It was like meeting a new man, yet one I already knew. The fresh and familiar wrapped up in a voice that used to say goodnight every night for years, and without which I didn't sleep as well.

"Thank you," I managed to say. I released his hands, stepped back and eyed him up and down. "And look at you, handsome." I used my *I suspected it all along* voice. Paul eyed me too, and when his eyes landed on my legs, he stifled a laugh.

"Does it still hurt?" he asked. The last time he saw me was in the immediate aftermath of my coffee table's attack. The scrape on my right foot had healed to a few scratches. The gash on my calf had subsided too, but it still required a bandage. It wasn't the greatest accessory with my short, pale-pink flirty dress and heels, but he'd already seen me at my worst.

"Yes," I laughed, "it still hurts." I had forgotten about my injury until that moment. In fact, I had forgotten about everything.

"You look absolutely amazing, Amanda. Not that I'm surprised."

"You do too, Paul. The coast agrees with you."

"Well, I've been in Manhattan for a few months now. I'm an East Coast boy at heart," he said as if I needed to be reminded. "Shall we?" he said, crooking his elbow.

I slid my arm through his and we walked toward the hotel restaurant. I felt people watching us, or I imagined they were. After we reached the restaurant entrance, Paul said, "After you," and placed his hand gently on the small of my back as we avoided a large group of people coming out.

He ordered two glasses of red zinfandel, obviously recalling what I used to like. It wasn't what I wanted that evening but I didn't say anything. I was flattered by his blatant purpose of proving how much he remembered about me. When the wine arrived, in glasses bulbous enough for goldfish to live in, we toasted "*to us*" at Paul's suggestion, just like we used to do.

"How long has it been?" I asked, still feeling warmth in my face.

"Since we last saw each other, or since we last spoke?" Paul said with a smile.

"Both, I guess." I didn't care about the answer but I felt compelled to talk.

Paul's skin was beautiful. It had always been perfect, but now he had one of those light tans that probably persisted year round. His hands were great too. I noticed his fingers around his wine glass. Even now that he was expertly coiffed and coolly dressed, a manicure would be too froufrou for Paul. But he had always been meticulous about personal grooming, even before he had any style—back when his lack thereof was one of his most endearing qualities.

"Ten years since we last saw each other," he said with certainty, and leaned back into the plush Deco chair. "A few since we last spoke."

"That's right," I recalled. "A few days after my birthday."

"But there've been e-mails," he added, almost as a question.

"Yes."

"I still have all of them," he said.

"Me too."

"Amanda, I'm just going to come out with it," Paul began, as the waiter appeared.

"Are you ready to order?" the man said. He wore nondescript black trousers, a black button-down shirt, and a maroon knit tie.

Paul asked him to come back in a few minutes, although I secretly wished he would stay and talk about the specials, so we could open the menu and delay whatever Paul was going to say. I wasn't ready to dive into our past. I'd spent too much time there. But Paul relished the past; he lived for it. Either that, or the future—our future. He rarely lived in between. That had always been a big difference between us. If this were the *Paul & Me* movie, I'd hit the Pause button and savor the present. He'd play flashback scenes on a continuous loop.

"Paul—" I said as he opened his mouth to speak.

"Amanda, just let me say this. It's been years in the coming."

"Okay," I said through a deep breath.

"I know what you're thinking," he began, looking down, running his index finger along the rim of his wine glass. "We've lived completely different lives for years. I'm sure you've had relationships. So have I."

"Paul, don't," I said gently.

The last thing I wanted to talk about was relationships we'd had with other people. Only Paul would remind you, in the midst of pouring out his heart, that you've both had sex with people besides each other.

"Just let me finish, please," he said.

"I'm sorry. Go ahead," I said.

"What I'm saying is, everything I want is right here." Paul laid his hand on mine as the waiter reappeared.

We laughed at the man's timing and decided to order. I wasn't hungry but my lack of food all day had invited the wine to start cozying in my head. Damn my low tolerance for booze! Gone were the good old days of tequila shots chased with beer. Now half a glass of good wine got me stupid. Or stupider.

"Amanda," Paul said, taking my hand the moment the waiter turned away. "I want to be with you."

Paul's expression was so sincere. He was an emotional soul who wore his heart on his sleeve.

"I know this seems out of the blue, but for me this is the culmination of all our years apart. Since the day we met, you are all I have wanted." He looked down at the table and nodded with a smile "Do you know I think about you every day?"

"You do?"

"Every day."

I felt the intense warmth of his hand.

Paul continued, "You don't have to say anything. Just know this isn't a game for me. I want us to get back what we had."

"Oh, Paul."

"Wait, just give me a few more seconds, then you can say everything on your mind." He took my hand again. "The way I see it, all these years that we weren't together are meaningless. They were important for careers, but on a personal level, meaningless. I always knew I'd make it back to you. I just didn't know when. I had to make something of myself, for your sake."

"Paul—"

"You were right not to marry me. Or stay out West with me. You were right that I needed to grow up. We were too young and I didn't understand it then, but now I do. Look at me. I work with Grammy winners, for God's sake!"

"I know," I said, proud of him.

"Can you believe that?"

"Absolutely," I said.

Paul nodded to himself. "You always believed in me more than I believed in myself."

I couldn't disagree with him there.

"Look at us now," he continued, staring into my eyes. "You're a big-time writer—"

"No," I laughed, "I'm not."

"See, that's what I love about you," he said with a sideways smile.

Whoa...love? He said it like it was nothing, like love equaled "like" and you can just toss it out there.

"You've achieved so much and you don't even know it," he said.

I slid my hand away from his. Suddenly I wasn't feeling well.

"Paul, I know what I've achieved and how hard it's been to achieve it. But I'm just a columnist. That's all. Trust me, it seems more impressive from the outside."

"You have your books, which I'm sure are brilliant," he said.

"My books? How do you know about my books?"

"Anne and Ravenna told me," he said with a shrug, as though they talked all the time.

"Paul, my books aren't published. That should tell you something."

He laughed to himself. "Amanda, this is just like you." He reclaimed my hand and squeezed it. "Arguing with me about whether you're talented. You're the most amazing person I've ever known. And funny. And beautiful. You're everything."

"Paul," I said.

"Amanda," he said.

"Thank you," I said. "That's very sweet."

"And?"

"And I have to go to the ladies' room."

10

• • •

The mixture of alcohol, no food, my past with Paul, and my uncertain present all conspired with the wine buzz to create a wave of nausea. I excused myself from the table and headed for the lobby. I looked back at our table and saw Paul finish his glass of wine, then happily butter some bread.

I couldn't accept Paul's grandiose buildup of my career, or my attributes. His fawning dredged up old feelings of having to live up to his "perfect" image of me. I actually felt faint by the time I reached the ladies' lounge. I sat on one of the floral-printed, tufted chairs, kicked off my shoes, and immediately conference-called Anne and Ravenna to ream them out for secretly talking to Paul over the years.

They calmed me down and told me they hadn't spoken to Paul in a long time, since before he and I last spoke, and that he must have been referring to old information. I apologized for even thinking they'd speak to him without my knowledge but they wouldn't hear it. They could tell I was anxious, but neither asked me any specific questions about the date thus far.

"Are you okay?" Anne asked.

"Yes, *mon amie*, you don't sound good," Ravenna said through puffs of a cigarette.

"I just need a minute," I said, leaning all the way forward, my head falling near my lap.

"A smoke would be good for you," Ravenna said.

I started to laugh. Then we all started to laugh, really hard.

"Would that make a good column or what?" I said.

"No, don't you dare tell zee world I tell you to smoke," Ravenna said, amidst exhaling.

"Shit!" I said.

"What?" they said in unison.

"My column, I haven't even started it!"

"It's okay," Anne said. "You have until Thursday, right?"

"Yes."

"It's only Tuesday. You have all day tomorrow and Thursday morning. You'll be fine."

"No, I mean I haven't even started it."

"It is okay," Ravenna said. "Do not worry. You will get it done."

"What the hell have I been doing? I should be ninety percent done by now and I have nothing!"

Thoughts of Daniel Perry belittling me in the glass cage started running through my brain. Not even a good word from Mia could prevent that from happening. I was the only columnist at the paper Daniel kept tabs on. I had never missed a deadline, but his hawk eye on me always made me fear that I would.

"And," I continued with a hard sigh, "Paul wants to get back together."

"Wow," Anne said.

"I knew zis would happen," Ravenna said.

"All this before dinner?" Anne added, not really as a question.

"No kidding," I said.

I had to get back to the table. To my date. With Paul. Though what I really needed was to get out of there. By the time I returned to the table, dinner had been served. Paul stood to pull out my chair and I noticed he hadn't touched his food.

"You haven't started?"

"I was waiting for you," he said. "Everything okay?"

"Yes, just not feeling a hundred percent."

"Is it the wine?"

"Yes," I lied.

Paul lifted my wine glass and moved it across the table, and then he set my water glass in front of me. "This should help," he said, resting his hand on my shoulder.

"Thank you," I said.

Paul started to eat with gusto, like a switch had been flipped. Minutes earlier he was pouring out his heart and now he was filling his stomach. I couldn't eat a bite. I was grappling with the realization of my looming deadline. I was grappling with the realization that Paul was sitting across the table from me, eating dinner like we did this sort of thing all the time. I was grappling with how to survive the rest of the evening without completely ruining the magic of it. Paul was perfect right now. So handsome, so attentive, such a gentleman. Like the old Paul but new and improved, freed from the shackles of his younger self and all the emotional neediness and insecurities it entailed.

"Paul," I finally said, "I hate to do this, but I'll have to go home right after dinner."

"What? Why?" He wiped his mouth with his napkin.

"I forgot I'm on deadline, I guess because of our date and everything. I haven't even started my column!"

"Your column?"

"Yes. Remember that thing I do so brilliantly?"

"You need to leave because of your column." He said *column* like it was a dirty word, not important enough to mention, and certainly not pressing enough to leave our date to attend to.

"I didn't say I need to leave right now. I'm just so behind."

Paul scoffed.

"You don't understand, Paul. The editor-in-chief, he hates me. I mean pure, unadulterated hate. If my column sucks, or worse, if I don't make deadline, he'll fire me. Like that." I snapped my fingers.

Paul's face would have been hard to read for someone who didn't know him. But I knew that look. Sadness mixed with annoyance, touched with a hint of *how could you do this to me?*

"Amanda, if you don't want to be here with me, just say so."

"What are you talking about?" I knew exactly what he was talking about. "Paul," I said with an inadvertent laugh of desperation to make him understand, "you really don't understand how awful this guy Daniel Perry is. He clobbered me the other day for a piece I wrote, and I really thought I was out of a job."

"Look, Amanda, I don't need this." Paul snapped his napkin onto the table and motioned for the waiter to bring the check. "Let's just go."

"Wait." I took his hand, trying to keep things calm.

"You know," Paul nodded sadly, looking at the table, not at me. "I come in from out of town, spend a fortune to stay here, pour my heart out to you, and you don't even care. You want to work."

"I don't want to work, I have to work. And I do care, more than you know," I said.

"Yeah? Well, you haven't said a word about anything."

"You asked me to let you finish before I said anything. Every time I tried to speak, you stopped me." I spoke in a gentle tone to quell his sudden change of mood.

Paul didn't respond. He just waved his hand as if to say *whatever, it doesn't matter.* The waiter appeared with the check and Paul signed it to his room.

He slammed shut the leather bill folder, then stood and stepped around the table to pull out my chair. Impressive; he was determined to act the gentleman he wouldn't have been years earlier if such a row had occurred. Which, on occasion, it did.

We left the restaurant and walked through the lobby in silence. We stopped at the valet booth and I handed my car ticket to a young man in a red jacket who then radioed to someone in the garage and gave us a generic smile. "It will be just a few moments, madam," he said. I wouldn't have minded if he had omitted the *madam*, but that was a gripe for another time. I turned to face Paul.

"We didn't have to leave, Paul. There are so many things I want to say."

"Amanda," he said with sudden sweetness and a deep breath, "I'm so sorry."

"No, I'm sorry. I ruined our date."

"Nothing could ruin seeing you again."

"I just need a few hours. Maybe we can meet for breakfast?" I didn't know when Paul was heading back to New York but I assumed it would be tomorrow. If I knew Paul, he wouldn't pay to stay at the hotel alone for much longer.

He took my hands. "There's no rush. Plus, you might remember I'm a late sleeper." He grinned. "Amanda, don't worry, I'm here for the week. Do whatever you have to do, I'll be here waiting."

The week?

"Wow, um, I'll call you later, then," I said.

"Take the evening to work and focus. Let's talk tomorrow. I'm going to take a walk and reacquaint myself with the city," he said with a smile.

Paul walked me to my car and kissed me gently and briefly. He held my face in his hands and we remained like that for what seemed like minutes. I was almost sad when my car arrived.

I got in, readjusted my seat to undo the position the valet had assumed, put on my seatbelt, and watched Paul walk down the street. He had his hands in his pockets and his posture was exactly the same as it used to be, ever-so-slightly hunched, a physical manifestation of old insecurities. I couldn't see his face but his silhouette looked lonely and bemused. Ironically, between the two of us, Paul was certain and I was the one at sea.

11

. . .

The next morning I got to the paper extra early. I enjoyed being in the main newsroom when it was quiet. Still, newspaper offices were never completely empty, a most endearing quality. There were always people paying attention to the happenings of the world.

John Mayes appeared at my desk as I slung my bag and purse over my chair.

"Surprised to see you here so early," he said. "It's barely seven."

"One of those days," I said.

"I would have expected you to be out today," he said as he casually rifled through papers on my desk.

"Why?"

"I don't know, maybe because of your hot date last night."

"Excuse me?"

I hadn't told John about my date. Nor would I, because I didn't tell John anything about my romantic life. We were good work friends and little more. John always referred to me as "a hard nut to crack" because of my insistence upon keeping my personal life to myself. We had the smoking connection, or more specifically the nonsmoking connection, the newspaper connection, and we lived in the same neighborhood. That was it.

"I gave a talk last night at the Markson Hotel, for that annual journalists' convention. Remember I'm on the board this year?"

I nodded *yes* even though I hadn't remembered.

"I saw you walking out of the lobby," he said. "You seemed very, uh, deeply engaged."

"Oh," I smiled.

"You looked great, by the way." John slid his hands in his pockets and swayed from side to side, obviously waiting for details.

"Thanks," I said as I got comfortable in my chair and opened my laptop.

"So, who's the guy?"

"I'm sorry, John, I really have to work. Deadline. You know how it is."

He kicked the air like a kid kicked dirt. "Yeah, sure. I know how it is. Let's grab coffee in a little while and you can tell me all the sordid details."

"We'll see. Got a ton of work ahead of me." I wasn't being totally honest. Surprisingly I had completed most of my column within a couple hours of returning home from my date with Paul. I'd switched into work mode and hit the keyboard running. It had been cathartic and allowed me a much-needed break from thinking about Paul. And other things.

"So," John said. "Did you smoke on this big date?" Of course he had to bring up smoking. It was classic John; he never took a hint.

"No, I didn't," I said, staring at my computer, not at him.

"Well, that's good." Still he stood at my desk.

"John, I really have to work."

"Sure, sure. Shoot me an e-mail and let me know about coffee. Or you can IM me too. Whichever. Or stop by my desk."

"Ooo-kay." I gave John a look that said *time for you to go* and he finally did.

I had zero intention of meeting him for coffee and even less of discussing my date with him. He was a very nice guy, a good-looking guy, and a great reporter—probably because he never left people alone—but John and I would never date. I often wished he could find someone who liked him back because I felt unendingly guilty that I wouldn't give him a shot.

John's coffee ask-out was apropos because my latest column was about how sometimes people just don't like each other, even if they want to. I avoided any sarcasm in the column because, just like so many of my readers, I knew the feeling of unrequited "like." Paul and Timothy were floating around my brain as I wrote, but the column felt pure, and I liked it.

My editor, Mia, often said she liked not knowing what I was going to write about. Daniel Perry thought I should choose one theme and stick with it, but screw him and the horse he rode in on. It is a nice feeling when your editor enjoys your work, and tells you so. I had worked with editors before Mia who didn't do that. Previous editors ranged from nothing special to mildly annoying to, in one case, a total witch. I had worked with non-newspaper editors as well, but newspaper editors took the crazy cake.

In my column's early years I survived the cake eaters by keeping my head down and my mouth shut (most of the time) and now I had to contend with only Daniel Perry. There was one witchy cake eater, Leona Vargas, but I didn't work with her directly, and for that I was grateful every day. Leona was Daniel Perry's third or fourth in command, and she had much bigger fish to fry than me. She had tried to sauté me on a few occasions, if not outright fry me, but generally we avoided each other. Poor Mia had to deal with her, and so did John Mayes. Leona sneered at me sometimes when I headed to the glass cage, but aside from nasty glares, she wasn't an issue.

By nine o'clock I had e-mails from Anne and Ravenna, both of them wanting to meet for lunch. There was also an e-mail from Paul and a forwarded "must-read" article from Timothy. I opened that e-mail first because I wasn't quite ready to communicate with Paul again so soon.

Was I fickle? Or heartless? Paul was ensconced in a hotel just a few minutes away, waiting for me, and I didn't feel like communicating with him. Single women everywhere would smack me for being so cavalier. They'd think me a fool for possibly throwing away the chance of a lifetime. *Was it merely Timothy's newness that made his e-mail more appealing than Paul's?*

No, I decided, it wasn't Timothy's newness. It was Paul's not-newness, his familiarity, my already knowing what he wanted and exactly how he felt about me. Our date had left an odd, yet faintly familiar, taste in my mouth. Like when, as an adult, you eat something you loved as a child. There is comfort in the scent and memory, but if you'd never tasted it at age six, would you like it at age thirty-six? The taste in my mouth was something like that. Ultimately I decided yes, I might still like it.

Timothy's e-mail included a link to a *New York Times* article about architecture in which his firm's name was mentioned prominently, with several paragraphs devoted to their cutting-edge projects and how clients all over the world clamored for their services. I was smiling by the time I finished the article. Timothy wasn't bragging, at least I didn't think he was. He was trying to impress me. He didn't need to. I was impressed with him the moment we met. He wrote briefly that he was coming home tomorrow (*tomorrow!*) but I didn't have time to think about that at the moment.

I had to finish my column, make plans with Anne and Ravenna and, shortly thereafter, with Paul. Besides, Timothy was returning home to Washington, DC. He would be jet-lagged and certainly not expecting us to see each other that coming weekend, so I could put any stress about him aside for a few days.

Lunch with my friends would kill the afternoon and I wanted

my column to be finished before I left the office. The Percy Hall benefit awaited me the following night and that was weighing on me. For the most part I was happy to help out Terry by attending; he'd been a good friend to me since I started at the paper. But knowing Daniel Perry would use a microscope to examine my coverage of the event put me on edge.

I shot John Mayes an e-mail declining coffee. Ravenna, Anne, and I agreed, via IM, to forego lunch and meet after work at my place. Then I made a quick call to Paul to solidify our date for the evening. He would come to my place and we'd go from there.

Go from there. The words hovered. Literally or figuratively, I didn't know where we'd go.

12

• • •

Ravenna and Anne were waiting outside my door when I pulled in my driveway. Luckily we had a couple hours to hang out before Paul would arrive.

It was rare for the three of us to be together, not only because Ravenna was in New York most of the time, but also because Anne and Ravenna were mainly friends through me; they spent little time together on their own. They were talking about that very subject as the three of us walked inside. Anne swore she and Ravenna had met for lunch six months earlier when she was in Manhattan for business, but Ravenna insisted it was even longer ago.

"No," I corrected both of them, "the last time was when we were all together in New York a few months ago. How could you forget? That's when I met Timothy."

Anne and Ravenna walked into the kitchen as I tossed my purse, bag, and jacket on the living room sofa.

"Yes," Anne called out, "but that wasn't Ravenna and me alone."

"Anne is right. I remember zees sings."

"See? Ravenna remembers *zees sings*," Anne said.

"Have Ravenna teach you French and you'll have an excuse to meet all the time," I said. "*Voilà*, problem solved."

I walked into the kitchen to find Anne taking three wine glasses out of the cabinet and Ravenna scavenging her purse for cigarettes. I didn't want a drink, which Anne probably knew, but she got a glass for me anyway and put ice in it.

"Yes, Anne, I teach you French, zen we can meet wissout Amanda. For lessons."

"No fucking way. I'm bad with languages," Anne said, pouring the first glass of white wine. "Besides, I want to learn Romanian."

"Well zen, zer is no hope."

Anne poured wine into the other two glasses and handed one to each of us. We clinked, and then they stood there, staring at me, waiting for the details of my date.

"You know," Ravenna said to Anne after a moment, "I don't sink I like you wissout Amanda. You are not a romantic."

"Try getting crabs from a lifeguard," Anne said. "Then talk to me about being a romantic."

Ravenna and I laughed so hard, we nearly spit out our wine. Anne had a very soft heart but she had been burned enough to force a practical perspective on romance. She had specific rules about what she would and wouldn't do in relationships and on dates. Unfortunately none of them included "not sleeping with a guy on the first date" so she tended to have a lot of them—first dates and guys. Anne got attached to men quickly, the early sex no doubt playing a role in her subsequent emotional connection, but she got over them quickly too.

We stood in the kitchen and talked about my date while Ravenna's smoke swirled overhead. I left no detail unmentioned. By the time I was done with the story Ravenna and Anne were intermittently looking at each other, unsure what to say.

Anne spoke first. "Is he expecting an answer tonight?"

"No," Ravenna piped in, "zis is not possible."

"An answer to what?" I asked.

"To his proposal, I guess," Anne said.

"Proposal?" I felt something brewing inside me I couldn't

identify. "He didn't propose. He talked about how he felt, what he sees for the future. But he didn't actually propose."

"Well, he might have, if you didn't take off," Anne reminded me.

"Yes," Ravenna said while exhaling, "I sink so too. Perhaps zis is why he was so mad. Perhaps he was going to ask you, and zen you ended zee date."

"Wait, wait wait. I didn't end the date. Paul ended the date," I said.

"But I can understand zat," Ravenna said. I gave her an inquisitive look. She touched my arm in consolation. "I am on your side, *mon amie*, but I can understand his reaction. You know he wants to marry you. 'Paul want to marry Amanda' is like a sign he wears."

"I can't talk about this anymore," I said.

"Did you tell him about Timothy?" Anne asked.

"Oh yes," Ravenna said, "I am dying to know zis."

"I didn't tell him anything about Timothy," I said matter-of-factly.

"No?" Ravenna said.

"What's to tell?" I said. "For all I know Timothy and I will die out in a few weeks, if I even see him again."

"Don't say zat," Ravenna said. Anne nodded in agreement.

"I can't help it," I said. "Long distance is hard enough when you're in a serious relationship, and we can't even get there. I swear I've never known anyone so busy. I really admire Timothy's ambition and I'm impressed with how hard he works, but I can't see him making enough time for anything more than a weekend or two every month. We have yet to spend time together when he hasn't worked, at least a little bit."

"You really like him," Ravenna said, handing me a cigarette.

"Don't give that to her," Anne said.

"Oh, stop. She need zis."

"I think I do," I sighed. I lit the cigarette and smiled at Ravenna. "You know, I really like Timothy."

"He is a great guy," Anne said. "I could see you two together."

"You don't even know him," I laughed. It was the truth. Whenever Timothy visited we spent all our time alone. Ravenna was usually in New York and Anne was usually on a date or working late.

"But he is different zan everyone else I see you wis. His personality is like opposite from Paul. Oof! And from Steven, for sure."

"Jesus, why would you bring him up?" Anne said.

"Fok," Ravenna said, in her botched pronunciation of *fuck* that always cracked me up. "I am sorry. I forget we are not to mention his name."

"It's okay," I said.

Now thoughts of another ex, Steven, began to creep in.

"You see," I said, walking from the kitchen toward the living room, "this is why I can't talk about all this. Because other stuff comes up."

"Talking is good," Ravenna said. "It opens everysing, like doing art."

"I'm a terrible artist," Anne said, which made all three of us laugh because she was an art director for a small advertising agency.

"Zis is not possible," Ravenna said. "Everyone is an artist with zee right tool. I see you wis clay because zis is good for aggression. And for Amanda, I sink charcoal or maybe watercolor because her mind flows. Of course, she is a writer and zat is art too."

Anne and I stared at Ravenna in mock judgment.

"Okay," Ravenna said, "I'll stop. But clay would be very good for you." She nodded toward Anne.

"I need to figure out what to wear," I said. "Not just for tonight but for the benefit tomorrow."

I headed upstairs while Anne and Ravenna talked about which art form besides clay would be best for Anne. They followed several steps behind me. I heard Anne whisper, "I can't believe you mentioned Steven!"

"Yes," Ravenna said, "zat was bad. Zis is cheap wine, I sink."

. . .

Ravenna and I sat on my bed—she with her glass of wine, and me with my glass of wine-water—while Anne rummaged through my closet. She held up random dresses and outfits to which we would say yes, no, or maybe. She'd pull a hanger off the rod, show the clothes to us, toss the yeses and maybes on the bed and rehang the noes. As yet there were many noes, several maybes, and zero yeses.

"Paul's going to be here in less than an hour, we need a yes here," Anne said with a muffled voice as her head was buried between clothes.

"Any of zees will do," Ravenna said, pawing through the pile on my bed.

"Wait, hold the phone, I've got it," Anne said. "Wow, this is amazing. Not for tonight but definitely for the benefit tomorrow."

Anne emerged from the closet a moment later holding my favorite dress. I hadn't worn it, or even looked at it, in over a year.

Anne stood in front of the closet with the dress as Ravenna got up from the bed, walked toward her, and agreed emphatically that it was perfect for tomorrow night's benefit at Percy Hall.

"I've never seen zis before. Zis is beautiful. You must wear zis."

I stared at the dress. Gazed at it. Pined for it, even though it was right in front of me. It was just as beautiful as I remembered.

"What?" Anne asked, trying to read my expression. "This is

perfect. Now that I think about it, I've never seen you in this." Anne removed the hanger and held the dress up against her body. She is several inches taller than I am, so the dress hit her mid-thigh. On me it hit just above the knee.

"Nobody has seen me in it," I said.

"Is it new?" Anne asked. "It's awesome."

I got up from the bed, set my glass on the bedside table, and then walked toward the dress now dangling from Anne's fingers. I ran my hand softly over the braided black satin straps and bodice textured with delicate appliqué satin ropes swirling in a random pattern. I was smiling without realizing it.

"What?" Anne asked again, though she was looking at Ravenna. "What's with this dress?"

"Nothing," I said. "I just haven't seen it in a while."

"Zis is gorgeous." Ravenna leaned around the dress and looked at the tag. "Ooh la la, is designer. When did you buy zis? Why do you not wear zis?"

"I got it in New York," I said.

I remembered the day I bought it. The dress had been a huge purchase for me, but I was floating on clouds that day. I had just come from a great meeting with a literary agent about a book based on my column and I was scheduled to fly home the next morning. My birthday was a few days away and I had very special plans awaiting me. I didn't even hear the traffic noise on Madison Avenue once I saw that dress in the boutique window. I walked into the store, headed straight for the dress, and immediately tried it on. It fit as if it were custom-made for me; it didn't need a thing, no hemming, no loosening or tightening. It was perfect. As I walked back to my hotel, carrying the dress, I happened upon a stunning pair of heels in the window of Barneys. Very high, but not quite stiletto, black peau de soie, with an ankle strap. Five

minutes later I buckled the straps around my ankles. The shoes fit
as though they had been molded for my feet.

"Yeah?" Anne said. "You bought it in New York, and…?"

"And nothing," I said with a shrug.

"Come on, you're looking at this dress like, I don't know, you're
all weird now."

"I just forgot that I had it." I was mostly telling the truth.

"Out with it," Anne said.

"Yes, out wis it."

"Okay, fine," I said. "I got it for my last date with Steven. Okay?"

Anne and Ravenna simultaneously breathed in a collective *oh*.
They looked at each other, unsure what to say, obviously feeling
bad now that Steven's name had come up twice after being verboten for months.

"Let's put zis away." Ravenna took the dress from Anne and
disappeared into the closet. I could hear her moving things out of
the way to shove the dress into the dark abyss at the back of every
woman's closet, the place where things go to lie in repose until
eventually found again and promptly given away.

"No, wait," I said. "Bring it back."

Ravenna reappeared with the dress and I took possession of it.

"It's time to wear this gorgeous thing," I said.

I looked at Anne and she smiled at me. Ravenna stepped back
and looked at me as I held the dress against me in front of the
mirror.

"Yes," she said. "It is time."

13

· · ·

Paul showed up right on time. Obviously punctuality was a habit he had learned during our years apart. Anne and Ravenna were still at my place, and it was nice to see their reunion with him. They had always liked Paul and the sentiment was mutual. Plus Paul spoke French (and Spanish, and a bit of German), so he and Ravenna prattled on while Anne and I talked quietly about how good he looked.

"You weren't kidding," she whispered to me in the kitchen. "He really looks good."

"I know," I said, smiling in his direction. He smiled back at me from the hall.

"You'd have gorgeous kids." Anne was certain she could predict what a couple's kids would look like. She had her own version of the Punnett square that was wholly unscientific. To her credit, she'd never been wrong.

"Paul always said that too," I said.

"I have a feeling," Anne leaned in close to me, "you might get a start on that tonight."

"I'm not going to sleep with him," I said.

"Why not? You always had great sex."

"True." Couldn't argue with the truth.

"Hey, are you okay?" Anne asked after staring at me for a minute.

"Of course. Why?"

Anne always knew when something was wrong with me, sometimes before I did.

"You don't seem excited," she said. "This is Paul. This is, like, big."

Anne was right. I had been more excited about getting Timothy's e-mail than I was to see Paul in my home. It didn't make sense but I didn't have time to ponder it.

Anne continued, "It's like you were more excited to get Timothy's e-mail than you are to see Paul."

"I am excited. I really am," I whispered. "It's just…"

"What?" Anne had a trace of concern in her voice.

Just then Paul and Ravenna walked into the kitchen.

"Ladies," he said, "it's been great seeing you again. Anne, you look great, as always."

"Thank you. Right back at ya."

"And I already told Ravenna she's looking fabulous."

"*Merci*," Ravenna said with a deep nod.

"But this stunner here," Paul stepped toward me and took my hands in his, "the only word is *wow*."

I felt tingly as I looked into Paul's eyes. His voice was still like velvet to my ears. I had settled on a pencil skirt, silk top, and sheet-ripping heels. Clearly the ensemble was a success.

"I sink we'll go, yes?" Ravenna said to Anne.

With that, my friends wished us a great evening and left.

• • •

Paul and I walked a few blocks to the bustling commercial section of my neighborhood. He had hired a car service for the night, but he told the driver to kill a few hours and remain on call rather than force the man to sit, bored, in my driveway.

"Sure you're okay to walk in those?" Paul asked, referring to my heels.

"They're not uncomfortable." Walking in high heels sometimes felt great and this was one of those times.

"Thank God because they look fantastic on you," he said.

"Thank you," I said, squeezing his hand. I could feel myself smiling and blushing again. Paul could still do that to me. I noted to myself, although I didn't mention aloud, his repeated use of the word "fantastic"; it was very LA.

A few minutes later we reached the main street. It was busy for a Wednesday evening. We strolled arm in arm, reminiscing about some of the weekend trips we'd taken years ago. He complimented my hands, my hair, even my walk.

"You've still got it," he laughed to himself. "You know, I used to imagine you walking."

"Walking?"

"Yeah." He looked at me sweetly. "You're blushing," he said.

"I've never known anyone like you, Paul. You always compli mented me on everything. I've never known anyone who notices and compliments so many things."

"I'm not really like that," he said.

"Don't be so humble. Let me compliment you for a change. I can still remember you complimenting my toes!"

"Well, they looked beautiful," he said. "Like bright, tiny poppies."

I stopped walking and tilted my head in amazement.

"You remember the color of my toes on one day out of a thousand?"

"I know exactly what day you're talking about," Paul said. "You came back from running errands and you looked great. Your freckles were out, and I noticed you got a pedicure. I wanted to eat those toes."

"Who else notices those kinds of things? You. That's it."

"Amanda, I'm really not like that," he repeated, quite sincerely. "Only with you."

I squeezed his arm against me and it made me feel warm. I had never forgotten how openly loving Paul was. Years and distance can muddle one's memories and it was nice to know I hadn't been wrong.

We decided on a little Italian bistro, a place I knew Paul would like. The owner saw me from across the small dining room and signaled he'd be right over to us. Outside of the restaurant the owner and I might not recognize one another, but in the restaurant he always remembered me. He and his wife often joked that one day they would "make an Italian baby outta me yet."

"I love this place," Paul said.

"You've been here five seconds!" I laughed.

"I love it." He turned to me. "It's perfect."

We were seated against an exposed stone wall with a painting of Venice hanging over the table. The restaurant was cozy, busy, and rustic. The waiter placed bread and complimentary glasses of Chianti on the table, told us the specials, and then disappeared.

Paul moved aside his wine and leaned forward over the table.

"Do you remember the first time we went to New York?"

"Of course," I said.

"I loved that trip."

"Now I know you're crazy," I laughed. "You were miserable on that trip. Stressed and depressed and tired. Going from studio to studio trying to meet with producers."

"I loved that trip," Paul repeated in earnest. He stared at me with his deep blue eyes. Their color was deeper than the night before.

Our trip to New York could have been weeks ago, I remembered it so well. Paul was a few months away from completing school and I offered to meet him in Manhattan, for moral support and company, as he pounded the pavement looking for jobs. At the time I was already living here, having moved back East after graduate school. But Paul was still living out West and our relationship survived mainly on frequent visits, e-mails, and many phone calls every day.

Paul took my hand and said, "I remember getting that meeting with Richard Whats-his-name and—"

"I remember," I said. "You couldn't believe he even took the meeting. Didn't he win an Oscar?"

"Yes," Paul said. "He's the one who offered me that job. Offered it to me himself."

"Which you didn't take," I reminded him.

"Right. But what I remember most is looking around his office thinking, 'I can't believe I'm sitting here talking to this living legend,' and I was also thinking of you waiting for me in the coffee shop around the corner."

I laughed wistfully at the memory. That long-ago afternoon Paul had already tried to meet with five or six studio execs who wouldn't give him the time of day. The last meeting was the longest shot of all.

Paul continued, "Whats-his-name was talking to me about my reel, and I pictured you sitting at the counter in that coffee shop, probably doing the crossword puzzle and talking to the waitresses, and I didn't feel nervous anymore. Just the thought of you made everything feel better. You were my lifeline."

"Paul—"

"Amanda, wait. Before you say anything, let me get this out."

I stopped myself from speaking and smiled.

"I know we had a rough time and I wasn't there for you like I should have been."

That's true. So very, very true.

"But I was young," Paul said. "My life wasn't together. I only knew a couple things for sure. One," he extended a finger, "I knew what I wanted to do for a living. Two," he extended another finger, "I wanted to be with you." He paused and stared into my eyes. "That's it, that's all there was for me. Now here we are. I know it's been years but I feel the same. That may sound crazy to you but we were so good together. You were so good for me. There's no way I'd be successful without you. Every time I walked on the beach, I thought about you. About how great things would be if we lived the good life out there together. I wasn't successful then, but I am now. Granted I'm in New York now, but I'd go anywhere you want."

It was a beautiful, romantic sentiment he'd shared before, that he'd follow me anywhere.

"Remember when I got that award and thanked you?"

"Yes," I said.

"Your name just came out," Paul said with a soft but incredulous tone.

"Everyone was talking about it," I said. "All my friends, everyone."

"No kidding! My girlfriend dumped me later that night," Paul laughed.

Huh? It was like hearing a record scratch.

"Your girlfriend?"

"Yeah," Paul laughed again. "Not that I blame her." He took a gulp of his Chianti.

I stared at him in disbelief and it took him several seconds to notice.

"What?" he asked casually.

I felt my jaw hanging, flies buzzing, crickets chirping.

"Amanda, come on," he said and squeezed my hand. "You and I hadn't been together in a couple years. You were seeing other people, I'm sure," he added with a slightly accusatory tone. I knew he was referring to the info he got from Ravenna when they met in New York, when she told him I was seeing someone.

"Of course I was seeing other people. Seeing. Dating. Nobody I'd call a boyfriend."

"That's just semantics," Paul said.

"You were still calling me!"

"But we weren't together," Paul implored. "We were living on opposite coasts. We hadn't even seen each other in a long time."

His casual treatment of the whole subject left me feeling a bit sick.

"Paul, why would you mention another woman right now?"

"She wasn't another woman. She was just a woman. It's kind of funny if you think about it."

"Funny?"

"Amanda, believe me, it was nothing."

"But you mentioned it, like it's significant to our story."

"You're overreacting," he said.

I felt deflated and slumped into my chair.

"I can't believe this," Paul said with a pissed-off tone. "I tell you about something great and…tell me this, how many guys are going to thank an ex-girlfriend in an award acceptance speech? Of course you have to twist this into something bad."

"Here we go again," I sighed. "You do something wrong, then blame me for reacting."

"Let's not go there, please."

"Fine," I said flatly.

"Did you expect me to live like a monk? You broke my heart, remember? You ended it. You said we would never be together."

Paul was right. That's exactly what I'd told him.

"But you kept calling anyway," I said.

"Yes," he said, taking my hand again and aiming his deep blues at me. "I couldn't stay away. I loved you. Not having you in my life was the worst thing I ever felt."

"But you're saying you had a girlfriend. A *girlfriend*. That's a commitment, Paul, and you were lying to her. And to me, kind of."

"I was not lying to you."

"Ugh, you always told me everything on your mind when, frankly, I could have used an omission here and there. Like now!"

"I can't believe this," Paul said. "I tell you I love you. I tell you I've been pining for you for years, and you're mad at me."

Paul and I stared at each other. I didn't want to speak until I was sure what I wanted to say, a trait I'd developed since my days with Paul.

"I don't deserve this," Paul said.

"Probably not," I said. "Paul, I'm not mad that you loved me. I'm upset that you're rewriting our history. Those years after we broke up—"

"After you dumped me," he corrected me, tapping his spoon against the table.

"It hurts to think of all our old phone conversations now."

"Why?" Clearly he was ignorant of the magnitude of my feelings.

"Because in those conversations, you were trying to get me back," I said. "When your ex calls you all the time to get back together, you assume he's single. Turns out, all that time you were screwing someone as soon as we hung up."

Paul nodded sadly.

"She meant nothing," he said.

"I'm sure she'd be thrilled to know that."

The waiter had been standing a few feet away, waiting for us to disengage from our apparently coo-filled, intimate conversation. I accidentally glanced in his direction and he hopped to our table and asked if we were ready to order. Paul said yes, looked at me, and then asked the waiter what he recommended.

"Do you know what you want?" Paul asked me.

Yet again I wanted to leave our date but I forced myself to stay and try not to sulk through dinner. With zero enthusiasm or hunger, I ordered angel hair with white clam sauce. Paul opted for one of the specials, which I knew he'd love and finish completely despite the pall hanging over our table. As we waited for our food, Paul talked about an Italian restaurant we had found by accident on that New York trip. We talked about a cab ride to the Natural History museum, during which he got into a lengthy French conversation with the Haitian driver. We talked about a two-hour walk we had taken through Central Park when he had asked me, not for the first time, if I would move with him to New York or come back to California, depending on where he took a job.

By the time dinner arrived, Paul had taken us on a reminiscent trip through that lovely chapter of our past. I smiled here and there, momentarily forgetting the present, and picked at my food.

We walked back to my place and the sounds of summer evening provided the soundtrack. Paul held my to-go bag and I could feel him looking at me while we walked.

"Should I come in?" he asked softly as we neared my front door.

"I don't think so," I said.

Paul looked defeated. And insecure. But still so handsome.

"You never told me what you've been thinking," he said. "That's my fault. I asked you to wait for me to finish, and I just kept talking. Like always, I guess. I'm surprised you could even understand me with my foot in my mouth."

Paul smiled, and so did I.

"Please say something," Paul said. "I don't want your last word to be *no*. It'd be like my proposal all over again."

"Which one?"

"Any of them," he said sweetly, then leaned his head down to be at eye level with me. "Just once I want to hear you say yes. Tell me any question I can ask that will get a yes."

"You can ask to kiss me," I said.

Paul's face lit up with surprise.

"Amanda," he stepped closer to me, "may I kiss you?"

"Yes."

The moment our lips touched, everything felt different. The evening around us disappeared and there was only that moment. No past, no future, just an amazing kiss.

14

· · ·

John Mayes walked through the front door of the newspaper one second before I arrived. He looked back, held open the door for me, and we entered together. There was an unusually slow-moving queue of employees waiting to swipe their ID cards past the sensor. As we inched, John told me about a series he was working on, about the plight of professional men in the dating world. He asked if he could interview me for the story. Of course I said yes. I was happy to help John, knowing he'd help me with anything.

The security guard at the front desk stood up and announced the ID sensor was on the fritz and everyone would have to sign in by hand. The announcement elicited a communal grunt and various irritated mumblings. The line grew quickly, along with the volume and number of complaints ranging from snarls about the outdated card-swipe system to grim forecasts about union negotiations to low pay to dwindling staff to whether or not to charge for online content. At a newspaper, such complaints become white noise after a while.

Instead of joining the group bitch-and-moan session, John and I talked about the inspiration for his article. Recently he'd been e-mailing and instant messaging with a woman from an online dating site and he had high hopes for their first date. It was great to hear John talk excitedly about a woman.

Suddenly a hush fell over the group. Daniel Perry entered the vestibule between the sets of front doors. He eyed the herd gathered in the lobby, then noticed me as he opened the inner set of doors. Naturally His Highness didn't get in line; he walked straight through us untouchables. God forbid he should stand and wait with us lest he catch our possibly contagious mediocrity.

Daniel more than brushed past me; he nearly shoved me. He held up his ID for precisely half a second, not enough time for the security guard to check it, and then headed for the stairwell. For security reasons, not even the editor-in-chief was allowed to enter the building without signing in properly, but nobody was brave enough to tell Daniel to spare a moment of his very important time. He opened the door to the stairwell and turned back, laid his eyes on me, waited for everyone to notice, then raised his voice to say, "Morgan, my office, five minutes," with a tone that sent a chill through everyone. After he disappeared I saw a handful of stares in my direction before the din of complaints returned.

"Whoa," John said. "What did you do?"

"I have no idea," I said.

"You still covering the benefit tonight?"

"Yes." I grimaced.

"Maybe it has something to do with that."

"Maybe," I said. "I think he just hates me."

"Impossible," John said with a sincere smile.

"People don't always like each other, John."

He grinned softly, no doubt assuming I was referring to my lack of romantic feelings for him. "What I mean is, Daniel just dislikes me, for whatever reason."

Finally it was our turn to sign in at the desk. A minute later, as we headed up the stairs, John asked if he could interview me that morning. The first installment of his series was slated to run the following week and he wanted to wrap it up. I said I'd be happy to, after meeting with Daniel Perry, of course.

John and I were quiet as we ascended three dimly lit floors of the stairwell. He tapped, poked, and otherwise fixated on his Blackberry while I thought about the building itself and tried to deduce how many minutes I had left before Daniel's five-minute countdown expired. The building's exterior was architecturally outdated but inside it offered a sense of strength and longevity. Each gray step in the stairwell had soft areas of depression from decades of use. Often I'd wished the walls could talk. What might they have heard during wartimes? Had trysts occurred here after the latest issue was put to bed? Had a reporter ever decided to run, or sit on, a big story while running down these stairs?

John and I entered the newsroom and he headed off in the opposite direction toward his desk.

"I'll see you soon," he said.

"What's left of me," I called out.

I reached my desk, hung my bags over the back of my chair, and opened my laptop to be ready upon my return from Daniel's office. Mia popped over to my desk.

"Love the column," she said.

"Thanks." I gathered my requisite never-go-to-Daniel's-office-without-it notebook in which no notes would be taken.

"Here's what we'll do," Mia said. "We'll promo it and run John's first installment the same day. He told me you're going to interview, which is great. It'll lend good weight to his piece."

"Happy to do it," I said with no happiness at all as I eyed the glass cage like a virgin about to be sacrificed at the altar.

"We'll link them online," Mia said. "It'll drive more traffic to both of you, not that you need it."

"Great."

"Everything okay?" she said.

"Shit!" I couldn't find a pen and my nervousness was building. "I've been summoned," I said, nodding briefly in the direction of Daniel's office.

"Ah."

"Why can I never find a pen?"

"Because you're a writer. It's part of the curse. Here." Mia handed me a pen and stepped aside so I could make my way to the lion's den. "Don't worry about him," she added, as though Daniel was a person of no consequence.

"What's the other part of the curse?" I asked.

"Having an editor," Mia said.

I forced a smile, clutched my notebook and pen, and headed to Daniel's office. I was about to knock on his door when he waved me in, like a waitress. On the bright side, it was the first time he didn't make me stand outside the glass cage like an idiot.

I entered gingerly and said, "Hi," with a smile that hurt my cheeks. Daniel didn't bother with a greeting, so I sat down, hoping it was acceptable to do so without permission. He was standing, leaning forward onto his desk, putting all his weight onto his fingertips.

"I got a call from Emily Richmond this morning," he said.

I didn't respond, partly because I wasn't sure where this meeting was going and partly because I had no idea who Emily Richmond was. I waited for elaboration. After a few seconds Daniel sighed, stood fully, and put his hands on his hips.

"She called me on my home phone, Amanda. My *home phone.*"

I nodded in a slow circle, still clueless.

"My home number is unlisted," Daniel said.

"Mine too," I said.

"You're missing the point," Daniel said as though he shouldn't have been surprised.

I was getting smaller. And dumber. It's what happens when someone disparages your intelligence and usefulness over and over and over again. I could feel my body shrinking, my legs shortening, my arms retracting. *Emily Richmond, home phone. Emily Richmond, home phone.* In five minutes I'd be tiny and brainless, unable to drive a car without telephone books to prop me up or dial a rotary phone without an instruction manual.

"Emily Richmond was the host of the *Go Green!* benefit. Ring any bells?"

"Oh yes," I said. "Emily Richmond."

I hadn't thought of her since I sent the apology note to her foundation. I forgot her the moment I stuck the stamp on the envelope.

"Seems Mrs. Richmond wanted to confirm your attendance at tonight's benefit. I can only assume she's still so pissed about your coverage of *Go Green!* that she couldn't sleep last night." Daniel began to pace. "She was so sleepless, in fact, that she was up calling me at six a.m. I hadn't gone to bed until three, but that's beside the point."

My face contorted into a combined expression of *that sucks, uh-oh,* and *I'm sorry* while I inadvertently pictured Daniel being awakened from a deep slumber. *What would Daniel Perry dream about? Bylines? Pulitzers? Bears riding tricycles? What do his pajamas look like? What if he sleeps in boxers? Or worse, naked? That's a vile thought. Don't throw up. Doodle something. Take a note. Imagine fields of daisies or puppies in a Red Flyer wagon.*

"I assured her that your presence would go unnoticed," he said. "That you'd be all but invisible."

"Yes, no problem." My mind was still wandering.

Daniel stopped pacing and stood behind his chair.

"What?" he said, staring at me.

"I'm sorry?"

"What the hell are you smiling about?"

"Was I?"

"Don't make me out to be a liar." Daniel's tone changed and softened, transitioning from anger to tiredness. "You'll go to the benefit for," he lazily checked a piece of paper on his desk, "famine. Yes, famine. You'll look the part, and you'll bring someone."

"Excuse me?"

"You heard me," he said.

"Bring someone? As in a date?"

"Yes."

"Daniel—"

He held up his hand to quiet me. "I don't want to hear it. The paper is in enough trouble as it is, and we can't afford to lose our biggest advertisers. Mrs. Richmond told everyone you're coming, which means they'll be watching you. We can't very well have our dating columnist show up alone." He said *dating columnist* as though he'd need mouthwash after speaking it. I wasn't strictly a dating columnist but Daniel most often referred to me as such. "If you're standing there alone, it'll make people uncomfortable. If you blend in and keep to yourself and your date, and cover it properly, everything will be fine."

"The thing is," I said, "I really don't like to mix my work world with my personal world."

Daniel looked at me like I had just spoken in Cantonese.

"What I mean is," I continued carefully, "I don't usually bring dates to functions like that, where there's media."

"You are the media, Amanda." He sat down. "I don't care about your goddamn worlds. Word has it you have some big boyfriend in from out of town. Bring him."

"Pardon me?" I said pointedly.

"What?"

"With all due respect, Daniel, I'm not comfortable with you talking about my personal life and ordering me to socialize with a man."

Daniel stared at me. I stared back. It was a stare-off of monumental proportions. I was definitely, positively, absolutely going to be fired. But Daniel had crossed a line and I couldn't fail to respond.

"Jesus, Morgan, it was just a suggestion. I don't care who you bring." He shuffled some papers. "Hell, bring John."

"John Mayes?"

"Nobody knows him and he could use a night out," Daniel said.

I sighed and thought about Paul sitting in his hotel room. How odd it was for Daniel Perry to mention him, even though it hadn't been by name. Somehow Paul had become my Big Boyfriend In From Out Of Town.

I had told Paul about the famine benefit and we'd planned to get together afterward. All things considered, he would be a great escort. He was personable and handsome and accustomed to big social events. But I feared taking an emotionally heavy date anywhere associated with work. There might be questions to answer and I wasn't prepared to give answers about Paul—to myself or anyone else. With my luck we'd go, have a fabulous time, everyone would talk about how the "dating columnist" was seen with a dashing man, then things would fall apart and Paul would disappear and I'd be humiliated.

"I suppose I'll figure it out," I said and began to stand. "Is that it?"

"That's it." Daniel leaned back in his big, leather throne and kicked his feet up on his desk. They landed with a clunk.

As I neared the door, I said, "How did you know about my boyfriend?" I air-quoted the *B* word.

"What is this, girl talk? We're done. Story's running Sunday. Get me something by tomorrow end of day."

15

. . .

The rest of my morning consisted of writing, deleting every word, being interviewed by John for his series about dating for professional men, getting calmed down by Mia, and leaving early. I texted Anne and Ravenna to give them the minutes of my meeting with Daniel Perry. I didn't know how long Ravenna would be in town and I was relieved to learn she would be staying through the weekend. Anne said she would come over later and hang out while I got dressed for the benefit.

I left the office and called Paul from my car. He suggested we meet for coffee and take a walk to vent and clear my head. Fifteen minutes later, we met outside his hotel. The sun was shining hard. Summer had laid its softness on the world and most people had a relaxed air about them. Paul and I meandered downtown and caught up on our years apart. Jobs, friends, trips we'd taken. During those years Paul had sent postcards to me, every now and again, from random locations in the world. He now recounted those trips with both fondness and sadness.

"Even after a few years apart I couldn't go anywhere without wishing you were with me," he said. The sun shined on his skin and hair, and he looked both pure and movie-like.

"I know what you mean," I said.

We walked along the water, holding hands. He stopped and turned to me.

"So what are you going to do?" he asked.

"Um..." I was so preoccupied with thoughts of work and the strange meeting with Daniel Perry that I was not prepared to give Paul definitive answers about our future.

"I mean about tonight," he said with a smile.

"Oh," I smiled in return. "I'm not sure."

"Let me come with you," he said.

Paul's sincerity and understanding was exactly what I needed. Was this a new Paul, one who considered his own needs second? I thought briefly about Timothy and how fun it would be to bring him to such an event. He might be home from his trip, back in his apartment in DC, settling in, fighting jet lag, and hopefully thinking about me. The thought of him was so fleeting I didn't have time to feel guilty about it.

Then, out of the blue, I thought of Steven. I tried to push his image from my mind but it persisted. In general, I didn't miss Steven, but thoughts of him were more frequent than I ever admitted to Anne or Ravenna. The fact that his name had come up twice the day before was probably the reason. Yes, that was the reason. I snapped to it and watched Paul stare at the river. His familiarity soothed me.

"Will you come to the benefit with me, Paul?"

"Really?"

"Really," I said.

"That's two yeses so far," he joked.

He took my hand and we walked back to his hotel.

"Your friend John Mayes will be disappointed," Paul said.

"I don't think John likes me that way anymore. He's just a good friend."

Paul laughed and said, "Women."

. . .

I had already showered and finished my hair by the time Anne got to my place. I needed extra makeup time, so Anne got a beer and settled on my bed to talk to me while I primped in the bathroom."I've been thinking about what Daniel Perry said to you," she said, taking a sip.

"Which part?" I curled my eyelashes. "That I'm pond scum who will go to the benefit and be seen and not heard, or that a dating columnist is as high on the evolutionary scale as a tick?"

"It's really inappropriate for him to refer to your personal life," Anne said.

"That's putting it mildly. And it tops my list of things I'd never want to talk about with Daniel Perry."

I brushed my eyebrows into shape, but it was a futile effort. My eyebrows angled downward just enough to resist the lovely arch most women could achieve. And my brows are blondish, so brow powders or pencils stood out in a bad way, yet not adding any color for *oomph* made them fade away if the rest of my face was made-up. Alas, life is unfair.

Anne had perfect eyebrows. Brunette, with a natural apex that aligned with her outer irises. She is also fair skinned, has no freckles thanks to her Italian roots, and she could drink more than one cocktail without becoming stupid. I envied that quality. Ravenna could drink well too. And she too had great brows, thick and dark, thanks to Moroccan genes in her French lineage. Furthermore, both Anne and Ravenna could get terrifically tan with little effort, while an hour in the sun turned me into a speckled lobster.

"It's good you said something to him, Amanda." Anne air-toasted me as a sign of support.

"I had to."

"That asshole shouldn't feel free to order you to bring a date anywhere. After all my years in corporate America, trust me, that'd be a serious HR violation. He crossed the line."

"Daniel Perry would have to look up *line* in the dictionary," I said. "He has no sense of boundaries."

"You know what else I was thinking about? How did he hear about Paul, anyway?"

"That's been bothering me all day," I said, applying a coat of mascara. "I guess word gets around, but Mia wouldn't talk about me. Certainly never with Daniel Perry."

"Did you tell her about Paul?"

"Come to think of it, no." I held up a big, fluffy powder brush like a baton. "And John Mayes doesn't know anything. Eww, it's creeping me out that Daniel mentioned Paul."

"Yeah," Anne said with a laugh, "and he doesn't know your rules about not mixing your worlds."

"He does now," I said with a laugh.

"You didn't," Anne said.

"I did. He probably thinks I'm a certified nutcase, but screw him. My worlds theory works."

"Guess what," Anne said as she took another sip, "Charlie called me."

I stopped makeup-ing and leaned out of the bathroom.

"This morning," she said. "At work."

Charlie was Anne's most recent guy. They were hot and heavy for a good while. After a few months she tried to have the "where is this going?" conversation with him and, as a result, she hadn't heard from him in a month.

"Wow," I said. This was quite a development. "What did he say?"

"It involves you, actually."

"Me? How?"

"Well," Anne said, kicking off her shoes and pulling her legs under her, "he said he'd been doing a lot of thinking. He said he panicked when I mentioned your theory of the big three."

"You didn't," I said.

"I did."

"Anne, you never told me that. Are you crazy? You can't mention the big three to a guy. Of course he ran away!"

Anne set her beer on the bedside table and smashed her face into a pillow. "I know!" she said, her voice muffled. She turned over and looked at the ceiling. "I didn't tell him he was one of my three. Your stupid theory just came up in conversation." She extended her arm to reach for her beer. I walked over and handed it to her.

"One, it's not technically my theory. Two, you can't talk about it in the same conversation where you're asking about your future. Three, I wouldn't call it stupid."

"I know," she said, "but I didn't bring it up right then to connect it to my future with Charlie. Argh, I'm an idiot!"

I couldn't help but laugh. "It doesn't matter. Guys don't distinguish between subjects. They lump everything together and assume you want a ring."

"Yeah, well, that's what Charlie did," Anne said. "He apologized and asked if we could pick up where we left off. I told him I'd think about it."

"Good for you," I said. "Make him sweat it."

I returned to the bathroom to continue putting on my face.

"I'm happy he called, though," Anne said, smiling to herself.

This was the soft Anne, and I was the only person who got to see it, other than her boyfriends, with whom she could be the occasional doormat. For all Anne's strength, she had a particular weakness for dismissive men. The old state of wanting that which we cannot have. Nobody would guess it about Anne, but when she really liked a guy, he could walk all over her.

Again I leaned my head out of the bathroom. "I'm happy too. I can see you together."

"So you're good with taking Paul to the benefit tonight?" Anne's abrupt change of subject caught me off guard.

"Sure," I said.

"Just checking."

Anne finished her beer and set the bottle on the table.

"Why do you ask?"

"It's been a big week for you," she said. "Like, you're dating Timothy and really happy about it, but you've also been upset that you've barely spoken since you last saw each other. Then Paul shows up like something out of a movie. You've got Daniel Perry breathing down your neck, and all the pressure of covering the benefit tonight. And—"

"And...?"

"Nothing," Anne said, waving casually.

I gave her a look that said *talk*.

"Maybe Steven is on your mind too," she said.

I pulled my head back into the bathroom.

"Why would you say that?"

"Well, Ravenna mentioned him, and now you're wearing the dress."

"Anne, this dress deserves to be worn."

"Absolutely. It's awesome," she said.

Anne got up from the bed, walked to the bathroom, and then stood in the doorway.

"But I don't know," she continued, "maybe Paul's expectations mixed with Timothy's sort of disappearance has, you know, conjured up some memories."

I turned and leaned against the glass vessel sink, which protruded a couple inches beyond the edge of the vanity.

"I thought of Steven today when Paul and I were out walking." As soon as the words came out of my mouth, I felt better. "He popped in and popped out, but the timing was weird."

"Have you told Paul about him?"

"No way," I said. "And I'm not going to."

"Haven't you two talked about relationships you've had?"

"Not really. You know how guys are." I turned back to the mirror, deciding not to share, at least for now, the story about Paul getting dumped by his girlfriend the night he thanked me in his award speech. "Men prefer to picture women as single. I bet it hasn't even occurred to Paul that I've had serious relationships since him."

"That's not possible," Anne said.

"He made a snide comment about knowing I've 'dated.' But that's only because of what Ravenna told him a couple years ago when they talked in New York."

"Oh," Anne said, nodding. "That guy, William."

"Yeah," I said. "Such a nice guy."

"Such a small dick," Anne said.

I laughed hard.

"Was he Irish?" Anne asked in all seriousness.

I laughed even harder. Just as Anne had her own system of determining what a couple's child would look like, she had a similar method regarding penis size and nationality.

Anne shrugged and let her question go unanswered. She stepped into the bathroom and leaned toward the mirror to inspect her pores.

"He must know you've had relationships," she said.

"Maybe," I said.

"Why not just tell him? Shatter the fantasy."

"Because it's not his business."

"But," Anne looked at me via our reflections in the mirror, "Steven wasn't just any relationship. And it was only a year ago."

"I know."

"And this thing with Timothy could get serious," Anne added. "It's already on its way."

"There's no point in talking about this, Anne. I just want to have fun and live in the now."

"Good idea," she said. We smiled at each other in the mirror. "Hand me that blush."

16

. . .

The driver pulled up in front of Percy Hall. Paul said, "Here we go," and then got out. He walked around the car, opened my door, took my hand, stood back, and said, "You look spectacular."

"So do you," I said. I'd never seen Paul look so polished.

I handed my invitation to a tuxedoed man inside the front door and allowed Paul's hand on my back to gently lead me past the small, unadorned foyer, through the more impressive lobby, and finally into the grand ballroom, which had been decorated to the nines. I knew little about event planning but I recognized a remarkable transformation of a space when I saw one. Percy Hall was a prime location for sizable functions, but its antiquated decor—if one could call old fleur-de-lis burgundy wallpaper, white wainscoting, tiny crystal sconces and brass chandeliers dispropor-tionately small for the space "decor"—required serious bucks to facelift it when occasions called for a modern, or truly impressive, aesthetic.

"Wow," Paul said, taking in the magnitude of the gala.

"This is gorgeous," I said.

Mrs. Emily Richmond and her cohorts hadn't spared any expense for the benefit. A room that had been built to suit the tastes of turn of the century (twentieth, not twenty-first) upper crusters was now contemporary but opulent. Swaths of cream fabric covered every inch of the walls and ceiling. Percy Hall's chandeliers had been replaced with simple but enormous white drum shades that hung like clouds. The crystal sconces were gone in favor of simple modern sconces with no visible bulbs, and each was pressed into the wall fabric, creating a tufted effect. A shiny, espresso-colored parquet floor now covered Percy Hall's original, discolored, scratched wood floor. Interesting flowers, meticulously arranged, perched atop modern pedestals at every wall section, with smaller corresponding arrangements on every table.

The angel and devil who occupied the two halves of my brain were already arguing. The angel insisted the beauty of the event was an inspiration to fight worldwide famine, while the devil reminded me that famine was hardly the topic on the mind of anyone gazing at—and grazing on—the enormous amounts of food and drink.

There was a surprising mix of people. Young and old, black tie and cocktail attire and after-work suits, rich and not-as-rich. The benefit had been highly publicized, due in part to my review of the *Go Green!* event.

I recognized a few faces as Paul and I made our way toward one of the bars. I didn't know Mrs. Richmond, but she obviously knew me, and I feared she would materialize suddenly and ruin the special feeling of the evening thus far. Some people could do that, ruin a lovely time with their mere existence. Still, I was much happier than I thought I'd be. It felt grand to be there with Paul.

I introduced him to a few people. All the ladies warmed to him immediately. Nothing new there. Paul had an infectious smile and, it bears repeating, he looked dashing, like a softer version of James Bond. We fell into conversation with a group of thirty-somethings, one of whom had overheard Paul talking about the music business with a seventy-something moments before. I didn't know the group of people with whom we were speaking, but a few of them recognized me from my picture in the paper.

"Music isn't big here," one guy said to Paul. "Production, anyway," he added.

"Yeah, it's still pretty much split between LA and New York," Paul said. "But technology is changing that. I could edit songs in Boise if I wanted to. Or here," Paul added, squeezing my hand for all to see. "With the right setup, you can master an album anywhere."

The group of listeners started to grow. This was not a city of music producers, and Paul basked in the attention.

"Amanda," someone said behind me. I turned to see John Mayes. He had an attractive woman on his arm. "Susan Marshall, this is Amanda Morgan."

"Very nice to meet you," I said, shaking Susan's hand.

"You too," she said. "John's told me so much about you, I feel like I already know you!"

"All good things, I hope." I winked at John.

"Oh yes," Susan said. "He told me you're part of the series he's doing," she elbowed him, "about how hard it is for guys to date. Like that's really the case!"

"You'd be surprised," I said. John looked rather dashing too, I couldn't help but notice. John was certainly attractive but I had never seen him dressed up. Ask anyone to describe what a typical reporter looks like, they'd describe the daily garb of John Mayes: khakis, white button-down shirt, comfortable shoes. "What brings you two here?"

"Susan is very involved in charitable endeavors," John said.

"I try," Susan said. "It's never-ending, you know. There's always a cause to get behind."

A burst of laughter came from Paul's group of admirers standing behind us.

"So that's the long-lost boyfriend?" John asked.

"Oh, uh, yes." I was unsure how to respond to the *B* word. John's face held an expression I couldn't read.

I turned and popped my head into the group to say I would steal Paul for only a moment.

"Heard a lot about you," John said while shaking Paul's hand.

"You too," Paul said. He then shook Susan's hand.

"So you're a music producer?" Susan asked, as though she were meeting a real-life wizard.

"Yes," Paul responded. "Excuse me, would you?" Paul turned back to the group.

Silence fell over John, Susan, and me in the wake of Paul's sudden departure from the conversation. I was appalled but I didn't say so aloud.

"Well," John said, sliding his hands in his pockets. "I think we'll wander around?" he said to Susan.

"Wait," I said to John, "do you know which one is Mrs. Richmond?"

"No. But don't worry, I'm sure she'll find you." John patted my shoulder.

Susan trotted off to say hello to a couple nearby and John followed her. He briefly turned back and gave me the "perfect" hand gesture, referring to my appearance. I reciprocated with a thumbs-up, referring to his tux and his date.

When I turned back to the group, Paul was still answering questions about his work. I had heard it all before—how he got started in the business, the backbreaking rise from gofer cleaning ashtrays and fetching sandwiches, to assistant, to learning the business from the inside out. I had not only heard it, I had lived it. I was there for the early years. I had talked him down from the proverbial ledge during his countless anxiety attacks. I had talked him out of quitting more times than I could count. I did much of it via phone from three thousand miles away. I was proud of Paul's success, but his rudeness to John and Susan was unforgivable, and it left me cold. And not a little pissed off. Nonetheless, I allowed Paul to slide his arm around my waist as the people continued to admire him and hang on his every word.

"Well, if it isn't Amanda Morgan," a woman's voice said.

I turned to see a stately older woman.

"Hello there," I said with a smile.

The woman waited while I suffered the distinct social embarrassment of not knowing someone's name. Tiny threads in her Chanel cocktail suit glistened, her classic red lipstick was strong but not overpowering to her face, and her shoulder-length blond hair didn't move. She was the quintessential woman of society.

"I wanted to make your acquaintance," she said with a lofty accent that hinted at British. "I'm Emily Richmond."

Oh crap.

"Oh! It's lovely to meet you, Mrs. Richmond."

"Yes, well." Emily Richmond offered me a tight smile without loosening her matriarch's posture. She took my arm and said, "Walk with me."

"Of course," I said, feeling afraid, very afraid.

I excused myself from Paul and the group, and allowed Mrs. Richmond to lead me slowly through the ballroom.

"I do hope you received my apology," I said, noting her firm grip on my arm.

"I did, dear, thank you."

"I am truly sorry for offending you. Your charitable work is," I waved my free arm around, "incredible, and I'm afraid perhaps I didn't give it its due credit."

"That's all in the past." She patted my arm. "I must say, I rather enjoy your writings."

"Thank you," I said.

"Oh yes," she said, occasionally waving in a *pshaw* way to random people swirling around the ballroom. "My friends and I always look forward to your column. We talk about it at the salon every week. Relations between men and women these days, so very different than in my day."

"That's probably not a good thing," I said with a laugh.

"There are plusses and minuses, you know. It was simpler then. Expectations were clear."

"I've written about that," I said. "About how it'd be better if people stated their intentions."

"You're right, although there is something to be said for a bit of mystery. Women now can be mysterious because they live independent lives, but lord knows they don't keep anything a secret these days. That's a mistake. In my day, mystery stemmed from not opening one's mouth."

"I completely agree," I said.

I was pleasantly surprised at the tenor of the conversation. I had envisioned my run-in with the infamous Emily Richmond many times since agreeing to cover the benefit, and here I was, enjoying her company.

"Yes," Mrs. Richmond said, "I've noticed you're quite the private woman. I admire that."

"Thank you. I can't say the men in my life have always appreciated it."

"Yes, they do, dear," she said. "Whether or not they know it."

Mrs. Richmond and I neared one of the bars. I asked if she'd like anything to drink.

"Kir Royale," she said.

A minute later Emily Richmond accepted her drink. She tasted it and nodded in approval, and then she introduced me to some of her friends. They mentioned my column, complimented my dress, and wandered off.

"So tell me," Mrs. Richmond said in a hushed tone reserved for lady talk, "is that your someone?" She tilted her flute in Paul's general direction.

"Well, uh, yes. For this evening, anyway." I hoped she would get my meaning. Hers was exactly the type of question I wanted to avoid, the whole reason I didn't like to mesh my worlds, at least until I was in a relationship that felt secure. *When was the last time I had that?*

"I see," she said, taking a sip. "Handsome."

"Yes, he is," I said. "I'm not sure he knows it."

"They always know their attributes, dear."

"Even the insecure ones?"

"An insecure man is a waste of time," she said.

I considered that point. She didn't wait for me to agree.

"I thought you might like to meet some of the younger philanthropists who are so active in the city," she said. "These benefits tend to glaze over their efforts in favor of, well, the old guard, but young professionals are instrumental in making all of this happen. They get the word out through the Internet and whatnot. Amazing, technology these days. Over the years it's caused quite a surge in giving. Meeting some of them might help your coverage of the evening. Perhaps spice it up."

"I'd like that, thank you," I said.

Mrs. Emily Richmond again took hold of my arm and walked me toward a group of "younger" people tightly engaged with one another.

She whispered, "I'll be frank with you," as she pointed a finger in the group's direction. "These sons and daughters give almost as much as we do." *We* obviously referred to the richest, older members of society. "The Jamesons, Monroes, you've seen the names."

"Here and there," I said. "I'm afraid I don't really follow the society scene."

"Yes, well."

We neared the group, and their backs were to us, creating a wall of expensive fabric and shellacked hair.

"This one," Mrs. Richmond said quietly, pointing her knuckle at one man, "he came out of nowhere for this benefit and gave a ton. Practically took over the whole thing."

"That's really something," I said, assuming I was supposed to be impressed.

"In fact he was the one who insisted you cover it. Even had me call your editor, Daniel Perry, to secure it."

"Pardon me?"

"Oh yes," Emily Richmond said.

I was suddenly more confused than I had been all week.

"I must confess," Mrs. Richmond said, "I felt rather awkward calling the poor man at home before dawn, but there was too much money at stake. Don't worry, I told him we were delighted to have you. I also promised full-page ads for the next month, but that's between you and me."

Oh. My. God. So Daniel Friggin' Perry had purposely scared me and led me to believe the fearsome Emily Richmond couldn't wait to tan my hide. All the while, she actually wanted me here! Daniel probably thought if he'd told me the truth, I'd get a big head about it.

I whispered to her, "But why would that man, or anyone, want *me*?"

"He must be a fan, dear," she whispered. "You know men. They so adore women with strong opinions."

Ah, a fan. Probably one of the freaks who sent me anonymous, sexually suggestive e-mails. Now it all made sense and the picture was coming together.

"Let me introduce you," she said.

"Of course," I said. *Yes, please introduce me to someone who probably signs his e-mails "Pants-less & Panting."*

Anger about Daniel Perry forced expletives to fly around my head. I might have seemed poised and ladylike on the outside, but inside I was a drunken sailor on a weekend pass.

Mrs. Richmond tapped the shoulder of one of the men in the group and said, "Excuse me, all, I'd like to introduce you to Amanda Morgan."

They all turned simultaneously and it took me a moment to register the man whose shoulder had just been tapped.

"Amanda Morgan," Emily Richmond said, "I'd like to introduce you to the real force behind tonight's event, Steven Jameson."

17
· · ·

There stood Steven with his hand extended to me. I couldn't breathe. I was frozen.

"Well," Mrs. Richmond said, quite pleased with herself, "I'll leave you two to talk."

"Thank you, Emily," Steven said. He leaned down from his six-foot-three height to give Mrs. Richmond a kiss on the cheek.

"This one's special, Amanda," she said. "And Steven, dear, make sure she meets everyone, would you?"

"That's my job," he said, staring directly at me. Mrs. Richmond laughed, patted his cheek, and walked away.

"You're not going to shake my hand," Steven said.

It was Steven. It was really Steven. Steven who had almost become a figment of my imagination, a memory that pulled at my heartstrings even after I stopped loving him. I forced myself to shake his hand, which felt strong and enveloping and immediately reminded me of…everything.

"Get you a drink?" he asked, tilting his head, trying to read me.

I shook my head ever so slightly.

"Not even to throw at me?" he said.

Our handshake had ended, but I could still feel the ghost of his hand wrapped around mine.

"How are you, Amanda?" Steven's voice was assured and he showed no signs of awkwardness. He projected the opposite of everything I felt inside: butterflies, nausea, an inability to think or speak coherently.

I couldn't stop staring at him. I never thought I'd see Steven again. His chocolaty brown eyes were deep and warm. His mousy brown, unfussy hair was thick, and I briefly remembered what it felt like between my fingers.

Pull it together. You imagined this scene a hundred times—what you'd say, how you'd put him in his place, and you wouldn't show how badly he broke your heart.

"I'm great," I finally managed to say.

Steven eyed me up and down. "You certainly are." He took a hefty sip of his amber cocktail without taking his eyes off me. I heard the ice move in his glass as he tipped it to his mouth.

We stared at each other for a good minute. Then I noticed his slightly pursed mouth, a sign that he too was affected by this moment.

"You did all this?" I said.

"The event? Hell no," he said. "I wrote a check."

"I mean, you were the one who insisted I cover this?"

Steven continued to stare down at me. His height had always been a defining characteristic, embodying his large personality. Even his tone of voice wouldn't fit a man of smaller frame, such as Timothy, who despite having a well-defined body, was not tall. Steven's personality wouldn't even suit Paul, who neared six feet. Steven was like a force of nature.

"Emily Richmond said—" I began.

"Okay, yes," Steven said, "I insisted." He straightened his tie and glanced at the floor. These small actions were as close to fidgeting as Steven got.

"Why?" It was all I could ask. In fact, *why?* had been the only question I had wanted to ask Steven for a year.

"I read your last piece, your coverage of that environment

benefit. Good stuff. Funny." He spoke casually but always with a strong tone. "Thought the old guard could use a dose of reality again. Not that famine's not important." Steven rolled his eyes.

"I don't understand," I said.

"C'mere," he said, shifting his posture to say *let's take a walk.*

I looked across the ballroom to find Paul still talking to his group of admirers. He seemed a million miles away. I then looked at Steven and we started to walk. The floor seemed unbalanced and all the people and perfume and hairspray made me feel like I might fall. I focused on my steps and sensed Steven walking behind me as we headed across the ballroom toward the lobby.

• • •

After exiting the ballroom, I could breathe a bit easier, but only a bit. Steven's presence was overwhelming. I was relieved when I saw a grouping of red velvet, throne-like chairs.

"I need to sit down," I said, already beginning to sit.

Steven remained standing, staring down at me.

"So how ya doin'?" he asked.

"There's only so long you can stand in these heels," I lied, trying to be casual, when casual was the last thing in the world I felt.

Steven had one hand in his pocket. With the other, he set his drink on a nearby table. He was exactly as I remembered him. His air was powerful even when he was silent. Unlike Paul, whose soppy nature weakened his presence, at least to someone who knew him as well as I did. And Steven was unlike Timothy, whose energy was positive and friendly. Steven was intense. All three men were well educated, but Steven was by far the most intelligent: fiercely smart, lightning quick, and with a biting wit.

Timothy would be put off to know I felt that way, since his

MIT education was a huge source of pride for him, and he seemed to rely on it to impress people. Paul would certainly be envious, because his nature was to feel overshadowed by people, particularly in my estimation of them. But I knew Steven could probably master any field. Yet he was "just a money guy," as he used to refer to himself, with a "run-of-the-mill MBA." Truth was, he was a business whiz who made his first million by the age of twenty-five, while he was still in graduate school.

"Sitting or standing, those heels work," he said.

"Steven," I said, pulling myself together. "I don't understand any of this." I looked across the lobby toward the ballroom door. "And I can't stay out here talking to you."

"You're here with someone," he said.

"Yes."

"The guy from California," he said matter-of-factly. "The old ex." Obviously he remembered Paul from old photos we'd shared.

"New York, actually," I corrected him with impatience.

"Okay, look," Steven said, stepping over my crossed legs to sit in the chair next to mine. "I didn't know how to see you again. I tried to find you, but you moved."

"What are you talking about? You know where I work. You have my number. I didn't change it."

"I know," he said. "I called."

"When?"

"A few months ago. I heard you on the radio. I knew you wouldn't be answering your phone right then, so I called to see if the number had changed. When your voicemail picked up, I hung up."

"What did you want?"

Steven didn't respond.

"What do you want?"

Steven didn't speak. Instead he settled his deep brown eyes on mine.

"Fine," I said, steeling myself. "You're not going to talk, then I'll talk. I don't understand this. I can't even begin to try. You dump me, over the phone, with no explanation, the day before our trip. My birthday trip. Then," I felt tears welling up but I held them at bay, "I never heard from you again."

"I know," Steven said quietly. His soft tone cut a small incision in my heart.

"What do you know? You don't know anything. You crushed me."

"I know." His voice cracked a little.

"I kept thinking, 'what did I do?'"

"I know," he said quietly.

"You begged me to go on that trip." My voice was growing in intensity, powered by old hurt and anger. "You knew I was hesitant, but you persisted until I finally said yes."

"I know," he said.

I lowered my voice as people walked by.

"You knew my rule," I whispered hard. "Don't make plans to spend your birthday with a guy unless it's serious."

"I remember," he nodded with his head hanging down.

"And why did I have that rule? Because they *will* disappoint you. And that's coming from a romantic!"

Steven looked at the floor and smiled to himself. "I know you are. That's what I loved about you."

"Excuse me?"

Steven leaned toward me until his face was inches from mine.

"That's what I loved about you," he said gently. "I should have said it before."

I fell back into the velvet chair. This was the moment women dream about that never actually happens.

"Yes, you should have," I said.

"Amanda—"

"I never said it either," I admitted. "But you knew it. And you still vanished."

"I know," he said.

"No, first you called me, cold as ice, said we needed to talk, and five minutes later we were over."

Steven rubbed his forehead, then his mouth. "I know."

"Sure, you know." I nodded sadly, remembering my heartbreak, the worst I'd ever felt. Getting over Steven was one of the hardest things, romantic or otherwise, I'd ever experienced in my life. For a long time afterward I truly believed I would never fall in love again. Months later I met Timothy and he had been like a ray of sunlight.

"Do you know where I spent my birthday?" I asked.

"Don't remind me," he said.

"I can't remind you, because you never knew it to forget it. And why? Because I haven't spoken to you since that day."

Just then I noticed a boisterous group, led by Paul, exiting the ballroom. He noticed me across the lobby and waved. I waved back, and even at that distance I could see Paul's observant expression; he noticed I was talking intimately with a man.

Steven turned to follow my eyes and saw the group moving slowly in our direction. He quickly turned back to me. "We can't talk here, Amanda. I need to explain all this," he said, staring into my eyes. "You deserve it."

Damn right, I deserved an explanation. Steven had never struck me as a man who made grand gestures. Bankrolling, or even attending, major society benefits was not his style.

"Your boyfriend is coming over," he said with a smirk.

"He's not my boyfriend. And he doesn't know about you, so don't say anything," I whispered so hard it hurt my throat. I surprised myself by stressing that Paul was not my boyfriend. I hadn't been so definite about our relationship a day earlier in Daniel Perry's office, or to Emily Richmond, yet here I was making sure Steven didn't think I was taken.

"Can I see you again?" Steven's face was as pleading as it could get. He looked rushed and almost desperate. I stood and smoothed my dress. Steven also stood, looked at the group closing in on us, and then said, "Don't say no."

"You're a bastard," I said, feeling like I just got a B12 shot.

"I know," he said.

"You haven't said anything, sitting here."

"I didn't think you'd be here with somebody. Please, Amanda. Can I see you?"

Steven's manner was so point-blank. So matter-of-fact. I hated it because it was an extreme turn-on. I smiled at Paul as he neared.

"Fine," I said, almost as an aside. "Call me." I stepped past Steven and brushed against his arm. I felt something akin to an electric shock.

"That dress is really something," he whispered. I could feel his voice wash over my skin.

"It should be," I said through a fake smile. "I bought it for you."

A few feet away Paul shook the hand of everyone in the group and wished them a good night before turning in my direction. Steven and I stood in silence, he with his hands in his pockets, me clutching my purse.

"Hi, beautiful," Paul said, kissing me on the cheek. "Hey there," he said, extending his hand to Steven.

"Hi," Steven said. He gave Paul a quick, firm shake.

Paul and Steven locked eyes in a testosterone-charged moment.

"Looks like you made some new friends," I said to Paul.

"Yeah, nice people at this thing." Paul's eyes darted between Steven and me.

"You two haven't met," I said. "Paul, this is—"

"Steven Jameson," Steven offered.

"Steven, good to meet you. Paul Smith."

"Like the brand," Steven said.

"Huh?" Designers' names were lost on Paul, despite his labeled wardrobe.

"Forget it," Steven said.

I could not imagine a more awkward moment. The two biggest loves of my life shaking hands, staring each other down. Although Paul had just kissed my cheek, I could sense Steven next to me, actually feel his presence.

"Well," Steven said with a loud clap of his hands, "time for me to go beddy-bye." He reached down to the table for his drink.

Paul laughed and held up his watch for Steven to see. "It's eight-thirty," he said.

"I need my beauty sleep," Steven said.

"Paul," I said, "Steven is one of the main organizers of the benefit."

"Oh, yeah? Great job," Paul said.

"Amanda gives me too much credit," Steven said.

"Does she," Paul said.

"I'm just a giver," Steven said. "Love to give."

"Well," Paul said, trying to size up Steven. "I guess we should let you go."

"Good meeting you, Paul." Steven shook his hand again. "Amanda, I'll be in touch." He nodded once to me and walked away.

The air changed after Steven left. The room felt lighter, like gravity had been lifted.

18

. . .

Paul escorted me back into the ballroom, where I spent a half hour schmoozing with Emily Richmond and her friends. Paul made a great impression; he was warm, complimentary, and friendly while keeping his arm tightly around my waist.

When we finally walked out of Percy Hall, I knew my job had been completed precisely as Daniel Perry had ordered me to do it. I thought briefly of Terry and wondered how his flu was treating him, and how everything would feel different—would *be* different—if he had been able to attend.

As Paul and I waited for the car, I remembered Terry's health status wouldn't have made a difference because apparently Steven would have made certain I attended the benefit.

"I can't believe I'm leaving tomorrow," Paul said, nuzzling my neck.

"It's been quite a week," I said.

"Should I stay at your place tonight?" Paul asked my neck.

"My place?"

"I'm not expecting anything, Amanda. I just want more time together."

"What time is your train tomorrow?"

Paul scoffed and said, "I see." The car pulled up directly in front of us. The driver got out to come around and open our door, but Paul waved him away, opened the car door, and stepped back so I could get in. But I didn't get in. I stood firm and stared at Paul.

"Whoa," I said, "what did I miss? Why are you suddenly mad? I only asked about your train."

"I know what's going on here," he said. "You don't want me to come over."

"What? Paul, no. Though I'm not sure we should spend the night together."

"Something was going on in there with that guy. Obviously I interrupted something."

"No, you didn't," I said. "You know this night was important for me. There was all this pressure riding on it. Can't I talk to one of the hosts without being accused of something?" I hated to use both my job pressure and Steven's role as benefactor as crutches, but when you're feeling unsteady you'll lean on whatever is nearby.

"Something was going on, Amanda. You two know each other?"

"Yes," I said with a sigh. "I know him."

"Uh-huh." Paul nodded to himself.

"So now you're going to snit?" I felt something brewing inside me. Paul tensed and sucked his teeth.

"I haven't done anything wrong here," I said, my voice unintentionally rising in volume. "You were unforgivably rude to my friend, John, and his date. Do you know how embarrassing that was for me? Then, when you finally decided to stop basking in glory, you came to find me, and now you're mad because I'm completely exhausted and unsure if we should spend the night together? I haven't seen you in years, and you're crazy if you think you can just knock on my door, flash your smile, and get me in bed."

I hadn't meant to unload like that, but it felt good. First I got to call Steven a bastard, now I got to empty some rounds on Paul. I took a deep breath and waited for Paul to fight back. That was our routine, after all, a wonderful evening turned sour because he got unjustifiably mad about something. I noticed Paul was grinning.

"What?" I snapped.

"I just fell in love with you all over again," he said.

Paul took two steps, grabbed me, and kissed me hard. I didn't fight it. I put every ounce of anger and exhaustion and confusion and excitement and pressure into it. The evening air had cooled and my arms felt a chill. But our kiss was hot, literally. It was forceful and passionate and absolutely fantastic, to use Paul's very LA word. I didn't want to argue or talk. Sometimes you need to shut up and kiss.

Paul and I made out in front of everyone entering and leaving Percy Hall, and I didn't care. It was the exact opposite of how I expected, or wanted, the evening to go, but sometimes that's how life plays out.

Paul didn't end up spending the night. He smiled lazily at me during the entire drive to my place, and then walked me to my door. He told me he loved me. He told me he'd call me in the morning and, if there was enough time, he would say goodbye in person. He promised we would see each other again very soon. He apologized for being rude to John and his date. He told me I looked amazing. He said our kiss had left him with a foggy head and he would be thinking about it all night. He said everything a man says when he is about to leave you.

• • •

I walked inside my place, threw the bolt, dropped my purse, kicked off my shoes, and headed upstairs to get out of my dress and wash my face. I put on a T-shirt and boxers—Timothy's boxers, left at my place the last time he visited. I went into the bathroom, turned on the water, and waited for it to get hot as I examined my face in the mirror.

My lips were swollen from the kiss with Paul. I expected my

skin to be chafed too, but Paul had been perfectly clean-shaven. I reminded myself it was Timothy's any-o'clock scruff that always left its mark. After all, he was the only other man I'd kissed in months. But Timothy wasn't on my mind as the steam from the tap started to rise. Steven wasn't on my mind either. Nor was Paul.

For the first time all week, no man occupied my thoughts. I breathed in steam and washed my face with gusto, twice, to make sure all traces of makeup were gone. By the time I pressed a towel against my face, my skin felt tight and squeaky-clean. I shuffled downstairs to the living room, grabbed the phone off the charger, and called Anne. I wasn't in the mood to talk, which was the first thing I said to her, but I gave her a quick summary of the night. After we hung up, I texted Ravenna to say: Anne has the story, I'm beat, talk tomorrow.

I hadn't looked at my cell phone since leaving my house hours earlier. If calls or texts had come in during the benefit, I wouldn't have heard any ringing or pinging. The week was replete with men, drama, big decisions, socialites, stress, a dress, and subterfuge from both Steven and Daniel Perry. I needed a break.

I put my feet up on the coffee table and noticed the wound on my leg was just about gone. Interesting how trauma disappears, only to be replaced by new trauma. My computer dinged, alerting me to new e-mail. My laptop seemed far away, even though it was just on the glass end table next to my sofa. I tried to return to my aimless mental drifting but the sound of new e-mail is a siren call.

I rolled across my sofa and grabbed my computer, placing it on my lap as I rolled back into position. Among the new messages in my inbox were notes from Terry, letting me know his flu was on the mend; John Mayes, saying how nice I had looked tonight and how happy his date, Susan Marshall, was to have met me; Paul, telling me he was sitting in his hotel room thinking about me and our kiss, and how he'd be damned if he'd leave town tomorrow without seeing me; and Timothy, letting me know he was back home in DC and he had so much to tell me and he couldn't wait to talk that weekend.

I was happy to see Timothy's name in my inbox but I also felt something else. *Deflation?* One cannot rightly go from a Saturday night alone, flipping through magazines, to intense emotional reunions with long-lost loves and not feel the weight of it. That made sense, of course, but I knew it wasn't the core of my problem.

At the core was Steven. And Daniel Perry. I had been manipulated by both of them and left to fend for myself. Dropped in the jungle, in high heels, with nary a toothpick to fashion an escape. My closest friends knew Steven was the most intense love, and heartbreak, of my life. Steven seemed to know it too, which weighed on me.

Truth was, I didn't have only leftover anger at Steven. I was presently irate that his covert plan had landed me in the glass cage with my despicable boss. Unintentionally, but still. I was also irate about Daniel Perry using his power to coerce me into covering the benefit, and convincing me I had to kiss Emily Richmond's ass, even though she turned out to be not so scary a broad after all. Her family business was a local empire—department stores, railroads, real estate—so she'd certainly had brutal run-ins with the media that would dwarf a little columnist like me. How could I not see all of it before?

I decided to write my piece about the benefit while it was still clear in my mind, because who knew what tomorrow would bring. Paul in person, Timothy via phone, and perhaps Steven as well, in what form I couldn't predict.

As I began to write the piece, I thought *screw Daniel Perry.* I would take Mia's advice and put my own twist on it. That's what readers wanted and expected, after all, and that's what I needed to do. I settled on the title, *A Feast For Famine*, and let it rip.

19

· · ·

I woke up Friday morning with energy and motivation. I called Ravenna during my drive downtown to the newspaper, and we agreed to meet after work. She was nearly finished supervising a small gallery's grand opening and she needed a break from the "impotence"—her version of "incompetence"—of the gallery's employees. She said *fok* at least five times in the conversation, and I was still laughing by the time I parallel-parked outside the paper.

As I searched for quarters for the meter, I thought it might be fun to write a piece about the English language, how it often sounded much better when spoken by a non-native. Then I figured William Safire and countless others probably beat me to it years ago. I got a text from Paul as I put the sixth quarter in the meter. I was rarely inclined to calculate how much time you got per quarter but years of experience said thirty-seven seconds. Paul said he'd meet me at the paper in an hour, which would give us a bit of time before his train departed for New York.

An hour was the perfect amount of time to do what I intended to do: face off with Daniel Perry. I was freelance, after all. He didn't control me! So they gave me a desk, so what? I had my own desk. Hell, my own office! If Daniel fired me, tough! I'd found jobs before, I'd do it again. I had a good rapport with editors from other newspapers and magazines. I'd knock on their doors, schmooze them up, buy them eggs Benedict, and convince them to run my column. Or I could publish one of my books, yes! I had several books in the pipeline and getting the ax would be just the motivation I needed to finish one or all of them and move on from this cesspool of inequity and underpayment. I'd be my own boss and never again answer to the Daniel Perrys of the world!

On my desk was a note from Mia asking me to stop by. I was fixed on having my standoff with Daniel Perry, but when I looked over to the glass cage, I saw he wasn't there. I headed over to Mia.

"Well?" I said.

"Love it," she said. "Love, love, love it. This is better than the last one."

"Thanks." It felt good to get a compliment from Mia since I respected her very much. She was among a small number of editors who were also great writers.

"*A Feast For Famine*, I love that," she said, then began reading my draft. "'Mounds of Ahi sashimi, oysters on the half-shell, and shrimp cocktail are just the right aphrodisiac to get people in the mood—to give.' The benefit people are going to flip. Ninety percent of the way through I'm still thinking you're going to let'em have it, but you found a way to support the idea without gratuitously applauding it. You missed your calling."

"What can I say, I was inspired." My eyes fixed on Daniel's office.

"I can't believe you got this done already," Mia said. "You're like a machine."

I smiled. *Yes, I am a machine. A thresher about to rip up Daniel Perry.*

"Seen Daniel this morning?"

"Don't worry," she said, "you won't have to face His Majesty's wrath. He's in DC."

"What? He's not here?"

"No," Mia said, confused at my apparent disappointment over Daniel's absence. "He's interviewing the Treasury secretary. It's a pretty big story. I guess they went to grad school together or something."

"Oh," I said.

Shit. Shit. Shit. Shit. Shit.

"Am I crazy?" Mia asked rhetorically. "You seem disappointed."

"I just expected I'd have to defend this," I pointed to my article, "and I had my argument all worked out." Good lie. Mia smiled at my gumption.

"Guess you have to save it for Monday," she said, then rolled her chair around to her desk to get back to work.

So Daniel Perry was in DC. The coward. Treasury secretary, my foot. He suspected I would find out Mrs. Richmond wanted me to attend the benefit, and he had tucked tail and ran. I spent a few moments enjoying his cowardice before snapping back to reality.

Hearing the mention of DC reminded me to e-mail Timothy and welcome him home. How long had it been since we'd spoken? Two weeks? My internal calendar was wonky and I couldn't remember. Then I remembered Paul would be stopping by soon. It would be hard to say goodbye to him, but knowing he was in New York, rather than LA, made the parting easier. We had said goodbye so many times over the years, but this time felt different. Not as heavy or dramatic as in the past.

"Hey, girl." A man's voice startled me and I swiveled my chair.

"Terry! How are you feeling?"

"All better," he coughed.

"It's nice to see you," I said.

"You too. And good to know you took my advice." He raised an eyebrow.

"Your advice?"

"I told you fancy parties are great for make-outs. Mmm, hmm, yes I did."

"How did you hear?"

"Girl, you can't suck face outside of Percy Hall, in front of all of society, without me hearing about it. I was like, 'you go girl!' I still say the coatroom is hotter but you're one of those exhibitionists, I guess."

I blushed thinking everyone knew about my kiss with Paul, but I had done more embarrassing things in my life. I supposed this news was the silver lining to Daniel Perry's being out of town. At least he probably hadn't heard about my public display of lip-locking.

"Terry, let me ask you a question."

"Sure."

"I didn't tell you about him, did I?"

"Your make-out man? No."

"Hmm." I chewed on a pencil that wasn't mine, then realized it, then threw it a four-desk distance. The newsroom was so empty from staff cuts, the projectile pencil didn't hit anyone.

"Why?"

"I've been trying to figure out how Daniel knew about him," I said quietly.

"I don't know. I haven't been here, remember. Hey, let's get some coffee," he said.

"Nah, I'm on a coffee hiatus." Caffeine was the last thing I needed.

"Herbal tea, then. My treat. We have to catch up. I want to hear all about this man of yours."

"Why not," I said.

I threw my screensaver on and grabbed my purse just as my phone pinged, signaling a text message. I knew it would be Paul saying he was on his way. But to my utter shock it was from Steven: You looked f'n amazing last night. Can't get you out of my head. Call you later.

My heart stopped. My breathing stopped. Terry and I walked toward the elevator but I could barely put one foot in front of the other. They were merely words on a cell phone screen but I could feel Steven behind them. Suddenly he was all I could see, all I could think of. So much for that morning's vigor and strength. Three sentences from Steven and I was a goner.

• • •

Grabbing tea with Terry turned out to be a longer endeavor than I had anticipated. I made numerous attempts to speed him up and head back upstairs, but he didn't take the hints. Finally I told him that Paul was meeting me at the paper to say goodbye before he left, but Terry kept talking. The flu had kept him out of the loop for more than a week, an eternity for a social butterfly. He said knowing I was covering both benefits gave him peace of mind and he owed me big, and he wouldn't let me get away with not giving him every saucy detail.

I told him about Paul without getting into detail about our long history. The text message from Steven had thoughts circling in my brain like planes trying to land at a busy airport.

"Wait," Terry said. "He's in the music business? I thought he was an architect."

"The architect is the guy I'm seeing now, Timothy."

Terry dramatically raised one eyebrow and laughed to himself.

"He doesn't live here," I added.

"He's in New York, right?" Terry dumped two sugars into his second cup of coffee.

"No, Paul is in New York. Timothy is in DC."

"Anyone here?" Terry asked.

"No." I shrugged. What else could I say? I certainly couldn't count Steven among men I "had." At least Timothy and I were a regular item, actually dating, probably close to commitment.

Before Paul's appearance at my door almost a week ago, my life was simple. I was dating a guy I was pretty crazy about, and he was pretty crazy about me, but we hadn't really talked since our last visit *and* he went to Scotland without calling me the whole time *and* I had been wondering if his busyness would ultimately spell our end. But that's normal, run-of-the-mill dating.

Now, a week later, I had enormous matters to contend with. Paul back in my life—to what degree, though, I wasn't sure. Steven back in my life—to what degree, though, I wasn't sure. Everything was up in the air. Part of me missed the simplicity of life without romantic drama; friends, work, waiting to hear from Timothy, and seeing where we'd go. That's the kind of stuff I wrote about—regular life, dating, relationships, work—and the kind of stuff I was comfortable thinking about. "I don't want any more drama," I nearly yelled without realizing it.

Terry looked at me with understanding, but he said nothing. I looked at my watch and knew Paul must be waiting at the security desk. The security guard surely would have called up to my desk, and when he got no answer, he would have told Paul to wait. Paul wouldn't dare text or call my cell because he would assume I was locked in the glass cage with Daniel.

"Terry, I hate to do this, but I really have to go," I said.

Terry looked at his brightly colored Swatch and agreed it was time to make our way upstairs. In the elevator he said, "You got some big decisions to make." He rubbed my back.

"What do you mean?" I asked.

"I can just tell," Terry said.

When Terry and I stepped off the elevator, the newsroom had

been transformed. Everyone, including employees I didn't recognize, was standing, grouped together, clapping, under a banner that read *Will You Marry Me?*

Terry hugged me as I noticed Paul standing in the middle of the group. He walked toward me as everyone clapped behind him. He was smiling, his face bright with excitement. In retrospect I probably sounded like people in design makeover shows whose only comment upon seeing the finished renovation of their home was "Oh...my...God," but it's the only phrase that came out. After more clapping and woo-hoo-ing the group quieted and Paul stood before me with a dark green velvet box in his hand.

"I thought this would be a more memorable goodbye than grabbing coffee," he said.

I was stunned. I smiled as a reflex, but I was stunned.

"Well," Paul said to me as he looked around at everyone, "say something."

"Is this because I wouldn't let you spend the night?" I asked quietly. Everyone laughed.

"No," Paul laughed, "it's because I love you."

He opened the box to reveal a beautiful antique ring.

"But you're leaving today," I said.

"I don't have to," he said sweetly. A collective *aww* filled the room and some of the women put a hand to their chests, swooning in the moment.

"I...I...don't know what to say."

Paul looked around at the group. "How about yes," he said. "Make it a big three?" he whispered, referring to the number of yeses he hoped to amass on this trip. Paul couldn't know what those words signaled to me.

"Um," I said as my eyes panned the room, "can we go somewhere and talk?"

Paul took in a deep breath and blew it out hard, then forced a smile. "You need a few minutes, I understand." He turned to the group. "Everyone, thank you so much for stopping the presses and helping me pull off the best surprise in the world. Yeah?" he said to me.

"Oh yeah. This is a surprise, all right," I laughed.

The group disbanded and wandered back to their desks and offices. Paul and I walked to my desk and we sat down, me in my chair, Paul in a chair he rolled over from an unused desk nearby.

"How in the world did you do all of this?" I said.

"I called Mia," he said, rather proud of himself. "Anne helped too."

"My editor?" I couldn't imagine a world where Mia and Paul would intersect.

"I told her who I was and she basically said, 'Sorry pal, Amanda gets calls all the time from guys claiming to know her,' so I had to prove it. I told her all kinds of things only friends would know, and I mentioned Anne and Ravenna. I had Anne call her too. That's when she believed me."

"Of course," I said. "I forgot Anne and Mia know each other." Anne had done some design work for the paper a few times when two staff designers split without warning. I had arranged the contract work because it made sense, in the end, since a few of the major local advertisers were clients of Anne's firm.

"So?" Paul said.

"Let's talk outside," I said.

We walked across the newsroom together past many watchful eyes. Outside the sun warmed me up from a chill I hadn't noticed until it started to disappear. Hand in hand, we crossed the street to a plaza with benches and pigeons gathered around an oxidized statue of a man on a horse. For a million dollars I couldn't tell you who the man was. Nice-looking horse, though.

"Paul," I said, looking into his beautiful blue eyes, which were darker today than yesterday. "This is so incredible. You're incredible." I placed a hand on his cheek.

"But," he said, taking my hand in his, "you're saying no."

"I'm not saying no. I'm saying we're just getting to know each other again."

"I know everything I need to know, Amanda. This is what I've wanted since maybe our third date. Believe me, I know I've screwed up a lot, but I don't want to make any more mistakes with you. I don't even care about that guy from last night."

Damn it, why did he have to mention Steven?

"Paul, I need—"

"To think," he completed my sentence. "I knew you'd say that. Just tell me, is it because of that guy?"

"No, I promise. This is a lot to take in. I just need to think."

"Take this while you think about it." Paul opened the box and placed the ring on my finger.

"It is so beautiful," I said.

"I got it in France."

"France?"

During one of our conversations over the past week Paul mentioned a work trip to France six months ago.

"I told you," he grinned, "I've always known what I want."

Paul and I kissed as he squeezed my ring hand. It felt powerful, his hand around mine, the ring around my finger, the sun, the kiss, all of it.

"Don't think too long," Paul said, walking away. "I'll call you when I get in."

20

. . .

I left the paper early because I was useless for work. Plus, everyone was watching me. My work and personal worlds had collided. I never saw the movie *War of The Worlds* but I felt like I could be the star of it. I was uncertain about what answer to give Paul, and I felt terrible that Steven had popped into my head even before Paul mentioned him.

I tried to clear my mind by driving around the city, but it was useless. I drove home and parked my car in front of my place. Instead of going inside I started to walk, going almost a half hour without noticing, to see Ravenna at the gallery she was helping to open. The gallery's neighborhood had been on the upswing for some time and it was uplifting to see a rundown area transforming itself.

I walked through the front door and heard Ravenna before I saw her. *Pull zat up...zis need to be moved...not enough light here... fok!...be careful wis zat*! Ravenna's richly colored clothes and flowing black hair looked like art against the stark white walls. She turned, noticed me, and then said, "Okay, zat's it. My friend is here. Get zis done wissout me."

"I'm sorry, I shouldn't interrupt you," I said, feeling guilty for dropping in unannounced but not guilty enough to leave.

"Are you kidding me?" she said, using one of her favorite phrases. She always said it with such gusto, it seemed like it should hurt her throat. Ravenna turned back to the workers. "I'm leaving to smoke and eat. I don't want one call on zis phone. If you call me, I will sleep wis you and zen you be sorry."

The men smiled, the women looked confused, and everyone got back to work. Sweeping, hanging, nailing, adjusting spotlights, patching, painting, and every other detail that made a gallery ready to be seen by the world.

Ravenna and I walked down the block to a modern outdoor café housed in the first floor of a Deco-inspired row house. The waiter knew her already, of course, and brought espresso for both of us. Ravenna lit a cigarette and held open the pack for me. I took one, she lit it, and I sank back into the bright red, twisted wire chair.

"*Mon amie*, you don't look good." We traded feelings without speaking. We could do that. It was a special bond. "Okay," she continued, "I know everysing except what happen after he propose." I knew Anne had been the source of Ravenna's up-to-date information. "Oh my God," she said as she took my hand to see the ring, "zis is gorgeous."

I nodded in agreement. "He bought it six months ago."

Ravenna raised one eyebrow, and then shrugged. "Paul knows what he wants."

"Apparently," I said.

"Do you?" she asked.

"I should know that, shouldn't I?"

"Zer is no rule zat says you must know. But see, *mon amie*," she tsk tsk'd, "you are wild in your heart but you like some rules. Zey keep you safe."

"I guess I do," I said.

"It is because you are afraid of making zee wrong decision."

"I could just get married!" The *M* word felt odd, though not entirely bad, exiting my mouth.

"Sure," Ravenna said. "People do zis every day."

"What if this is my only chance? I've never been in a rush to get married, but I wonder about it, like any woman. I never even thought seriously about marriage, except, well—"

"Wis Steven," Ravenna said.

"Yes. I thought about marrying Paul a thousand times, but it was always off in the distance, and now it's been so many years."

"Time does funny sings to people," Ravenna said.

"And what about Steven?" Everything was occurring to me at the same moment. "I'm supposed to talk to him tonight. And what about Timothy? We're dating right now!"

Ravenna glanced around to see if my raised voice had attracted attention.

"Look at it zis way," she said. "Forget about Steven and Timothy. If zey did not exist, do you want Paul?"

"I can't forget about them!"

"Okay, okay." Ravenna patted my hand. "But zen you have your answer, yes? If zis were a question to answer in your column, you would say a person can be sure when no other love feels important."

Ravenna had a way of simplifying everything.

"Tell me what is going on wis Timothy," she said.

"We're supposed to talk this weekend. I'll ask him about his trip and his work, which is the most important thing on the planet," I said sarcastically. "He'll ask about my week and I'll say, 'Everything's great, thanks, I'm engaged!'"

Ravenna nearly spit out her espresso and we enjoyed a much-needed laugh.

"And Steven?" she asked with raised eyebrow. "What does he want?"

"Yes," I yelled, "what does he want? I guess I'll find out tonight.

No, scratch that, I am finding out tonight. Ravenna, I can't get him out of my head. Look at the text he sent me earlier." I held up my cell phone and Ravenna leaned forward to look at it.

"Ooh la la. Zis is very Steven. Zis is a good text."

"It's a great text," I said. "It's sharp and sexy and just this side of profane."

We both leaned back in our chairs.

"I'm sorry," I said. "We haven't even talked about the gallery opening."

"Oh, fok it," Ravenna said. "Zey are all zee same, but zer are nice people in zis one. Zee owner did an internship at MoMA, which is how I know her. She is very good. You know what, we should eat."

Ravenna's change of subject didn't surprise me. In Ravenna's world, food was an integral part of every meeting. She didn't eat much, but if you met for coffee, there would be cookies at the very least. If you met for drinks, there would be something salty. If you met for a meal, there would be several courses.

"Can you believe I'm going to talk to Paul, Timothy, and Steven?"

"Zis is big, no?"

I knew what Ravenna was referring to: the big three. Or maybe she wasn't and I was just obsessing.

I looked at the lovely ring on my finger.

"I'm not ready yet to make a decision," I said.

"You will be soon, *mon amie*."

21

· · ·

After nearly two hours at the café I walked Ravenna back to the gallery and talked to the owner for a few minutes. Turns out she was a big fan of my column. I told her I'd try to get her some good press for the opening. She was so appreciative that she offered me a painting. I declined several times but she insisted, so I could expect delivery of a framed who-knows-what in a few days.

I called Anne on my long walk home and learned she had a big evening ahead—a date with Charlie. I was happy to hear the news. Charlie had seemed a decent guy, all things considered. Gentlemanly and together, until his panic and subsequent disappearance at the prospect of getting serious. After all, who was I to judge such reactions?

Anne apologized for not telling me about Paul's surprise proposal. There was no need, I told her. That's what best friends do; they help to plan huge surprise proposals for one another. Anne reminded me how I had often complained that despite Paul's many proposals, none were ever "official," and now I couldn't say that.

Paul called the moment I stepped inside my front door. He reported that his train ride had been fine and he missed me, and was I still wearing the ring? Yes, I told him, of course I'm wearing it. Paul had returned to his world and for that I was thankful. After we hung up, I wondered if he would change his mind, if the old insecure Paul would return and insist that my taking time to think meant only bad things, and therefore he must rescind his offer. That sent fear through me and suddenly I didn't want to lose him.

Still, I was excited to talk to Timothy. He hadn't specifically said we'd talk that evening but why would he wait another day to call me? His freshness and newness were like a cool drink on a hot day. Just thinking of him made me feel lighter. Timothy was exactly my age, while Paul was a couple years younger and Steven was a few years older. Timothy loved his career, as I loved mine. But unlike me, he loved his career to the point that he wanted to work every minute of every day, and he couldn't imagine doing anything else with his life.

I had already tried several career paths and still had ten ideas for my future, but I was content. Timothy was more than content. He was ecstatic, all the time. He didn't need to work every day, he wanted to. He couldn't wait to get to the office, even on weekends, and he talked about his work the way cinephiles talked about their favorite movies. In most ways Timothy's habit was quite refreshing, since most people complained about their jobs. We enjoyed talking to each other, and we seemed to enjoy the same activities. However, we didn't actually engage in too many activities together since our first few dates. It bothered me, but not to the point of worry, only to the point that I'd taken notice. Timothy and I tended to talk about plans rather than act on them, and we always ended up in the bedroom.

Timothy and I differed most in regard to our perspectives on how life should be lived. His intensely technical engineering education from MIT permeated his being. He considered himself to be creative, but he was ultimately hemmed by an engineer's mindset. He and I hadn't experienced any relationship problems as yet (save the fact that we hadn't spoken lately), and occasionally I wondered how he might handle emotional turmoil. Amazingly, he didn't seem to have any. Absolutely none. He was romantic and energetic and ambitious with a healthy ego, but did he feel things deeply? He was physically passionate, but was he truly passionate? I did not yet know. I *did* know that before my life was upturned almost a week before, Timothy was on my mind every few hours and I couldn't wait to see him again. From the tone of almost every one of his communications, he felt the same.

I changed into comfortable hang-out clothes and grabbed a beer from the fridge. It was a beautiful early evening. For the first time all week, I didn't have anything to do but wait—for phone calls, for clarity, for answers to come to me. I ambled into the living room and assessed the placement of my furniture and decided it was time to reconfigure it.

I knew Anne would call before her date, and Ravenna would call to check up on me, so when my home phone rang a few minutes into my furniture-moving, I didn't pay attention to the number.

"Hi." Steven's voice was like a clap of thunder.

The world stopped turning, air molecules ceased circulating, the taste of beer overtook my mouth, and I couldn't move.

"You there?" he asked.

"Yes." I had to force words out of my mouth. "I'm here."

There was silence on the line. I couldn't hear Steven breathing but I could feel him there. Suddenly I worried he was calling to tell me he'd changed his mind, that he'd acted on a whim and it was too sudden, and he was sorry, he couldn't do this. Again.

"What are you doing?" he asked.

"Moving furniture."

"Why am I not surprised," he laughed a little.

"I'm still me," I said.

"Good."

"Steven—"

"Can I see you?" he said, cutting me off.

"See me? Uh, when?"

"Now."

I needed air. His insistence, his intensity, the mere sound of his voice left me unable to move another chair or shove the big sofa another inch. I grabbed my beer and headed out the door to sit on my front steps, take a deep breath, and consider what to do.

"You're not saying no," he said as I gently closed the front door behind me, careful not to lock myself out.

"Steven, I don't know."

I sat on the top step, took a swig of beer, and gazed across the street. And there he was, leaning against the hood of his car. A four-year-old Porsche Carrera Cabriolet, in black, with beige leather. Talk about a still from a movie. That damn car. I loved that car. Because it was his, because it was fast, because he drove it hard, and because he used to hold my hand between shifting the gears. If the choice were mine, I would opt for a rich gunmetal with black interior, or deep mahogany with beige interior, and I wouldn't go for a convertible. Not in that car. But it wasn't my choice. One day, hopefully, but not yet.

I watched Steven slide his phone into the front pocket of his jeans and cross the street. His posture and gait hadn't changed. Neither had the excitement it caused inside me. I didn't stand up as he made his way up my front walk. I wanted to stand, but I thought it best to stay put.

Steven stopped at the bottom of my steps, of which there were only five, and motioned with his head to ask if he could sit. I nodded *go ahead*. He sat sideways a few steps below me and looked up at me, then he turned to stare at the street, just as I was doing. Silence fell upon us, as though gravity had pulled our conversation below our reach.

"I thought you were getting rid of that car," I finally said.

"Tried. Couldn't find anything that felt right."

I nodded.

"It's a little long in the tooth," Steven said.

Four years old is hardly old for a luxury car but, again, Steven drove hard.

"So," I took a drink from my beer bottle, "how did you know where I lived?"

He grinned just barely. "Mrs. Richmond knows the chief of police."

"Ah."

"So were you going to say yes?" he asked, still gazing across the street.

Jesus, he knows about Paul's proposal too?

"Say yes to...?"

"To letting me see you," he said.

Oh. Phew.

"I didn't have time to think it over. For me this is all out of the blue."

"I must say, you're handling it quite well," he said.

"Thank you." I stifled a laugh.

We watched cars drive by, people walk past, dogs sniff important invisible things.

"Want one?" I asked, holding up my beer.

"Yeah, sure," he said with surprise. "Thanks."

I stood and then looked down at him. Steven looked smaller than I'd ever seen him, but still very solid. I went inside to the kitchen and grabbed a beer, opened it, and headed right back outside. I was vaguely aware that I didn't look great but, to my surprise, I didn't care. I leaned down and handed Steven the beer, then retook my spot on the top step.

"That's new," he said.

I looked at him for clarification. Our eyes met, which caused me to forget what he had just said. His index finger flipped away from his beer and pointed at my ring hand.

"Oh, yes," I said.

Steven air-toasted me, then downed a third of his beer in one gulp. *How do men do that?*

"Are congratulations in order?" he asked, staring at the street, not at me.

"Not quite," I said.

"Why's that?"

"Is this really what you want to talk about?"

"Not in the slightest. Mr. California-Now-New-York doesn't blow my skirt up. By the way, you said something last night that made me curious."

I looked at him and waited.

"You said he doesn't know about me. Yet I know about him."

"Wow," I said with zero exuberance, "you were listening."

"I remember every word you ever said, darlin'."

"Darlin'?"

"Yeah, fuck, that's cheesy. But I'm a hick at heart."

"Steven," I said strongly enough that he turned and looked at me. "What do you want?"

His head was tilted down but his eyes were up on me. If I could freeze him in a moment, that would have been it.

"I want you to come car shopping with me," he said.

We both loved cars, especially test-driving. Damn it, it was so like him to surprise me.

"Sounds like a blast, but I'll pass," I said.

"Because?" he asked slowly, waiting for me to jump in. I didn't. "Because you're about to become Mrs. California? Pardon me,

New York. Or because I'm a piece of shit who doesn't deserve your help?"

"Getting warmer," I said.

Steven turned and looked at me head on. "Because you're over me. Because I was an unconscionable asshole who left you with no understanding of why it was over. Because you trusted me, and that was everything for you, and I broke your trust."

"Give the man a prize," I said.

"So you'll marry Mr. California, then," he said casually.

"For your information, I'm dating someone."

"Someone in addition to Mr.—"

"If you say Mr. California one more time. Yes, someone else. And Mr. Calif—"

"See, it's hard not to say it," Steven said.

I laughed. I couldn't help it.

"And *Paul* doesn't know about that guy either," I said firmly.

"And what state does Mr.—"

"He's in DC," I said.

"Come on, that's not even a state."

I laughed again. Only Steven would mention DC's lack of statehood.

"And what does Mr. DC do?" he asked.

"He's an architect. Er, an engineer." I fumbled for words. "He's both."

"Right up your alley." Steven obviously remembered I liked architecture.

"How'd you meet? During one of your trips there?" Steven also obviously remembered—and was one of the few people who knew—that occasionally I did writing work for a think tank, unbeknownst to the newspaper. "Or did he go to school there?"

"MIT," I said rather proudly.

"Oooh wee, a smarty. I don't see him facing off with me like

Paul did last night."

"No, that wouldn't be his style," I said.

Both of us avoided the biggest thing that transpired the night before, the fact that Steven admitted he'd loved me.

"So you're dating one guy, engaged to another—"

"I'm not engaged. I'm...thinking."

"Well, think on this while you're thinking. I need a new car and nothin's better for thinking than test-driving a Porsche."

22

. . .

Saturday morning brought more gorgeous weather. When I hadn't been fantasizing about Steven, I slept fitfully through the darkest hours of the night and only fell into a deep sleep once I saw the sun start to rise. As I washed my face, brushed my teeth, and pulled my hair into a ponytail, I felt different than I had in previous days. Not better, exactly, but different.

I headed downstairs to make tea, check and send e-mail, and enjoy the morning, when there was a strong knock at the door. I fumbled with the keys to unlock the bolt. When I pulled the door open, Anne was already standing inside the screen door, holding two cups of coffee and a bag filled with breakfast treats, I assumed, from the butter stains seeping through the paper.

"You're up?" I said, in shock. Anne was a late sleeper.

"Please, I haven't been to sleep yet." Anne walked past me toward the kitchen.

"The slut is dead, long live the slut," I said, shutting the front door with a whoosh.

"No, but Charlie and I had a good time. He's very talkative now." Anne popped the lid off one of the coffees and leaned against my kitchen counter. She handed me the white paper bag and I unrolled the wrinkled top to look inside at the assorted pastries.

"Want one?" I asked.

Anne waved me off and said, "Coffee first."

I hopped up on the counter and reached in the bag to pull a section from a huge cinnamon roll. "So he's talkative. That's good, right?"

"Yeah," Anne took a sip of her coffee, "I just don't remember him being so talkative. It's like, in the last month when I wasn't hearing from him, he learned ten million new words and I heard nine million of them last night."

I laughed. "Funny how we remember people, even if they haven't been gone long. Maybe he was talkative before, but then he split, and now you remember him differently."

"No," Ann said pensively, "he's ultra-motivated now. He was normal before."

"I guess being away from you lit a fire under him."

"Get this, he's moving to New York," Anne said as she reached into the bag of pastries.

"New York?"

"Yep. I learned that at the eight millionth word. We were on the couch, making out, everything was good, and bam! 'I'm moving to Manhattan,' he says. Just like that."

"What the hell?" I wondered for the umpteenth time why men do the things they do.

Anne nodded. "And he wants us to get back together."

"Well, New York's only a train ride away," I said. "Or a short road trip. You can easily do it."

"So marry Paul, and I'll get back with Charlie, and we can hang out in Manhattan."

Anne looked at my ring hand, which was shoving pastry into my mouth.

"You took it off?" she asked.

"I didn't want to scratch my face while I slept." Anne nodded as if to say *that makes sense*. "And, I'm not engaged, technically," I added.

"How was your night?" Anne asked.

My phone rang in the living room. "Saved by the bell," I said and ran for it.

Anne followed me in. I smiled widely and held up my phone for her to see Timothy's name on the phone screen. "Yay!" she said quietly, and plopped down on one of two big puffy white chairs.

I couldn't stop smiling as I answered and said, "Hi!"

"Amanda, hi!" Timothy said. "How are you?"

"I'm great. How was your trip?"

"It was crazy! Good but crazy!"

"Tell me all about it," I said. "We haven't talked in forever."

"I will, and I want to, but I have news. I'm coming there!"

"You are? That's so great! When?"

"Tomorrow," Timothy said. "I know it's like no notice but, long story short, our Edinburgh client is collaborating on the new university museum there."

"I've read about it in the paper. It's a pretty big deal," I said.

"Oh yeah. And, drum roll, we got the project! So I have to be on site ASAP. Well, Monday, technically, but I'm coming tomorrow to get a jump on meeting everyone, and familiarizing myself with the landscape. And I'm dying to see you! It's been weeks. I'm sorry about that."

"That's okay," I lied. "But, wow, this is huge. Congratulations."

"Thank you. This is pretty much a dream project. I have no idea how I'll balance it with all my work here, but I'll be working with top people and I couldn't say no."

Just a few weeks earlier, Timothy and I had been cuddled on his sofa when he said to me, "Don't let me say yes to anything else," because he was stretched thin and feeling overwhelmed. Happy, but overburdened, time-wise.

"So," he continued, "I was thinking I'll drive up early so we have the day together. Wait, are you free? I didn't even ask."

"For you? Of course I'm free. I can't wait to see you," I said.

I felt much better after talking to Timothy. Lying in bed the night before, I had considered with a bit of sadness that I hadn't heard from him since he got back from Scotland. I had made excuses for it—*he's so busy, he's been traveling, he's not officially your boyfriend so there's no obligation on his part to call,* blah blah blah.

Then I remembered all the lovely and romantic things he'd said throughout our time together, and during countless hours on the phone when we weren't together in person. How he never before felt this way, how he couldn't believe someone as wonderful as I am even existed, how happy he was about our relationship, how he would find himself smiling about our dates even days later. He was a tremendously sweet guy whom I happened to meet smack dab in the middle of a meteoric rise of his career and, like it or not, it was something with which I had to contend.

"Well," Anne said, "that answers my question about whether you talked to him last night."

"Nope, not until just now." I sat down on the sofa across from Anne's chair.

She smiled curiously. "You're different when you talk to him. All cheery."

"Am I?"

"If I read a transcript of that conversation, there'd be exclamation points every third word."

"Timothy's very peppy," I said. "It's nice. Most people complain all the time."

"You really like him," she said.

"You know, I really do."

After relaxing for a few minutes in a stream of morning sunlight, Anne finally asked if I'd heard from Steven. Yes, I told her, not only heard from him but saw him. Anne shot upright in the chair to hear the story. Afterward she grabbed the pastry bag and both coffee cups and carried them into the kitchen, talking as she walked. "I know you're over him, but do you think you could ever fall for him again?"

I shrugged. It was easier than responding. I then reminded Anne we were meeting Ravenna for the gallery opening at noon, so she went upstairs to take a nap in my small second bedroom and I hopped on my computer. I didn't get any work done. I thought about Timothy and basked in the positivity that emanated from him. I was afraid to become attached, but Timothy made it feel fun, like it should be. I didn't know a ton about him and that was the best part; I *wanted* to know him.

Then I thought about Paul. He was loving and romantic but I already knew him inside and out. There was no mystery with Paul and that was comforting. Not thrilling, but comforting. He was passionate and wrote poetry and gave me antique French engagement rings. There wasn't a doubt in my mind that Paul had, in fact, loved me all these years, and I knew that wouldn't change.

But then goddamn Steven crept into my head and everything in me responded. My breathing became shallow, my stomach flexed, my mouth twitched. It was like standing near lightning, when the hair on your arms stands up. But only an idiot stands near lightning, especially if she has been struck before.

23

· · ·

I had to practically pummel Anne to wake her up. She took a quick shower and changed into one of my dresses, a simple flesh-colored sundress that, according to Anne, "made her look like a corpse." Even though Anne and I are both fair-skinned, she could pull off certain bright colors that washed me out, and I could pull off certain neutrals that did not flatter her. She is a few inches taller, so my dress didn't hit at quite the right spot, but she didn't care. She was too tired to change.

We arrived late to the gallery by my standards, though lateness was a relative term by Anne's standards. A lot of people were already there and the space looked great. Sun-filled and vibrant with huge colorful paintings adorning every wall, odd sculptures on pedestals, and several small installations on the floor, each cordoned off by reams of white thread.

Ravenna saw us and said, "Sank God you're here, I want to shoot everybody." She smiled and waved and mouthed "hi darling" to several people every minute. Mimosas and hors d'oeuvres floated on colorful trays carried by attractive male servers wearing black T-shirts, slim black pants, and red sneakers. The gallery owner rushed to me and thanked me profusely for the newspaper's presence. I humbly accepted her thanks and told her truthfully I had very little to do with it; I had merely shot an e-mail to the arts and entertainment editor, Katrina Something-long-and-Russian, to suggest they send someone (not me!) to do a little write-up. Obviously they had received the e-mail and decided the gallery opening merited a few inches.

Before we knew it, an hour had passed, and I was beyond done looking at and talking about art, artists, and the gallery. Anne, Ravenna, and I stepped out back to a small courtyard to escape the fray.

"I don't know how you do this," I said to Ravenna.

She lit a cigarette and said, "I don't do zis much anymore. Zis was a favor. As I said, zee owner is a good artist and very hard worker."

Anne piped in, "I can't count how many of these I attended back in school. After the third or fourth one, I'd had it. I hate artists. They're prima donnas."

"Zis is true," Ravenna said.

"You're both artists!" I laughed.

"I never fit in that world," Anne said. To be sure, Anne was much happier in charge of creative services in the professional world than she would ever be wearing paint-splattered overalls, struggling with her inner muse.

"I did," Ravenna said, "but I hate zem, and most are not good. Some are magnificent but most, oof! Horrible."

My cell phone rang. I apologized as I took it out of my purse to turn the ringer off.

"Get it," Ravenna said, waving to someone inside. "I have to run in zer. Be right back."

I looked at the phone. "It's Steven," I said to Anne. My voice almost cracked.

"Get it!" She nudged my arm.

I walked to the back wall of the courtyard and answered the phone.

"Hi," he said. "What are you doing?" I was about to answer him when he added, "Where are you? I hear funky music."

"I'm at a gallery in the south end."

"Hip," Steven said.

Silence fell on the line and I felt a nervous need to fill it.

"Ravenna's in town to help with the opening," I said, "so Anne and I came to meet her."

"And how are Anne and Ravenna?"

"Terrific. I'll tell them you asked about them," I said.

"You having a good time?"

"At the gallery opening or standing here talking to you?"

I heard Steven laugh a tiny bit.

"Let me put it this way," I said, "I'm standing next to a six-foot, neon-orange sculpture of a man pulling gum off his shoe."

"So you're not having fun. Speaking of, what shoes are you wearing?"

I ignored his shoe question. "Quite the contrary," I said. "This is stimulating and inspiring. I might switch careers."

"You want to tear your hair out," Steven said. "You're feeling the minutes of your life inch past. You want to smack every pre-tentious, angst-ridden one of them."

"You like art," I said.

"Art. Not artists," he said.

Ravenna came outside and noticed me on the phone. She sidled up to Anne and I could see Anne reporting that I was talking to Steven. I held up my index finger to suggest *one minute*.

"I should probably get back in there," I said to Steven.

"Yeah. I'll pick you up in a half hour."

"Make it an hour," I said, and hung up. My arms felt like noodles and I had to catch my breath. I'd just made plans with Steven. He didn't even have to talk me into them; we just fell into our old habit of working off each other in a conversation. Wherever the conversation headed, I went.

Anne and Ravenna walked over to me.

"She is blushing," Ravenna said, elbowing Anne.

"He's picking me up in an hour," I said. I felt flushed and excited.

"Zis is good," Ravenna said.

"I don't know what I'm doing!" I was getting more flustered by the second.

"You're going to drive zee cars, yes?"

"That was his suggestion last night," Anne said.

"Oh, that's right," I said. "I forgot."

"Go get ready," Ravenna said to me, then turned to Anne. "You go wis her. She is all up in zee air now."

"I'm fine," I said, faking it badly. "Just a little nervous. I mean, it's *Steven*."

"Yes, you need time before you see him. I would come but I must stay here until zis stupid sing ends."

"Okay," Anne said, "we're taking off. I have to get some sleep anyway. I'm seeing Charlie again tonight."

"Zis is a big day for everyone." Ravenna kissed my cheek. "I talk to you later."

• • •

I dropped off Anne at her apartment and then rushed home to change. And pace. And wait. It was exactly an hour after Steven called me at the gallery that I stood at my front window and watched him park his car across the street, climb out, wait for cars to pass, then cross. He spun his keys swiftly around his finger as he walked. There was an unmistakable energy to his stride, a sense of real purpose. Watching Steven for even a moment brought back a mountain of old feelings.

He knocked on the door instead of ringing the bell. I took a few deep breaths before walking down my front hall. I opened the door and he was leaning one arm against the frame as though he'd been waiting a long time.

"Hi," he said with a knowing smile.

"Hi." We stared at each other for a moment. "Want to come in?"

"Really?" he said.

"No."

He grinned, and then said sincerely, "I'd like to come in."

"I'll come out. Just a second." I went to get my purse. When I returned to the front door, he was sitting between small pots of flowers on the low brick wall surrounding my outside entry area.

"Ready?" he said.

"That depends. Ready for what?" I closed the door behind me.

"For a drive," he said.

"In that piece of crap?" I nodded toward his car.

"To start," he laughed.

"You were serious?"

"Who would suggest going for a test drive as a joke?"

"Good point," I said. "Okay, let's go."

We walked across the street without speaking. When we reached his car, Steven opened the passenger door for me and, after closing my door, he remained there for a moment. I worried he might be having second thoughts. Then I decided not to wonder anymore; from now on if I had a question I was simply going to ask it, and when he got in the car I did just that.

"Having second thoughts?"

"About what?"

"This," I said.

"No."

I nodded.

"You?" he asked.

"Every second," I said.

Steven turned on the car. The sound of the powerful engine made me smile but I did my best to hide it. I refused to let Steven see my joy, though his ego probably knew better.

"She likey," he said, throwing the car in gear and nearly screeching out of the parking spot.

"So we're going to drive a...?"

"I told you."

"A Porsche," I said in an unimpressed tone.

"'A Porsche,' she says, like it's a Pinto. We're going to drive *the* Porsche. Nine-eleven Turbo."

Steven was referring to his dream car.

"No more convertible?"

"No more convertible," he said.

"It has a spoiler," I noted without enthusiasm.

"Damn straight. Cuts the wind resistance."

"Okay, Mario Andretti."

Steven smiled, which pinched the skin around his eyes in an indescribably sexy way.

"I've been waiting to do this," he said.

"Waiting for what?" Steven was a man who didn't wait for anything he wanted.

"For you," he said.

He placed his hand on mine, and then quickly withdrew it to downshift as we neared a red light. I couldn't respond to what he said, or to his hand on mine. They say time travel is impossible but I flew briefly to the past. A momentary trip back in time to one of my favorite days of my life.

That long ago day we had planned to take a test drive but we never made it to the dealer. On the highway heading out, just before the exit where we should have pulled off, we spontaneously decided to take a day trip to a historic house an hour outside the city. We toured it, ate a late lunch on a terrace overlooking unspoiled wilderness as far as the horizon, and then stayed at the attached inn for the night. We talked until morning, in a squeaky bed heavy with quilts. Though both of us would normally choose a fancy hotel over a rickety inn, it was twenty-four hours of bliss.

24

...

Steven and I drove mostly without talking, with the top down and good music playing. We drove for a half hour, out into the country, arriving at an exotic car dealer frequented only by true aficionados. The owner had a racing past and no need for money. He traded and sold cars because he loved them—their past, present, and future. He gave us a warm welcome, having met us together once before. Steven must have called ahead because the owner threw him a set of keys and said, "It's out back."

We admired a number of cars in the main showroom and then exited to a clearing out back that wasn't visible from the road. There sat the car of Steven's dreams in a stunning cobalt blue. There might be a few cars in the world as sexy, but none more so.

Steven held up the keys and said, "Well?"

I snatched the keys from him and got in the driver's side.

"It's only got two thousand miles on it," he said. "The previous owner had it about a minute, then went Italian."

I adjusted the seat and took a minute to familiarize myself with the bells and whistles.

"Two thousand is brand new," I said.

"Time to break it in," Steven said.

"Where to?" I asked, completely uninterested in the answer.

"Giorgio told me a great several-mile route."

I turned on the engine, revved it, smiled, put it in gear, and said, "Just tell me when to turn."

Nothing could have felt better than ripping that magnificent car around country roads, past cows and horse fences. Steven sat back and enjoyed the ride. He didn't chitchat or ask inane questions like, "How does it feel?" He took in the bucolic scene as we raced through it at eighty-plus miles per hour. I was a slow driver compared to Steven.

I felt exhilarated by the time I pulled into the dealership's small front parking lot. Driving a car of that caliber pushes fog from the brain, clears the sinuses, and opens the eyes. It's a rarefied experience.

I turned off the ignition and handed the key to Steven. "Your turn."

We switched seats and I watched him out of the corner of my eye. I wanted to see his expression upon hearing and feeling the first growl of the engine. Yet he merely smiled, that was all. No intensity, no "Hell yeah!" Just a smile.

We started off on the same roads, but two or so miles into the route Steven turned off to blaze his own trail. I'd wanted to do the same and just keep going until the car, or I, ran out of gas. But it was Steven's test drive more than mine. Being with him again after so long was seductive, yet once I was a passenger again I reminded myself not to confuse the present with the past.

"Steven," I finally said.

"Yeah."

"What's going on?"

He didn't answer me.

"Tell me now or turn this heap around and take me home."

"I want…," he began but didn't finish. Instead he stared ahead at the road.

"What?" I could tell my sudden impatience was unnerving to him. It felt good.

"I want you to come with me," he said.

"Not unless you spell it all out. Right now."

"I mean, I want you to come with me everywhere."

I tried to process, digest, and breathe.

Steven continued, suddenly impassioned, almost angry. "It doesn't matter where the hell I go, I want you there. For a fucking year, that's how it's been. I see a movie, I want you there. I come home from work, I want you there. I go on dates, I want you there."

"Not helping," I said with a warning tone.

"I thought I had to end it. Do you understand?"

I shook my head *no*. Hearing him mention the end of our relationship stole my voice.

"And then right after, like a minute later, I thought, 'Holy shit, what did I just do?' I picked up the phone to call you but I stopped halfway through dialing your number. I could still hear your voice, your crying. You were fucking blindsided and confused." He ran a hand aggressively through his hair and I became incensed.

"You make it sound like I was hysterical," I said.

"You weren't at all, that's the thing. I could tell you were crying but you were trying to hide it." Steven looked sideways at me. "I never heard you cry before."

I said nothing, not wanting to relive those awful minutes.

"I couldn't believe I did that," he said.

"You've probably made a hundred women cry," I said with a scoff.

"Yeah, I probably have. But this was different. You said, 'If you don't really want to be with me, then you shouldn't be.' I kept hearing it over and over in my head."

"So it's my fault? Because I didn't beg you to stay. Fucking egotist."

Steven gripped the steering wheel so hard, I thought he might pull it off. Then he put his hand on mine and looked down at them stacked one on top of the other. He turned the car onto a road without a sign. It was most likely a private road because there was a farmhouse in the distance and a matching horse fence on either side, stretching the length of the road.

"It's my fault." Steven looked at me. Into me. "You didn't do anything wrong, Amanda. I got close when I didn't want to. Christ, it was the last thing I wanted."

"I see," I said.

"No, you don't."

Talking about our relationship, specifically the end of it, made me feel pangs of old heartbreak. I couldn't go through it all again. I was about to tell him so but he spoke before I got the chance.

"You knew I lost my mom," he said.

The statement startled me. It was completely unrelated to the subject of us. Steven had lost his mother to cancer two years before we met.

"I couldn't call you back," he said. "I tried dialing your number, but," he shook his head with frustration, "if I had called you back, that would have been it. We would have been together. I couldn't do it. I just couldn't do it. I couldn't lose you."

"Lose me? You're not making sense. You wouldn't have lost me."

"Yes, I would have. Eventually. Fifty fucking years later, maybe, but I would have."

So sometimes it was true. People really panicked and pulled away even when they loved you. It was a famous excuse used by jilted people everywhere, but sometimes, just sometimes, it was true.

"When my mom got sick..." Steven stared at the horizon.

"You left Wall Street and moved back here," I said.

Steven nodded. "When she got sick, that was everything. I sold my book," he said, referring to his client list, "left behind my entire life and didn't care. I had to be here for her, and for my dad."

"How is your dad, by the way?"

"He's great," Steven said somberly. "He's out in Arizona near my sister."

We sat for a few moments and digested all that had been said.

"Why didn't you tell me all of this back then?"

"It wouldn't have made a difference," he said. "If it was swift, you'd hate me but it would be over. If I told you all that, I couldn't have ended it. I needed to end it."

"But you didn't have to do it like that. Over the phone. It hurts just thinking about it. You were so cold."

"If I'd been nice, like Mr. California or Mr. DC—"

"Stop it," I said.

Steven sighed. "You can't break up with someone nicely, for fuck's sake."

We let a few moments pass as Steven's words floated in the air. I wanted to say, "So I was just someone to be broken up with?" but I knew he didn't mean it that way.

"What do you want now?" I asked.

"A chance. That's all. I don't deserve it. I'm an asshole. You don't trust me, which you shouldn't, based on the past. But I'm asking for a chance."

"Tell me this," I said. "Why did you do the whole benefit gala? You landed me in hot water with my boss, and to say he's a prick who hates me would be an understatement."

"I didn't know that. I'm sorry." He laughed a little bit.

"It's not funny, Steven. The man is a bastard of epic proportions. He makes my life a living hell. He terrified me into thinking if I didn't cover that benefit, he'd fire me. He lords my column over me and getting rid of me is always implied."

"I'm not laughing because it's funny." His face still registered mild amusement.

"What?"

"You were never supposed to find out I was behind that. I subscribe to your feed, so any time you publish something I know it. I read the piece about the environment benefit. Loved it, by the way. People were talking about it and blogging about it. I'd contributed to that foundation before and the only meeting I ever attended was one where Mrs. Richmond was freaking out about 'that damn Morgan article.' She said she was going to get you fired. She's a haughty bitch, and a powerhouse. I knew she'd try to do it. So I talked to her afterward, buttered her up."

"Jesus, Steven, that must have cost you a fortune." I tried to imagine how much it would take to placate a woman like Emily Richmond. Steven neither confirmed nor denied it. "All that for me?"

"It's just money," Steven said.

"That's why she was so nice to me on Thursday night. You bought it. You *bought* niceness."

"How else am I gonna get it?" Steven said.

• • •

Steven and I didn't say much during the drive back to the dealership. He pulled into the back lot, turned off the ignition, and looked at me.

"You getting the car?" I asked.

"I don't know. What do you think?"

"It suits you."

"Suits you too," he said slyly.

He got out of the car and walked around the front, stopping to admire it from that angle. Even though I had been sitting for most of the afternoon, it felt good to slow down and stop moving. I tried to fix my hair, as the windows had been down for the entire drive, but I gave up and leaned my head and arms lazily out the window. Steven stood in front of the car and we shared a look that said *this car rocks*.

"You're not wearing the ring," he said a few moments later, not looking at me, leaning every which way to assess the car from every vantage point. "You give Mr. California the heave-ho?"

Oh shit. I'd forgotten to put on Paul's ring. And Paul hadn't entered my mind, not once, since Steven called me at the gallery a few hours before.

"No," I said. "I'm just not wearing it right now."

Steven opened my door. I got out, stretched, and then strolled to the edge of the grassy clearing while he went inside to talk with the owner. A couple minutes later they came outside together and walked toward me, talking as they walked. Giorgio was explaining something when Steven said, "Aw, shit and shove me in it."

I hadn't heard one of his signature outbursts in a long time. I knew something had happened but I couldn't tell what. Then, with an awkward posture, Steven lifted his right leg slowly to look at the sole of his shoe.

"There are many cows around here," the owner said. He patted Steven on the back. "Sometimes they wander. What can you do."

25
• • •

Steven kept the top down as we drove back to the city. By the time he dropped me off at home, my face was flushed from wind and sun, and my hair looked like a colony of builder ants had moved in and erected monuments. Our conversation on the return trip was surprisingly normal, as though nothing significant had transpired, yet his admission of why he'd ended our relationship was a dramatic turn of events. The fact that I had just spent hours with Steven was notable, to say the least.

He walked with me to the bottom of my steps, but not up to my front door. That was the better move. He didn't kiss me goodbye. He didn't even try. He didn't say anything prosaic like *I'll call you later*. We were in new and unfamiliar territory.

Once inside I went to the kitchen and splashed cold water on my face, and then went upstairs to change. I took off my bra, my most favorite act of undressing, and noticed Paul's beautiful ring sitting on the dresser. I put it on, looked at it on my hand, then took it off.

I changed into jeans because of the slight chill from the air conditioning, and added a tank top and flip-flops. I walked out of my bedroom and turned back to see Paul's ring sitting on my dresser, abandoned. I felt like I had cheated on it by spending time with Steven. I walked across the room and put the ring on my finger.

I headed downstairs and went straight to my computer, which

was sitting as usual on the end table next to the sofa. The message light was blinking on my home phone. I dialed in to my voicemail. While I waited for it to connect, I entered the password on my computer to wake it from sleep.

There was one message each from Anne and Ravenna, both saying they would have called my cell but they assumed I was still out with Steven. There was a message from Paul, inquiring about my weekend thus far. He too said he would have called my cell but he assumed I was at the gallery opening. His voice was kind and warm, but I knew it well enough to know he was holding back. He wanted an answer.

I called Anne and Ravenna to tell them I had survived my test drive with Steven. I laughed at the irony. Both literally and figuratively, Steven and I had taken a test drive. Anne was on the other line with Charlie when I called, and she said she'd call me back in a bit. Ravenna was on an impromptu date with the curator of the city art museum, Malcolm Werner, who had attended the gallery opening. Turns out he knew Ravenna's mother and learned of Ravenna's help with the little gallery just days earlier. All of this Ravenna whispered to me while Malcolm was in the men's room.

As one needs time to digest a big meal, I needed time to digest my outing with Steven. I grabbed my laptop and went outside to sit on my front steps and write for a while. It was too soon to call Paul. Not that he'd given me a deadline for my answer to his proposal, nor did I give him a specific time at which he could expect an answer, but there's only so long you can "think" without the proposer getting impatient.

I sat on the top front step, looking at the world, not knowing what I intended to write. It was a normal circumstance. Drinkers drink. Eaters eat. Shoppers shop. Writers write, or think about writing. When properly inspired, I wrote "letters I'd never send."

Over the years I'd amassed a ton of them—love letters, angry letters, analytical letters, resignation letters, catch-up letters. Often I'd think on a man and write to him, to connect in the way people did before the advent of phones, e-mail, and texting. I never sent the letters but writing them made me feel like I had sealed them, addressed them, stamped them, and slid them into a mailbox.

The sun was no longer high in the sky. The street buzzed with the transient activity of a summer Saturday. A soft breeze carried the scent of grilled food, reminding me I hadn't eaten since breakfast with Anne. What might she and Charlie be planning for the evening? Would Ravenna end up in bed with the curator? I thought of Timothy and felt a mixture of excitement and relief that I'd see him tomorrow. He had unwittingly taken a back seat to my week's activities. Whether or not my heart had grown fonder as a result of his recent absence, I was thrilled at the prospect of seeing his smiling face.

Dear Timothy, I typed, when a familiar voice startled me.

"Doing a final edit on the benefit piece?" John Mayes said as he headed up my front walk.

"Hi there. You scared me," I laughed.

"Sorry," John said with a smile. "So?"

"That piece is done. It's running tomorrow, I think."

"Wow, that was fast," he said.

"I was inspired."

"Thought maybe you decided to skewer them at the last minute," John said.

"Nah." I patted the step next to me.

"Whatcha writing?" he asked as he sat.

"Nothing. Just thinking mostly."

"I'll bet." John pointed his gaze at the ring on my finger. "There'll be a lot of broken hearts out there."

"Maybe mine will be one of them," I said.

"What do you mean?"

John's assumption that I was now engaged made me feel something new. Or was it something old? Perhaps something new wrapped in something old. Oh yeah, I was a great writer. My gut said it was fear at the prospect of getting married. *Married.* It was a foreign concept, but I was warming to it. My trust issues would be a thing of the past. Right? I could sow a few oats, like going on that test drive with Steven, and seeing Timothy one more time, and then I could wrap myself in a marriage blanket embroidered with the words, "No more dating. No more wondering. He loves me. I love him. The end." Put a bow on it and lay it across the bed.

"I'm just kidding," I said. "How are things with Susan?"

"Pretty good. You know, she's nice," John said.

His enthusiasm was overwhelming. Not.

"Since we're on the subject of our love lives, let me ask you something," John said. "I thought you were dating someone. Not Paul. Someone else."

"Yes, I was," I said, hoping that would end the topic.

"So you're not dating him anymore," John said, not quite as a question.

I didn't know how much I wanted to share with John. The ring on my hand said, "I'm engaged," but I didn't *feel* engaged. Despite our friendship, I worried about my image, how it'd look for the paper's "relationship columnist" to be considering marriage to one man while still dating another, especially when neither man knew of the other's existence.

"It's not important," John said, rescuing me from having to answer.

Just then I saw Anne turn the corner onto my street. She was about thirty feet away and waved when she saw me sitting outside. I loved that we lived in the same neighborhood; we were at opposite ends of it, but it's great to have your best friend so close.

"Hey, you two," Anne said when she reached the bottom of my steps. John stood and said hi.

"Hey yourself," I said. "What are you doing here? Shouldn't you be getting ready for your date?"

"No." Anne gave me a flat look.

John sensed the *girls need to talk about something private* vibe between us and asked if he should leave. Anne urged him to stay and suggested the three of us grab dinner.

"Hey," I said. "Did you know Ravenna's on a date right now?"

"With who?"

"Malcolm Warner. I think that's his name."

"You mean Malcolm Werner, as in the curator at the museum?"

"Yes, I guess."

"Wow," Anne said, clearly impressed.

"You know him?" I asked.

"He used to be at MoMA back when I was in school. Oh wait, I bet he knows Ravenna's mother. You don't know his name?" Anne was shocked at my ignorance.

"Even I know that name," John said.

"You do?" Fancy that, John Mayes was in the know about the art world.

"What rock have I been living under?" I said.

"Mia did a piece on him when he came to the museum to head up the modern wing," John said.

"Pardon me. I'm not in the art world," I said, twirling my hand. "How old is he?"

"I'd put him at about fifty," John said, looking to Anne for confirmation.

"Yeah," Anne said. "Sexy, though."

"Ladies, you're killing me," John said. "Fifty is the next decade I'll hit. You don't want to hear you're hot for your age."

I stood and roughed up John's hair, then we all went inside so I could plug in my computer. I was suspicious about Anne's apparently cancelled date with Charlie but I didn't say anything while John was around. We made plans to walk down the street and try to score an outdoor table at our favorite neighborhood bistro. I went upstairs to change (namely, put a bra on), but when I came downstairs John was leaving.

"Where are you going?" I asked.

John held up his cell phone. "Susan," he said.

"Everything okay?"

"Everything's fine. I'll take a rain check on dinner. I thought she had plans for tonight but she just called."

"She should come too," I said and Anne nodded in agreement. "The more the merrier." Suddenly I liked the idea of having a group dinner. It would get my mind off serious things, like fantasies of spontaneous sex with Steven on a country road, against a Porsche, with cows staring at us.

"That'd be great, but I don't think so," John said. He looked hesitant and uncomfortable. "Susan is uncomfortable with me hanging out with you."

"Oh." I couldn't blame a woman for being uncomfortable with her new boyfriend enjoying the company of single women she barely knew. "Well, I understand. Hopefully we'll all hang out together soon." I hugged John.

"Sure," John said during our hug. "Great to see you, Anne."

It wasn't more than one minute after John left that we heard a knock on my front door. Anne answered it while I kicked off my flip-flops and slid my feet into nicer sandals.

"Look who's here," Anne said.

Ravenna walked through the door.

"Hey! What are you doing here?" I said.

"I need an evening wis my friends." She handed me two bottles of wine.

"What happened to Monsieur curator?" I asked.

"He knows I am leaving tomorrow and I must be wis my friends."

"So he came back from the men's room and you just took off?"

"No, no, he knew all day I would not be wis him for zee evening. When you called he was in zee shower."

Anne and I looked at each other.

"The shower?" we said simultaneously.

"*Oui*," Ravenna said.

"You said he was in the men's room," I laughed.

"I said bathroom." Ravenna's *bathroom* sounded more like *bass-room*.

"Same thing," Anne said.

"No, a men's room is public," Ravenna said, walking past me into my living room. "A bathroom is at home."

"You went to his house?" Anne and I said in tandem.

"Of course not. We were at his hotel," Ravenna clarified.

Anne and I mouthed the word *hotel* to each other.

"He doesn't live here in the city?" I asked.

"Yes, he does," Ravenna replied.

Anne and I looked at each other in confusion.

"He likes to spend days at hotels," Ravenna said.

"Is he married?" Anne asked.

"Oof, please," Ravenna said. "He like to leave his home sometimes, so he doesn't get sick of it."

"Not a bad idea," Anne said.

26

. . .

Anne and Ravenna set the table in my backyard as we waited for the grill to get hot. Ravenna had talked us out of going to the bistro down the street in favor of staying in for her last night in town. The two of them had raced down the street to a gourmet market to buy food, which gave me a chance to call Paul. He was on his way out for the evening and said he wished I was there with him. I agreed, which was sort of a lie, but a tiny white one. I did miss Paul a bit, but since I wasn't yet accustomed to having him back in my life, I couldn't miss him a lot. We asked about each other's day. Paul spent his in the studio; I spent mine at the gallery with Anne and Ravenna. Little white lies never hurt anyone. When you start lying in different colors, then you have something to worry about.

After Anne and Ravenna returned from the market, I told them about my conversation with Paul as we tended to preparations. After twenty minutes the table was set, the wines were breathing, the grill was hot, and we were ready for our night.

"Lying is good," Ravenna said.

"I don't know about good but sometimes it's necessary," I said.

"Of course it's good," she said. "Zer is lying in all healthy relationships." Interestingly, Ravenna could hit the "th" in certain words, like *healthy*, which strangely disappointed me. I would have preferred to hear *hellsy*.

"You have to lie sometimes," Anne said. "Like, you had to lie to Paul. Steven came out of nowhere and he's not relevant to your choice about marrying Paul."

I sifted the coals in the grill. I could feel my friends eyeing me.

"Zis is crazy. I'll ask her," Ravenna said to Anne. "Okay, tell us about your day wis Steven."

I turned around with tongs in hand, grinned, and launched into the story. Both Anne's and Ravenna's jaws were hanging by the time I finished.

"Zat is incredible."

"That's, like, I don't even know!" Anne said.

"Yes," I said. "But I'm telling you this story with Paul's ring on." I turn the ring slowly around my finger. "And Timothy's coming tomorrow! I'm a bitch, aren't I?"

I went to sit next to Anne on a dilapidated wood bench that I adored. It was soft, and creaked when you sat on it. It could hold two moderately weighted people, any more would destroy it. Ravenna sat across from us in a newer all-weather chair, the kind you buy in sets at home improvement stores. Now that I had a backyard I couldn't force my friends, or any other guests, to sit on the ground.

"*Mon amie*, you are zee most honest person I know. You would never hurt someone on purpose."

"What are you going to do?" Anne asked.

"Nothing until after I see Timothy," I said.

"Good. You take time. Sleep wis all of zem." Ravenna held up her index finger to proclaim the most important point.

Anne and I looked at her.

"What?" Ravenna said. "You must know before you make zis decision."

"She's got a point," Anne said.

"I've already slept with all of them," I said.

"Zat was zen, zis is now. You sleep wis Steven over a year ago. And Paul? A decade can turn a boy into a man, or do zee opposite. Oof, I've seen zat too."

"Timothy's the only one you're sleeping with now," Anne said. "And you said he's...?"

"Good," I said. "Not mind-blowing. But very good."

"And Paul was always good, *oui*?"

"Paul was big," Anne interjected.

Ravenna and I laughed. Anne had a knack for remembering men's sizes with the same accuracy as baseball fanatics remembered players' stats.

"Zees sings don't get smaller," Ravenna said with an encouraging tone.

"Paul was extremely giving in bed," I said. "Highly sexual, but very loving."

"All your guys have been sexual," Anne said. "I've had so many duds and small penises."

"How's Charlie wis sex?" Ravenna asked.

"He's good," Anne said with a shrug.

"Oh fok, zat's bad." Then she asked me, "Which one was zee best lover?"

"There's no question," I said.

"Steven," Anne and Ravenna said in unison.

I didn't need to confirm their guess.

"So we've covered Paul, Steven, Timothy, and Charlie," I said. "What about Mr. Werner?"

Ravenna topped off our glasses, even though I had barely touched mine, then poured herself more wine and detailed her afternoon. Malcolm Werner had arrived at the gallery after Anne and I left. He made a beeline for Ravenna and they quickly fell into conversation about New York, Ravenna's mother, Europe, art, and marriage. Ultimately he convinced her to ditch the party and accompany him to his hotel for tea. Shock of all shocks, they never made it to tea. They did, however, barely make it out of the car with their clothes on.

"Where does it stand now?" I asked.

"He wants to see me tomorrow," Ravenna said.

"What's it like being with a man in his fifties?" Anne asked.

"If zey have a good body, it's zee best," Ravenna said. "His body is great." Ravenna made the *perfect* symbol with her fingers.

Neither Anne nor I questioned Ravenna's allusion to having slept with more than one man in his fifties. Ravenna was a woman of secrets, which meant even though she was a dear friend, that status didn't guarantee I'd know everything about her life.

I couldn't stand it anymore. It was high time to learn about Anne and Charlie. Ravenna and I didn't want to pry but...that's a lie, yes, we did. Usually Anne was forthcoming about her romantic situations, so her silence thus far about her cancelled date was looming over the conversation.

"All right, that's it," I said. "Anne, what happened with your date tonight? Did he cancel on you?"

"No," she said, pulling her legs under her and rocking on the bench. "I cancelled it."

This was an unexpected turn of events worth hearing about. Ravenna and I looked at each other, and then stared at Anne until she spilled the details.

"Both of you know what you don't want," Anne said. "But I know what I *do* want. A relationship."

Ravenna and I nodded. Anne continued, "I'm sick and tired of this pattern where you get into a relationship and the guy just changes his mind. Charlie and I were almost like you and Steven. Not quite as serious, but definitely getting there. Then, boom, he's gone. Like if the conductor said, 'Next stop, monogamy, before our final stop, commitment' and Charlie jumped off the friggin' train."

Anne often used trains to illustrate her feelings about relationships and people in general; her most common reference was to bisexuals, whom she ardently believed were "one stop away on the train to Gaytown." She continued her story as she grew visibly more frustrated. "And now Charlie decides he wants me back? I'm not sure I want him back."

"Wow," I said, impressed with Anne's fortitude but also a bit surprised at her feelings.

Anne was a woman who really, openly wanted to be in a relationship. I did too, much of the time, but I was quiet about it, fearful that even the slightest mention of wanting a relationship would make the chance of it disappear.

"I thought you were excited about Charlie," I said.

"I was," Anne said. "But as we were making plans for tonight, I felt kind of stupid."

"You are not stupid," Ravenna said.

"I know!" Anne yelled to the sky. "But remember, right in the middle of our get-back-together date he told me he's moving. If I went out with him tonight and we ended up in bed, which we probably would, then yeah, I would be stupid. It dawned on me that I was making a plan with a guy who ditched me, then didn't hesitate to call me up like nothing happened. I'm sick of it."

"Did you say all this to Charlie?" I asked.

"No. I didn't want to get into it until I know what I want."

"But you just say you *do* know what you want," Ravenna said. "A relationship, no?"

"Yes," Anne said. "But I'm not sure anymore that I want one with him."

Anne's words resonated with me. She must have sensed it because she looked at me.

"Have you been wondering that?" she asked me. "About Steven?"

That wasn't the name I expected to hear.

"Actually," I said with a sigh, "I've been wondering that about Paul."

"Zis makes sense," Ravenna shook a cigarette out of a box and handed me one. I took it. She gave me a light, and then let hers hang out of her mouth. "You love Paul. He is a wonderful guy who loves you. But you are wis Timothy now. And he is coming here tomorrow."

"For work," I added, feeling the need to remind my friends that Timothy wasn't, in fact, making the trip just to see me.

"So what?" Ravenna said. "He is excited to see you all zee time. He smiles and he is positive and he want to travel wis you and he talks about a future." She exhaled a long stream of smoke. "You love him, no?"

I felt myself blush. "Love him? I don't know."

"Zat is good! Zee future wis him is a mystery. You know what it is to be wis Paul. And you know what it is to be wis—"

Ravenna stopped before saying Steven's name because, in truth, I didn't know what it was like to be with Steven long-term. He hadn't given us that chance. This fact did not escape Anne or Ravenna's notice.

"You were with him for months," Anne said.

"Yes," I said. The best months of my adult life. Followed by the worst.

"Here's what you do," Ravenna continued, undeterred. "You see Timothy tomorrow like nussing has changed, because nussing has. Spend time wis him, have sex wis him, and when he goes back to Washington, you decide. If Paul does not like waiting, fok him."

I almost spit out my watered-down wine at Ravenna's dismissal of Paul. No matter how unpleasant the news, Ravenna's *fok* always cracked me up. If she were to say "a fokking meteor is heading straight for us," I would die laughing.

27

• • •

I woke up early Sunday morning and wrote a letter I'd never send—to myself. One, to allay my guilt. Two, to admit selfishly that I was happy Ravenna would be coming here more often if she continued her new affair with Malcolm Werner. Three, that I was glad Anne didn't jump back into a relationship with Charlie. I also wrote about John Mayes and his sudden exit because of Susan's "discomfort" with me. Then I wrote briefly about Daniel Perry: I wrote *tear him a new one* at the top of my to-do list for tomorrow morning. The supreme bastard of the universe would be back from Washington by then, after interviewing the Treasury secretary and getting his ego polished.

I was fed up with not knowing why Daniel Perry hated me, fed up with his attitude, fed up with his maliciousness, fed up with his purposeful belittling every chance he got, and fed up with not smacking him in the face. If I had to do so with words, so be it.

The girls' night had been cathartic for me. Anne and Ravenna had polished off three bottles of wine, the two Ravenna brought plus one from my stash, while I drank one twice-refilled glass with ice cubes tossed in. My friends didn't hold it against me that I was an alcohol lightweight. As good friends do, they sufficed in areas where I was lacking. Our long conversation opened me to considerations that the week's frenetic pace hadn't allowed me to see. I was quite affected to learn that Ravenna truly enjoyed her time with Malcolm Werner, the fifty-something curator with the great body, and that Anne had cancelled the date with Charlie rather than the other way around.

I finished the letter to myself and filled the remaining morning hours with prettying up my face, straightening up my place, and deciding how we'd spend the day. I thought taking a drive around the city would be great. Timothy and I hadn't seen each other in several weeks, and we had talked so little that I felt distant from him. It was a distance I didn't like, one that left a little hole I could feel when I thought about him and breathed at the same time. I couldn't wait to kiss him again and I no longer felt guilty that I had kissed another man in the interim. I had only kissed Paul, after all. Yes, it was a great kiss, but you have to kiss your long-lost ex-boyfriend when he reappears and proposes years later. It's the law.

I did not feel guilty that I'd wanted to kiss Steven. Really wanted to. Still wanted to. Timothy and I weren't committed. If we lived in the same city we probably would be, but as it stood, we hadn't had "the conversation" yet.

The minutes ticked away and I became more and more excited about the prospect of touring Timothy around. I planned the day in my head: We'd stop at the museum so he could get a sense of it, then we'd stop for food, which we would take along as we drove around the city, and eventually we would go to my favorite park for an "impromptu" picnic. In my fantasy, the day was already perfect.

Take off Paul's ring. Take off Paul's ring. Take off Paul's ring. I forced the mantra through my head until I physically removed the ring, too afraid I'd forget to do so before Timothy arrived.

I heard a knock at the front door. It was probably too early for Timothy. He was a late sleeper anyway and most people rang the doorbell. Knocking was the distinct domain of certain personalities. *Please don't let it be Steven. Please don't let it be Steven. Please don't let it be Steven. Okay, let it be Steven but only for a minute.*

I opened the door to see John Mayes.

"Hi," he said. "Sorry I didn't call first."

"That's okay." My eyes darted to the clock.

John looked tense.

"Everything all right?" I asked.

"Yeah, I guess." He shuffled his feet. "Susan dumped me."

I stepped outside and motioned for John to sit with me against the low brick wall outside my front door.

"Amanda," John said, nodding sadly, "you hear relationship stuff till it's coming out of your ears."

"John, it's okay. What happened?"

"Last night I went over to her place to pick her up, and I could tell she was mad. Well, I knew she was mad when I talked to her from your place. That's why I left so suddenly. Sorry about that, by the way."

"No problem. I understood."

"Anyway, she was really mad when I got there." John sighed. "Funny about women," he half-laughed, "you can't always tell what they're really feeling. Even if you ask them outright."

"Yep, we're a pain in the ass." I nudged him. He smiled.

"She said it's unacceptable for me to have single female friends."

"Unacceptable?"

"Unacceptable," John said.

"But we work together," I said.

"I know. And she was so excited to meet you at the benefit. I think that's part of the problem."

"I don't understand," I said.

"That night, when we met Paul and he was, um—"

"Rude as hell?"

John laughed. "Yeah. When he snubbed us, Susan got it in her head that something had happened between us." John motioned his hand back and forth suggesting *the two of us.*

"What? That's crazy," I said.

"I told her that," he said.

"You didn't."

"Yeah, telling a woman she's crazy isn't the smartest thing. Hey, you might want to mention that in your column sometime."

"Oh, John, I'm really sorry," I said. "Susan seemed nice."

"She is nice. But I had to tell her that I wouldn't date someone with the provision that I can't have female friends. I mean, we've only been dating a few weeks. Most of it on the phone and online. She can't tell me who I can or can't hang out with. I've known you for years, I just met her." John was so calm in his retelling of the story. I was impressed.

"John, when you start dating someone, all your single, opposite-sex friends become threats. It's part of the dating game. An annoying part, but a big part."

"You'd know better than me," he said.

"Wait a second," I said.

John looked at me.

"You said you told her that you couldn't keep seeing her?"

"Yes," he said.

"A minute ago you said she dumped you."

John looked confused, and then said, "You're right. I must be so used to getting broken up with. Well, this should make an interesting entry in my series about men in the dating world."

We both leaned against the brick wall as the sun moved higher in the sky.

"It's none of my business," he said, "but I can't help but notice you're not wearing the ring."

Before I could come up with an explanation, John and I were distracted by a bright blue BMW Z3 pulling into my driveway. I was so excited at the sight of Timothy's car that I ran down my front steps and raced the length of the walk. By the time I got to his car, he was stepping out and we snapped together like magnets.

"Hey, you! I missed you!" Timothy said, squeezing me in a bear hug.

"You're early!"

Timothy kissed me with fun passion and I was so wrapped up in it that I didn't notice John standing at the end of the front walk. Timothy did, though. He paused mid-kiss and said, "Amanda?"

"Oh!" I laughed. "Timothy, this is my friend, John."

Timothy, ever-courteous and happy to meet new people, stepped in front of me to shake John's hand. "Great to meet you. I've never met any of Amanda's friends."

"Good to meet you," John said.

"John is a reporter for the paper," I said.

"Oh, cool," Timothy said to him. "That makes you the second newspaper person I've ever met."

"Nice to be distinguished for something," John laughed.

Timothy squeezed my hand and said, "I'm going to get my stuff out of the car. Good meeting you, John. Maybe we'll see you later."

"You too," John said.

John gave me a skeptical look, obviously wondering who this guy was, and why I was racing to hug him and kiss him like a boyfriend.

"You guys have a good time," he said. "I'm going home to work on an article explaining why I'm single."

I gave John a hug.

"You'll tell me about him later?" John whispered during our brief embrace.

I patted him on the back as he turned to walk away.

"Probably not," I said.

• • •

"Ahhh," Timothy said, sinking into my sofa. I stood in front of him. He reached forward, grabbed my hips, and pulled me onto him. "I haven't been away in so long."

"You were just in Scotland!" I said.

"That was work," he said, kissing me between each word.

"It didn't have to be." I kissed his forehead, eyes, cheeks, jawline, and neck. "You could have taken time to wander around and explore, eat great food, climb up Arthur's Seat."

"Great food in Scotland?"

"Sure," I said. "At any French restaurant."

"What's Arthur's Seat?"

"Oh my God, man, you have to get out more," I joked.

"No kidding," he said.

"You could have trained to London and tried to make the Beefeaters laugh."

"Try to make the what *what*?"

"The guards," I said. Timothy looked at me curiously. "At Buckingham Palace and the Tower. They won't laugh, no matter what you do. Trust me, I've tried everything."

"Mmm, I'd like to see that," he said.

Timothy's hands were all over me, insistently making up for lost time. Before I knew it my top was off and he'd pulled his T-shirt over his head and we were pressed together. He whispered how much he had missed me, and how amazing I felt against him, and how this was all he thought about on his drive from DC.

"I thought about you the whole time I was away," he said. "I really wished you were there with me."

"You did?"

His light, almost icy blue eyes were bright and sweet. They were so different from Paul's, which were a deep ocean blue. Timothy's blues were fresh and exciting while Paul's were richer and filled with history.

"Of course I wanted you there." He devoured my mouth between every sentence. Then he stopped and said with a smile, "You sound surprised."

"Well, I barely heard from you since the last time we saw each other. So..." I trailed off. I didn't want to complain even though I wanted to complain.

"Amanda, you were on my mind the entire time." Timothy held my face in his hands and kissed me. "I would have loved it if you were there. Though it's better you weren't," he laughed.

"Why is that?"

"Because I'd want to do this." He slid his hands down my back. Far, far down. "And all I did was work."

Our chemistry hadn't changed in the weeks since we last saw each other. Our mouths complemented each other, the rhythm of our kisses perfectly synced. Our breathing grew harder, our skin got hotter, our hands couldn't touch enough fast enough.

"Next time," he whispered into my ear, "come with me?"

I smiled, and he pulled away for a moment to view my face. Then he pulled me to his chest and cuddled against me.

"How long are you in town?"

"I'm not sure," he said. "A few days."

"That's great!" Timothy and I had never had more than forty-eight hours together. I pushed myself up and he ran his hands through my hair. "I was thinking today would be perfect to take a drive. Though I know you've been on the road for a while." He waved it off, indicating the drive from DC was nothing. "We can stop at the university museum and then I can show you around."

"Sounds perfect," he said, kissing me.

"Then tonight we could watch a funny movie." I ran my finger in a circle around his chest.

Timothy smiled big. "There's no place else in the world I'd rather be right now." Timothy's sheer happiness at simply being in my presence always made me feel wonderful. "There are a couple calls I have to make later," he added guiltily. He played with my hair and looked at it like it was a rare, gorgeous sight.

"No problem," I said.

"So how have you been?" he asked. "What was your week like? I've been so overloaded that I don't know what's going on with you. How's your boss, the asshole?"

"Ugh, Daniel. Let's not talk about him. Otherwise my week was fine. The same. You know."

"That's it? I'm jealous," Timothy said, ignorant of the irony.

"Please, if you weren't going at a hundred miles an hour, you'd be miserable."

"True." He clapped his hands around mine. "I'm really psyched about this museum project. There are some heavyweights involved. I'm not leading the project but it's a dream collaboration."

"I'm really happy for you," I said. "The paper's run a few stories about it. The sketches look beautiful."

"They do, don't they? I'm only on the engineering end of it, though," he said.

"You're not designing any of it?"

"No, but there isn't architecture without engineering." He gave me a knowing look.

"Right," I said. Spending time with Timothy had afforded me a free education about his field.

"The lead architects are from that firm I told you about in Chicago," he said.

I nodded, remembering him mentioning it on our first date. "The 'rock stars' in Chicago?"

"Right," he said. "Those guys are ridiculous. Brilliant. I'm dying to work with them."

"The whole project sounds fascinating."

"It's exactly the kind of thing I've been waiting for," he said. "The connections I'll make, unbelievable. But then I think maybe I should slow down a little."

"What?" I was astonished to hear such words from Timothy.

"I'm not all work," he said.

I looked at him skeptically.

"Okay, maybe I am," he conceded, "but I don't want to be. I don't like not knowing how your week is going, and feeling like we have to catch up."

"I don't either," I said.

We kissed gently.

"I hardly ever see my friends anymore! Of course, they're crazy busy too."

"And your parents," I added as an obvious point.

"Eh, I don't see them anyway," he said. "But, yeah, I should make more time for things like that."

"You don't see your parents?"

"No. We're not really close," he said.

"But you get to Boston fairly often and that's where they live, right?"

Timothy nodded and looked at me with wonder and interest, as if he were assessing a piece of art.

"And you talk to them," I stated, like an attorney leads a witness on the stand.

"Not really," he said with a carefree grin. "I haven't seen them in a few years."

Timothy was nonchalant, as though we were talking about the last time he saw *Seinfeld*. I was confused. "But you just said they're in Boston, and you go there almost every month, right?"

He nodded again as he leaned forward and grabbed a bottle of Gatorade from the coffee table, which I always bought for him before his visits.

"My mom actually called me the other day," he said.

"Oh, that's nice. How is she?"

"Fine, I guess." He took a big gulp. "I haven't called her back." He noticed my confused expression. "Like I said, we're not close. She calls me sometimes," he said with a shrug.

"You don't call her back?"

"Nah." He kissed me on the nose. "We just don't have anything in common."

"Besides the fact that she's your mother?" I said jokingly. This was all news to me, that Timothy had essentially no relationship with his parents.

"It's no big deal." Timothy wrapped his arms around me and we kissed for a long time. When we finally stopped, my lips and chin were red and swollen from his eleven o'clock shadow.

28

• • •

Once Timothy and I made it off my sofa, he took a quick shower so we could go about our day. He had wanted me to shower with him but I knew if I did, we would never leave the house. It had happened before, during my trips to visit him and vice versa; on more than one occasion we didn't get out of bed until four in the afternoon.

Within an hour we were walking around the perimeter of the university museum. Timothy explained where the new modern art addition would be built. He described the use of different materials, chosen specifically to set the new building apart from the original while retaining a cohesive aesthetic. Timothy explained that since the city's main art museum, headed by Ravenna's new beau, was only a few neighborhoods away, there would be collaboration rather than competition; any and all efforts to draw attention to our city as a premier destination for art. Straddling the Mid-Atlantic corridor, he explained, the city was a prime location for new interest. New York would always be the main go-to destination, but smaller cities were investing more money in projects like these, he explained with enthusiasm.

We meandered around the university grounds, eventually circling back to a large fountain in the plaza facing the expansive front entrance. I reached into my purse and grabbed two pennies. I handed one to Timothy.

"Make a wish," I said.

Timothy smiled, leaned in, and kissed me. "I don't have to."

"You can't have too much luck," I said.

He took half a second before tossing his penny in. I thought hard about my wish before tossing my penny in.

"Tim!" A voice said from behind us. We turned to see a dapper man walking in our direction. "Tim, my boy! Good to see you!"

"Malcolm," Timothy said, extending his hand.

"Thought you were due in tomorrow," the man said.

Timothy placed his hand on my lower back and said, as a means of presenting me, "I had a reason to come early."

"I should say so," the man said with an approving smile as he extended his hand to me. "Hello."

"Hi," I said, shaking his hand. "Nice to meet you."

"You as well." The man's handshake was strong and enveloping.

"You two are colleagues?" I asked.

"I'm sorry," Timothy said. "Amanda, this is Malcolm Werner, curator at the city museum. Malcolm, this is Amanda Morgan. She writes a column for the paper, among other things."

"Amanda Morgan, of course," Malcolm said. "Ravenna's friend!"

"And so are you!" I didn't know how much knowledge to admit.

"You two know each other?" Timothy said.

"Well," I said, searching Malcolm's face for a helpful clue, "yes, sort of."

"I've heard that about this city," Timothy said. "Everyone knows each other, at least by degrees. I guess it's true."

Malcolm turned and yelled, "Ravenna, look who's here!"

Timothy looked at me with surprise. "I'm finally going to meet the famous Ravenna?"

I leaned around Malcolm to see Ravenna shaking hands with a young man she had been talking to, and then she turned toward us.

"*Mon amie!*" She sped up her pace.

"I thought you were leaving today," I said, hugging her.

"I convinced her to stay one more day," Malcolm said with a satisfied grin. "Amanda, please help me convince her to stay longer. From the way Ravenna goes on about you, I feel like I know you already. If anyone can convince her, it's you."

"Ravenna, *this* is Timothy," I said.

"Great to finally meet you," he said.

"You too," Ravenna said.

"Tim, as long as I have you here," Malcolm began and then stopped. "Oh, I'm sorry, ladies, do you mind if we talk shop for a few minutes?"

We told the men to take their sweet time. Ravenna grabbed my arm gently and led me for a stroll around the fountain.

"He's handsome," Ravenna said, referring to Timothy.

"He's handsome," I said, referring to Malcolm. "You weren't kidding about his body."

It was easy to discern Malcolm's physique from his posture, energetic stride, and the way his clothes fit. His expensive jeans fell perfectly, just as his linen jacket fit his shoulders in a not-too-tight way. His white linen button-down shirt was unbuttoned enough to allow a clear view of his strong neck, prominent collarbone, and tan skin.

"Yes. And he can't keep it off me. Timothy is very pale. Where is he from?"

"Massachusetts," I said.

"Zat explains it." Ravenna took cigarettes out of her purse. "What are you doing here?"

"Timothy wanted to drop by and get a look at things before his meetings tomorrow."

Just then my phone pinged, indicating a text message. I pulled it out of my purse and saw it was from Paul. I showed it to Ravenna. It read: I woke up thinking about you and wishing you were here. I love you.

I texted him back the same message, pretty much.

"Zat's lovely. He's being very patient, no?"

"It's weird," I said.

"Maybe he is changed."

"Maybe," I said. "If I don't say yes I'll lose him forever, won't I?"

"You have not lost him yet," Ravenna said.

Timothy and Malcolm walked toward us.

"Why don't we all get together tonight?" Timothy said.

"Terrific idea," Malcolm said. "Let's set it up later this afternoon. Amanda, you have a terrific man here. Top notch. The team's lucky to have you," he said to Timothy, shaking his hand. Ravenna and I smirked at each other that the men had made an evening plan without consulting us, but we let it go, and parted ways.

Timothy and I walked back to my car and I couldn't wait any longer to ask, "How in the world do you know Malcolm Werner?"

"He's consulting on the project," Timothy said.

"As curator of the city museum, isn't he too busy to help the university with a fabulous new modern wing?"

"This is a collaborative project," Timothy stressed. "It's awesome! Malcolm's a big deal. He consults on lots of projects, mostly exhibits, but this isn't unusual. Besides, this university museum will never really compete with the city museum. The scale alone, there's no comparison."

"But you two really seem to know each other," I said. "How did you meet him? He lives here. You live in DC."

"He was in Edinburgh when I first got there," Timothy said. "We all got smashed one night. It was great."

I remained super-duper positive to match Timothy's constant

excitement but it bothered me that I didn't know he'd already met such a prominent person from my city. When it came down to it, I didn't know too many details about Timothy's life. I'd heard countless fun and funny stories, and I knew all his friends' names and had even met some of them, and I knew Timothy had told them all about me, but I didn't know he had met, and gotten smashed with, the city museum's art bigwig. And I didn't know he was the type of man who wouldn't bother calling back his own mother.

"Plus," Timothy continued, "Malcolm's a Harvard man, so we have the Boston connection. He's way into art and I'm not, but he's a really good guy."

"Seems like it," I said.

Timothy and I drove to a café down the street from the university and picked up lunch. As I drove us to a park just outside the city I felt something less than positive but I couldn't put my finger on it.

Timothy and I sat under a tree and ate. We talked about everything from politics to fashion to travel. Eventually we ended up sharing college stories, which was his favorite non-work subject, and we laughed at each other's long-ago drunken antics.

"What are you most proud of?" I asked him.

"I'm pretty damn proud of the diplomas hanging on my wall," he said without hesitation.

"You should be," I said, though I'd been hoping for a non-scholastic answer.

"And you?" he asked. "Very few people get to do what you do."

"I suppose. But I'd have to say my friends and family. They're incredible people and I'm proud to have them in my life."

"Hmm," he said and smiled at me.

We sipped cool water, took a stroll, then headed back to my place for a nap.

• • •

We met Ravenna and Malcolm at a BYOB restaurant in my neighborhood. They brought the "B" which included a couple bottles of great wine from Malcolm's collection. He explained without braggadocio that his wine cellar was the finest private collection in the city. We scored the last available table on the patio and relaxed in the evening air as Malcolm told us the history of his wines.

Ravenna and I had called Anne to invite her and she joined us by the time appetizers arrived. I was happy she and Ravenna would finally know Timothy; it's hard to talk about your relationship when your friends have never met the guy. Naturally, within ten minutes, Timothy and Malcolm were heavy into work talk, so we fell into girl talk.

"No Charlie tonight?" I asked Anne.

"Nope," Anne said, clinking my glass. "I told him I needed time to think and that's what I'm doing."

"Good for you," Ravenna said. "If zat is what you need."

"What I need," Anne said quietly so Timothy and Malcolm didn't hear, "is someone who won't just take off."

"Like Paul," I blurted without thinking, and then spooned a few ice cubes into my wine. When I looked up from my glass, Anne and Ravenna were staring at me. "Well, he's done it before. It's what he does!" I half-yelled, catching the men's attention.

"What have I done?" Timothy said, taking my hand and kissing it.

"You really surprised her," Anne said as cover.

"Yes, like wis coming here today," Ravenna said.

"I told you I was coming today," he said sweetly to me.

"But you only give one day's notice," Ravenna said. "Zis surprised her. It was sweet."

"She's more than worth it," Timothy said.

"Here, here!" Malcolm added.

As quickly as we'd attracted the men's attention, we lost it again. Malcolm and Timothy fell back into their conversation about flying buttresses or the manipulation of negative space or whatever art-architecture-structural engineering types talk about. I whispered to Anne and Ravenna, "And not just Paul. Steven did it too. Way, way, way worse."

Timothy turned to me, kissed my check, and courteously poured more wine into my glass. He couldn't know I had just achieved my ideal wine-to-ice balance but it didn't seem an important point to mention. He then resumed his conversation with Malcolm.

"What do you mean zat is what Paul does?" Ravenna asked. "He always wants to be wis you."

"Paul used to break up with her all the time," Anne offered casually.

Ravenna looked at me with concerned interest. This was news to her.

Anne continued, "Then he'd call a few hours later. Sometimes a day later, right?" She looked at me for confirmation. I nodded.

"How did I not know zis?"

"It was before you and I were friends," I said. "In my first couple years with Paul. Whenever he got upset he would talk about breaking up, and often do it, then he'd come back and apologize."

"I'm sorry, *mon amie*."

"It's fine, really," I said. "It was his pattern, and it hurt me a lot. Then I got used to it. But eventually I got tired of it."

"I would too," Ravenna said. I could tell by her expression that she was shocked to have been unaware of such an important detail about my relationship with Paul. Ravenna and I met when Paul and I were in our final months, and I started dating a new guy soon after I finally broke it off with Paul.

"He loves to go on about how harshly I ended our relation-ship," I said. "But technically he had ended it a hundred times. I just ended it for the last time."

Ravenna looked at me with understanding.

"Anyway," I said to Anne. "I'm sorry about you and Charlie."

"Me too," Anne said with a sigh. "But it's summer, the season for breakups."

"Zis is not true," Ravenna said. "Oof, Anne and her seasons."

"She might be right," I said. "John Mayes just broke up with his woman."

"I'm tellin' ya," Anne said. "She writes the relationship column," Anne tilted her glass at me, "but I know this stuff. Sorry to hear about John, though. He's a nice guy."

"I'm sorry too," I said. "He and I talked this morning and he seemed pretty depressed about it. Maybe I should invite him out, make us an even six. He's probably just sitting at home, and he lives only a couple blocks away."

Anne and Ravenna thought it was a great idea, and so did Malcolm and Timothy when I ran it past them. I knew Timothy was happy to be with my friends, and Malcolm was happy to be anywhere with Ravenna. I had another, secret motivation in mind, but I didn't share it with the table.

"I'm going to go call him and hit the ladies' room," I said. "Be right back."

I snaked around the crowded terrace and entered the restaurant. I found a quiet spot beyond the bar and called John. As I suspected, he was sitting at home, working, in the middle of a wicked case of writer's block. He was thrilled for a chance to step away and clear his head. After we hung up I walked further into the restaurant, to the back wall where I could still survey our table outside. Then I called Paul.

"Hey baby," he said. "Where are you? It sounds noisy."

"Out with Anne and Ravenna, and her new man. And John, my friend from the paper."

"That's cool," Paul said. I knew he barely remembered John, if at all.

"He just broke up with that woman, the one you met at the benefit."

"Right," Paul said, not remembering either one of them enough to make a dent, which irritated me because he'd been so rude to them.

"Anyway," I continued, "John's bummed so I thought he could use an evening out. Plus, I was thinking maybe he and Anne might hit it off." My irritation switched to mild excitement.

"Sounds like a plan," Paul said, not joining in my enthusiasm.

"Did I catch you in the middle of something?"

"Just watching a movie," he said. "Call me later, okay? I love you."

After we hung up, I decided to hit the ladies' room after all.

29

• • •

I woke up Monday morning wrapped in Timothy's arms and pret-zeled in his legs. He felt me stirring and tightened his embrace and pulled me even closer.

"We should wake up like this every morning," he mumbled into my ear. "You're the first thing I think about every day." He kissed my cheek, pressing his face into mine. I could feel the scratchiness of his seven o'clock shadow. It was comforting and familiar after months of dating.

I laughed sleepily. "You think about work the second you wake up."

Timothy smiled with his eyes still closed. "I think about you right after." I did love Timothy's honesty; he was who he was, and it was refreshing. Exactly who he was, though, I was still learning. That made me happy too.

He purred deeply, squeezing me even tighter.

"I don't ever want to leave this bed," he said.

"This might be the most comfortable any two people have ever been," I said. Then reality hit me. "Ugh, I have to see Daniel Perry today."

Timothy opened his eyes and pulled his head back to look at me.

"Who?"

"My boss," I reminded him.

Timothy closed his eyes and nuzzled against me.

"Oh, him," he said. "Don't you see him every day?"

"Most days. But today I have to have the talk."

"What talk?" Timothy kissed my face, moving toward my ear, making my cheek tingle.

"*The* talk. Where I let him have it for—"

"For what?"

I suddenly realized I hadn't told Timothy about the recent happenings with Daniel Perry because one, Timothy and I had barely spoken in weeks, and two, explaining the story would require lying about, or omitting, Steven's involvement in the famine benefit.

"For the way he treats me," I said. "It's time I did something about it."

"Good for you. Now," he said, as his hands began gliding over my hips, "let's not think about work for a few minutes."

"If it's only going to be a few minutes," I said with a smile.

Timothy laughed and kissed me. I was in the mood, but not as much after thinking of Daniel Perry and the day ahead of me. Once that ghastly man entered my mind, bad thoughts began percolating in my head and good things stopped percolating elsewhere in my body.

"Hey," I said softly as Timothy kissed my neck with warm, morning lips. "I wonder what happened with Anne and John."

The evening before, as Ravenna, Malcolm, Timothy, and I left the restaurant, Anne and John were engrossed in a conversation about dating and relationships. Specifically, about ending them.

"They looked like they were hitting it off," Timothy said. "What happened to that other guy she was seeing?"

"Charlie?"

"I guess. You said they were pretty serious. But that was a while ago." It was only a few weeks earlier but Timothy had no sense of time. "Did he hit the road?" he asked, continuing to kiss me softly and trying to tempt me with his hands under the covers.

"Pretty much," I said. "Then he came back."

"Mmm." Timothy was only half listening. "Sounds like he panicked."

"That's what I think. I told Anne not to mention the big three," I laughed.

"The what?" Timothy said lazily.

"The big three," I said.

Timothy looked at me, waiting for an explanation. I was certain I'd mentioned the idea to him before, but he merely grinned sweetly at me and waited for elaboration.

"The theory that everyone will have three great loves in life," I said, and then decided to return to the subject of Anne and Charlie. "I'm just saying, I can't blame Charlie for panicking. He probably thought Anne was hinting in a big way—that she loves him, that she wanted to get serious, all of it."

"That shouldn't make him run away," Timothy said. "Anne seems great." He moved hair out of my face and gazed at me. His lack of panic was comforting. He propped himself up on one elbow. "The big three, huh." He considered the notion as he rubbed his eyes. "That's a romantic idea. Sounds like you," he added with a warm smile.

"Thanks, but I adopted it. A man said it to me years ago. He was a family friend who'd just married his wife for the second time. They were married for many years, got divorced, and then got married again. He was telling me their story and mentioned the theory. His theory, I should say. Then again, maybe it wasn't his theory, just like it's not mine. Anyway, I don't know if his wife was number one, two, or three, but the idea touched something in me and I never forgot it." I smiled at the memory. I hadn't heard about that man in years. I hoped he and his wife were still happy.

"So Anne told Charlie about the big three," Timothy said, fully digesting the information.

"Yes," I said. "She just mentioned it and didn't mean anything by it, but Charlie probably got spooked."

Timothy looked at me with intense affection. "I'm glad I'm getting to know your friends."

"Me too," I said.

Incorporating a love interest into your life is hard enough if you live in the same city, but Timothy and I faced the distance barrier as well. Now that barrier seemed to be coming down.

I let Timothy shower first because he had an earlier start to his day. He had wanted us to shower together but I knew where that would lead and I needed to get my day going. Plus, I wasn't feeling quite as, uh, motivated as the last time we saw each other. I was very attracted to Timothy, but our most recent spell of weeks apart had taken a slight toll on my libido for him.

I could hear water running through the pipes behind the wall. I started to make coffee and warm a bit of milk in a pot. I set out cereal, yogurt, and bread for toast. I planned to offer eggs or French toast if Timothy wanted them, but I suspected once he was showered and raring to go, that's exactly what he'd do. I bumbled around the kitchen until my head was swimming hard enough that I had to sit down and make a few notes, knowing if I didn't, the ideas would vanish, and they felt too important.

I went into the living room and opened my computer, typed in my password, and woke it from sleep mode. I walked around the airy, sparsely-furnished room and opened the shades on the tall windows. Within a few seconds my computer dinged, indicating new e-mail.

I expected the usual junk and spam and all manner of press releases in my inbox, so instead of checking it I wrote down the thoughts I needed for my writings, and then went back to the kitchen to make myself a café au lait.

I worked as a barista in college and I could still make almost any coffee beverage. Café au lait was my favorite. So simple, so soothing: half coffee, half steamed milk. I didn't steam the milk when I made it at home, but hot stirred milk tasted the same, maybe better. I put four teaspoons of sugar into my oversized mug and carried it into the living room.

I could no longer hear the shower water running. Now I heard Timothy walking around my bedroom upstairs, dressing, primping, and readying for his big first day on his dream project. I was happy he was here, in my place, in my presence, and would be for days. We needed this time together. Our lives were so different, which kept our relationship fun and fresh, but there was a distance between us, caused partly by geography and partly by his fixation on work.

I scanned my e-mail inbox with disinterest as I waited to see Timothy walk down the stairs. Spam. Junk. Spam. Press release. Press release. Junk. My eyes halted abruptly when they landed on Steven's name. My chest got tight. My stomach sucked itself inward. I forgot to blow on my coffee before taking a sip and burned my lips and tongue. The subject line of his e-mail: *5am.*

I was frozen. Afraid to double-click the e-mail and open it. I didn't want Timothy to come downstairs in the middle of my reading. If I had any brains I wouldn't still react this way to Steven. His appearances—in a text message, an e-mail, a crowded ballroom, or leaning against his car across my street—always startled me. Scratch that, they paralyzed me.

I snapped myself back and noticed e-mails from Anne and John Mayes. I opened John's to find a lovely thank-you for dragging him out of his funk and showing him a great time, "especially talking to Anne," it said. *Hmm, seems John is dealing with his breakup rather well.* I closed his e-mail and opened Anne's as Timothy appeared at the top of the stairs.

"I just got an e-mail from John saying it was especially nice talking to Anne last night," I called up to him. "I'm about to open one from Anne."

Timothy walked downstairs, came over to the sofa, sat on the arm, leaned down to kiss my head, and read the e-mail over my shoulder. He began to read aloud as I jumped ahead to the words *he kissed me.*

"They kissed!"

"See?" Timothy said, and then he stood and walked to the kitchen. "Looks like it worked out. Wow, that coffee smells great."

I followed him to the kitchen. "Want a café au lait?"

"I don't know," he laughed, "what is it?"

"Coffee and steamed milk." How funny, I thought. Timothy had traveled across much of the world and he didn't know café au lait? I wrapped my arms around him and we kissed. "I'm sorry, I taste like coffee," I said.

"You taste amazing." He ran his tongue around my lips. "If zat is zee taste of a café au lait," he said with a terrible French accent, "give me a double."

I made him the drink and stirred in a few teaspoons of sugar. He said with an apologetic look, "Any chance you have one of those to-go cup things?"

"Actually I do." I pawed through a cabinet for one of several insulated mugs I'd collected over the years. I chose the nicest one, made of stainless steel, and poured his coffee into it. "I could give you the one with puppies on it but I don't want the other boys to beat you up."

"I can't wait," he said. "This project, at my age, at this stage of my career, I'm so psyched." His exuberance was palpable. "I checked my e-mail upstairs and Ted, one of the guys in my firm, said two other guys on the project went to MIT."

"Good, so you'll have that in common," I said. "That always helps."

"Totally! That's the best news I could get," Timothy said, hopping with excitement. He looked like a little kid on his way to something really fun rather than a man about to start a backbreaking job that would tie him up at least twelve hours per day. I knew the MIT connection put it over the top. Even years after completing school Timothy talked about it all the time. Every chance he got. Whenever there was an opening.

"I'll text you the directions to the university right now, just in case you need them," I said. For all Timothy's smarts, he was terrible with directions. The fact that I had taken him to the university just yesterday did not guarantee that he would remember how to get there. "This early in the morning it'll take you less than ten minutes." I unplugged my phone from the charging cord I kept on the kitchen counter and began to text him the information.

He slid his arms around my waist and said, "You're wonderful."

"And you haven't even tasted my French toast," I said.

"I can't wait to see you later," he said, resting his forehead on mine.

Timothy's energy and positivity and nice words permeated the air around us. He kissed my cheek, walked to the hall, grabbed his computer bag, and headed for the front door.

"By the way," he said, "was that an engagement ring I saw on your dresser?"

Ho-ly shit.

Timothy searched his pockets for his keys and, unable to find them, kneeled down to open the outer flap of his computer bag.

"Yes," I said.

He looked up at me. "Uh, something happen while I was away?" He felt around his bag for his keys.

I kneeled down so we were eye to eye. "Actually, an old

boyfriend showed up and asked me to marry him."

"Oh yeah?" Timothy said as he finally found his keys. "And what was your answer?"

"I told him I'd think about it," I said.

"Hmm, I almost believe you." He kissed the tip of my nose. "But there's a problem with that story."

I raised an eyebrow.

"That ring isn't nice enough," he said, staring into my eyes. We shared a brief moment of unspoken fantasies about what might happen between us in the future. "A really smart guy would give you a ring you wouldn't have to think about."

Timothy gathered his workbag, to-go cup, and keys from the floor. We stood up together. I didn't know what to make of his assessment of Paul's engagement ring.

"So, really," he said, hoisting his bag up on his shoulder, "where did you get it?"

"It's Anne's," I said. "A gift from her grandmother. It needs to be cleaned and the best jeweler is right near the newspaper so I told her I'd take it in."

Timothy pulled me gently to him. "Thank you for an incredible night. Let's do it again tonight! I'll call you later."

"Good luck today," I said.

We shared one more long kiss before he walked out the door. As I stood in the front window and watched Timothy drive away, I felt more compelled than ever to write a piece about truth—how we long for it, and how we so often deny it.

30

· · ·

I had two important items to accomplish that morning: One, read Steven's e-mail, and two, confront Daniel Perry. The moment Timothy's car was out of sight I made a beeline to my computer. I brought up my inbox and again felt short of breath just seeing Steven's name. The e-mail's subject, *5am*, had lingered in my head during my conversation with Timothy, even as we kissed good-bye. I remembered Steven to be a late sleeper. The only time he saw five o'clock in the morning was at the end of a night out. But sure enough, the time stamp on the e-mail was 5:02 a.m. I clicked to open it.

```
Amanda,
It's five in the morning and I'm up thinking
about........the Porsche. You thought I was going
to say I'm thinking about you. Fucking egotist.
-S
```

Three sentences. One expletive-laced joke insult, stolen from me. One huge smile across my face. At that moment I realized something rather profound: Steven hadn't changed. He was exactly the same, and my excitement and happiness at the thought of him losing sleep over me made me realize I hadn't changed either.

His e-mail didn't ask for anything. No dates, no *I'll call you later*, no chitchat. It was just Steven, sharing a moment of truth. Instinct told me to rustle up some anger or resentment but neither came. Since the benefit gala, and especially since our test drive, our history was being rewritten, and my feelings right along with it.

I looked at the clock and saw I'd lost time musing about Steven. Now I had less time than I'd need to write anything worthwhile. I didn't want to arrive at the paper before Daniel Perry. I wanted him to be sitting at his desk in the glass cage so he'd see me walk across the newsroom. I'd walk with purpose, stare him down, give him a *don't mess with me* face, and he'd know the storm was a-comin'.

I quickly jotted some notes about truth. I'd always prided myself on being an honest person but I really wasn't, was I? I had an engagement ring upstairs. The giver of it, Paul, knew nothing of my current romantic predicament. Was I obligated to tell Paul that I'd been dating someone for months? Likewise, was I obliged to tell Timothy another man just proposed to me? Of course, I *had* told Timothy about the proposal; he simply chose not to believe it. As for Steven, he was the only party who knew the truth. He knew Mr. California, aka Paul, wanted to marry me. And he knew I was dating Mr. DC, aka Timothy.

I had to choose one of them. I couldn't keep Paul waiting much longer for my answer. And now that Timothy had his big project in my city, he and I would be getting much more serious. *Right?* He'd told me a few weeks into our dating that he wasn't seeing anyone else. I had told him the same because it was true at the time. Now I had to choose just one. The pressure was substantial.

These were men of substance and significance, not casual dates or hookups. Each of them wanted a relationship with me, and since I took relationships very seriously, I had to make a choice and stick with it. The truth as I knew it: Couplehood isn't simply a decision two people make to be exclusive; it's a state of mind.

Timothy would be returning to my place that evening and staying for a few days. He would be in my bed while Steven was in my inbox and Paul was around my finger. Three men, three very different relationships, and one woman who needed to make a big decision. Wow, I thought, that would make a great tagline for a book.

• • •

I took the stairs up to the main newsroom floor. I breathed slowly and methodically, keeping my heart rate steady. An hour earlier, just before I hit Save on my notes about truth, I made a decision that could change the course of my life. I didn't write about it, or call a friend to talk about it. I simply decided it, and the resolve was empowering.

I didn't stop at my desk to sling my bag over my chair. I didn't set up my computer for a morning's worth of work because I hadn't brought my computer with me. I gave John Mayes a wave and tapped Mia on the shoulder, but I stopped for nobody and nothing in my pursuit of Daniel Perry.

I saw the wanker in his office. Unfortunately I saw two other people in there with him. One person I didn't recognize, the other was Leona Vargas. I couldn't deal with her right now. *What should I do?* If I stopped for any reason, especially nervous hesitation, I might not go through with it. Several years of cowering in Daniel Perry's presence had hobbled my bravado. It took all my available strength to keep my head up and my resolve...resolved.

I stopped ten feet from the glass cage. It was Monday morning and the paper was abuzz with the sights and sounds of important things being reported, laid out, formatted, edited, snipped, rewritten, fluffed up, and cut out. I didn't want to make a scene.

I surreptitiously glanced around to find not a soul acknowledging my presence. It was exactly as I'd wanted.

Using my thumb I felt for Paul's ring on my finger. Crap, it wasn't there. I had meant to put it on. Timothy was a few neighborhoods away, scaling his new mountain of a project, but he might as well have been back in DC for as close as he felt to this moment in my life. And where was Steven right now? Day trading, perhaps. Or on a conference call, pardon me, con call, talking about hedging and buying long (or is it short?) and hostile takeovers and liquidity, or whatever investor types talk about. Or maybe he was test-driving a Maserati through fields of cow poo.

If I had asked each man to come with me that morning, for moral support, which one would say yes? Which one was the best kisser? Which one of them had the best taste in music? If I were sick, which one would make me a cup of tea without being asked? If I were in labor, which one would be pacing outside the delivery room? (There's no way I wanted any of them in the room with me.) Did I want children? Jesus, I was in my midthirties, I had to figure that out soon. I didn't want to be old and crinkly when my kid graduated high school. Timothy liked cars, but did he like cars as much as Steven? Paul didn't care about cars, but he knew I loved them, so that wouldn't be an issue. What if Steven only wanted "a chance" and nothing more? What if I chose him only to find he didn't actually want a serious relationship with me, rather just the option of having one? And what did Timothy see happening between us? Would he always be so happy and excited about everything? He was like a dog in that way—even if you left the house for twenty minutes, when you returned his reception was as if you'd been gone a week. How could anyone be *that* happy and sweet, yet not bother to call his mother? Steven was abrupt and intense and often surly, but when his family needed him, he dropped his entire life and ran to them. Paul was an emotional bag of tricks. Romantic, loving, gentle, needy, but was he strong enough for life's big stuff? Was I thinking too much? Are other women so torn? Was my car getting ticketed right now?

Daniel Perry finally looked up and noticed me. His meeting was ending, and within seconds the two people walked out of his office. Leona Vargas darted a glance at me but it was meaningless. Everything about her was darty. I took a deep breath. Forget writing about truth, I was about to live it.

I walked to the glass door and almost hesitated, out of habit, but I depressed the cold steel lever and pushed the door open. Daniel Perry said nothing. I closed the door behind me and he looked at me as though it were any other day.

"I'm busy," he said. "What?"

"We need to talk," I said.

"About?"

"About why you hate me," I said. "About the future of my column. About why you lied to me about the benefit. About why you made me think Emily Richmond wanted to skin me alive when she was actually dying for me to attend that benefit. And," I stepped closer to his desk, "about why you're such an intolerable prick."

Daniel's mouth hung slightly open. I had never seen him speechless. Then I noticed a slight movement in his brows; they moved toward each other as his anger surfaced.

"Who the hell do you think you're talking to? First off, we'll talk when I want to talk to you. And we'll talk about what I want to talk about, which will only ever be one subject: work. It ends there."

"Not anymore," I said.

Daniel scoffed and leaned back in his chair.

"What does that mean?"

"You will talk to me," I said. "Or—"

"Or what?"

"I'm gone," I said.

"Don't make me laugh, Morgan."

I stared him down. "Fine. Goodbye, Daniel." I turned and walked to the door.

"Wait a second, drama queen."

I didn't turn to look at him. I waited with my hand on the lever of the door. Daniel's image was reflected in the glass.

"What do you mean 'lying to you'? How dare you accuse me of that."

"How dare I? You sound like a woman," I said.

I stood still, staring out of the cage.

"My, my, someone's panties are in a bunch," he said.

Daniel Perry just mentioned my panties. To throw up or not to throw up, that is the question.

"What happened, Amanda, somebody dump you?" Daniel's tone was patronizing, much like the voice in my head when I made fun of his fire truck pajamas. It took everything in me not to turn, hurdle his desk, and throttle him. I'd seen enough movies to know it was possible to kill someone instantly. Patrick Swayze in *Road House*. Arnold Schwarzenegger in *True Lies*. Arnold Schwarzenegger in *Predator*. Arnold Schwarzenegger with the English language.

But it was unlike Daniel to be that nasty. That base. That crass. Then it hit me.

"I can't believe I didn't see it before," I said.

"What?" Daniel said. "What didn't you see before?"

I watched his reflection in the glass. He leaned forward on his desk and spoke to my back.

"That not everybody cares what Amanda Morgan thinks? That not everybody thinks you're 'all that'? That just because you write a popular fluff column, you're actually not important at all? That despite your big fantasy of storming into my office and laying down the law, you're nothing more than a ten-cent columnist, replaceable at a moment's notice?"

I felt like crying. I felt small. A knot pulled at my throat. *Do not cry. Whatever you do, do not cry.*

"Impress me," Daniel Perry said. "Wow me. Bowl me over. Tell me what light bulb just went on in your head that will change the outcome of this meeting, because from where I'm sitting, it looks very bad. For you."

"It's personal," I said.

"What's personal?"

"You. This. The way you treat me. It's personal."

I turned to look at him. Daniel stared at me as he gnawed on a fat pen.

"Morgan," he said with the sigh of a genius explaining something to a simpleton. "You drink too much of your own Kool-Aid. Nothing here is personal. This is business. Truth is, I'm hard on you because you're not very good."

There was that word again—truth. Daniel Perry was so matter-of-fact with it. So cavalier with such an enormous insult. I had thought I left the subject of truth back at my place, in jotted notes on my computer, but it shows up everywhere. And everyone has their own version of it.

"Then why keep me around?" My voice was weak.

"Because people are idiots, and newspapers cater to the lowest common denominator. People would rather see a front-page photo of a kitten stuck in a tree than a war zone. They want recipes and celebrity gossip, not business news. Well, some do, but they're a minority. And most people would rather read about dating blunders than the truth about their own government."

"I disagree," I said.

"I don't give a good goddamn," Daniel said.

"I think people prefer to read the truth," I said.

"They don't know what that is."

"Yes they do. You just don't know what it looks like." Daniel inhaled to respond but I cut him off. "You think you do, but you don't." I could feel my strength growing by tiny leaps and bounds. "You think interviewing the secretary of the Treasury is important to Joe Schmo's life? It could be, if it were real, but it's not. Those interviews have caveats and verboten subjects and entire topics you're not allowed to ask about. It's a scrim to create the illusion of transparency. I may write about dating and relationships, and you may call it gruel for the masses, but it's serious work, and it's my photo and byline out there. I actually care about the people who write to me. You care only about yourself. My opinions are raw and unswayed, despite editors who've tried to bully me into writing what they considered to be good advice. What I write is honest, and that's why people read it." Daniel knew I had not been referring to Mia, rather to editors I had survived before she was put on my column.

"That wouldn't make a bad op-ed," he said.

"Excuse me?"

Daniel placed his pen in his mouth again, and spoke without removing it. "The holes in interviews, taboo topics, etcetera. Get to work on that. We'll run it Sunday."

I looked at him as though he'd just pulled off his human skin to reveal a cyborg underneath.

"Look," he said with an irritated sigh. "I don't hate you." Daniel looked like he had indigestion. "The future of your column is secure as long as you don't pull another stunt like this. And I didn't lie to you about anything regarding the benefit. And I'm a prick because I can be. Satisfied?"

"No," I said.

"Jesus H. Christ. You're not satisfied. Tough, because that's all you're going to get."

"I'm sure this isn't the first time you've said that to a woman."

Daniel raised his brows. I had stunned him. Yes, I hit below the belt with that one, but if he insisted on painting me as a fluffy, ten-cent, replaceable chick, he'd get an earful of what that kind of chick would say.

"You did lie to me," I said. "You told me Emily Richmond was sleepless at the thought of my covering the benefit. You purpose-fully made me believe she hates me. You told me the paper would lose tons of money if I didn't write a glowing review of the benefit. You threatened my column. Turns out," I raised my hands halle-lujah-style, "Emily Richmond loves me. She and her friends, they *love* me."

"What in hell are you talking about, Morgan?"

"Don't play dumb, Daniel. The gloves are off now. I know all about it. Mrs. Richmond didn't threaten the paper. She begged you to have me at the benefit. She told you about my, uh, the guy who paid tons of money just to make sure I'd be there."

"What?" Daniel's face registered honest ignorance. It was a face I'd never seen before.

"You're a liar," I said. "And I quit." I turned to walk away.

"Amanda." Daniel stood from his chair. "Emily Richmond told me exactly what I told you. Some guy paid for you to be there? I don't know anything about it." Daniel Perry was telling the truth, damn it. I could hear it in his voice. I turned to face him again.

He continued, "You might've heard the newspaper business is in trouble. This might be news to you but our industry isn't exactly on the upswing. Mrs. Richmond is a very powerful woman, a huge political supporter, and along with her friends, a good twenty percent of our local advertising. As far as I know, she wants your head on a stake."

"Oh," I said. "But that doesn't change how you treat me."

"For Christ's sake, you want me to put you over my knee and burp you?"

"Don't make me ill," I said.

Daniel sighed.

"What do I have to do to get you out of my office?" he asked.

"Just tell me why. I'm just one columnist. And I'm freelance. I'm nothing. Yes, my readers like me, but there are big syndicated columns out there you could get for cheap. Even cheaper than I am, though it's shocking that's possible. Readers would like them too. I hate thinking it, but it's the truth. If you dropped me and put someone else in my spot, readers would get pissed, and then they'd get over it. I'd fade away and that would be that. I shouldn't even have contact with the editor-in-chief, yet you summon me to your office all the time and treat me like a peon. What did I ever do to you?"

Daniel rubbed his eyes. "You did nothing, Morgan."

"You tell me I'm a drama queen. That I'm not very good. That I'm fluffy and people only read me because they're not smart enough to have taste." Daniel rubbed the bridge of his nose. I continued, "Let me tell you something, you egomaniacal blowhard, my column is good. It's a labor of love. I could be making bank in the world you love so much—the big, bad world of politics—but that's just a trough of sweaty hogs all jockeying for position. I know that world. Oh, I know that world."

"I know you do," Daniel said.

He does? I looked at him and waited for more.

"You're an employee," he said. "Of course I know about your

background."

"I'm not an employee, I'm freelance. You've made that distinction crystal clear."

"Whatever." Daniel brushed the air with his hand.

"Nobody here knows about my background. Nobody here knows about anyone's background unless they've been here twenty years. Okay, some people know I did my undergrad in DC, but that's it."

Daniel Perry looked at me—really looked into my eyes.

"Fine, I'll go easier on you," he said. "Will that make you happy?"

"No, but I can tolerate it."

"Terrific," he said as though nothing could be less terrific. "Now go."

"There's something going on, Daniel. I know it. I can feel it."

"Feel this," he grumbled as he began to shuffle papers on his desk. "Get that op-ed to Editorial by Thursday."

I opened the door to leave, and he said, "I take it you said no."

"Pardon me?"

"You're not wearing an engagement ring," he said. "Did you say no?"

I was about to lambast him when I remembered Paul's proposal took place at the paper.

"No, not exactly."

"Then you said yes," he said.

"No."

"Well, which is it?"

"What is this, girl talk?"

Daniel smirked and I walked out.

31

. . .

After walking out of Daniel's office, I felt better but still confused. I'd thought him a liar, but I was wrong. I thought he'd be thrilled for me to quit, but I was wrong. I thought he'd fire me just for confronting him, but I was wrong.

I still knew there was something bigger behind his mistreatment of me. One can sense such things. So he knew I'd done political consulting in my DC days, that shouldn't be a big deal. Tons of beltway undergrads work in government before discovering the stasis and futility, and then move on to other fields and cities. Maybe Daniel Perry knew I'd consulted occasionally in recent years. It's possible; he was pretty connected.

Mine was a simple story. I was a very good analyst. A great analyst, my professors always said. I liked studying policy and bloated government and complex situations, and then reducing them into manageable piles of information that the nitwits who held public office could comprehend. After a few internships and low-paying jobs, a former professor recommended me for a job at a nonpartisan consulting firm where I spent a couple years before hightailing it out of the Capitol and off to California for grad school, where I met Paul. Simple, clean, easy story.

Those years were like another life, and I rarely thought about them or talked about them. In many ways, my political background trained me well for my current profession. I liked to peel the onion, pull back the layers of an issue, and get to the root of it. I liked taking first a macro, then a micro, view of things. I liked thinking both practically and romantically. And I liked finding humor in—or injecting it into—serious topics. Writing my column was the perfect vehicle for my kind of thinking. I wasn't enigmatic, I was merely private, but Daniel Perry made me feel like I was a mystery he'd solved, and one that wasn't very interesting after all.

The longer I sat in my car outside the paper, the more I calmed down. The sun beat down and the day was getting hot. Thinking about my earlier life brought Paul to mind. When we first met I was planning on life in academia. Writing was a pastime—a hobby, not a career. But grad school required me to write all the time and eventually I became motivated to write for a living.

Just as the thrill of analyzing policy for the consulting firm's clients became stale, eventually I also grew tired of analyzing policy and politics just for the sake of grades. It was compelling intellectually, but the work itself didn't make me feel good. I felt best in the wee hours when I put the textbooks away and wrote by hand and candlelight. Whether or not I was great at it, it made me feel good. I felt more accomplished writing a personal piece the world would never see than writing a heavily researched, incisive analysis of democratization, or coercive diplomacy, or the European debt crisis that might be published.

In those days, when Paul and I argued, I'd go back to my apartment and write about it. When we were happy, I'd write about it. When I was upset or frustrated, I'd write about it. If a professor gave me a hard time, I'd write about it. After all, Aristotle said man is a political animal, and it's not a huge jump to apply political theory to the non-political world. I had so much experience analyzing situations from every vantage point, eventually my written analyses of my own relationships, and those of my friends, became second nature.

When I moved to this city and scored my column, Paul felt threatened. He never used that word, but his lack of happiness for me was obvious. He was convinced my new career would change things between us. I insisted he was wrong, and I resented his perspective, but maybe he was right. He needed to stay in California to move forward in the music business, and I encouraged him to do so, saying we'd work it out somehow. But he never encouraged me. In the end, we didn't work it out.

All of that history flooded back in the wake of my face-off with Daniel Perry. I was about to turn on the ignition in my car when I got a call from Ravenna.

I answered, "Please tell me you're still in town."

"Of course," she said. "Malcolm wanted me to stay. What is going on wis you? How is Timothy? Did you see your boss? Where are you?"

"Sitting in my car outside the paper," I said.

"Let's meet, *mon amie.* I need coffee."

As soon as I hung up with Ravenna, I got a call from Paul. I almost didn't answer but I knew that wasn't the right thing to do. Perhaps I'd told him about facing Daniel today, and he was calling to see how it went.

In the past week I'd said so many things to so many men, I had trouble remembering what I'd said to whom. I answered the phone. Paul and I talked about our weekends, but I was preoccupied with the previous half hour of my life. Before walking in the door of the newspaper, I had decided to quit my column. I assumed I would walk out of there needing to find a new career. Now, not only was I still a columnist, I had even more work to do.

I told Paul about my big Daniel Perry confrontation but he didn't grasp the magnitude of it. He wanted to know if I was still "thinking." He wanted an answer to his proposal and I knew he was entitled to one. Thankfully, he preferred to get my answer in person. I told him we would talk later and make a plan to see each other. I had no idea how I would speak to him later, what with Timothy in town, but I couldn't grapple with that now.

• • •

Ravenna and I sat outside at our regular bistro where the waiters were always thrilled to see us. They brought us espresso but caffeine was the opposite of what I needed. Instead I ordered a beer, the first time in my adult life I'd ordered a drink in the morning. Ravenna didn't comment. She merely toasted her porcelain demitasse cup to my glass.

"Okay," she said, lighting two cigarettes and handing me one. "What is going on?"

"That prick," I said. Whatever level of calm I'd achieved sitting in my sun-warmed car outside the paper had faded after my conversation with Paul, and it was fast being replaced by unsettled feelings and building pressure.

"Which prick?" Ravenna asked.

"Daniel Perry."

"He fired you!"

"No."

I told Ravenna what had unfolded in the glass cage. "He knows something, or thinks he does. It's probably not even important. And," I sighed with frustration, "Paul wants an answer. And he wants it in person. I mean, of course it should be in person. We're talking about marriage here." I took a long sip of my Samuel Adams.

"How can you talk in person wis Timothy here?"

"Exactly! But I don't know how long Timothy's going to be in town, and it's not fair to make Paul wait for another guy to leave."

"Why not?"

I pondered Ravenna's question. She leaned forward on her elbows, her cigarette releasing smoke in a twisted upward trail. "I like Paul so much, you know zis. But he comes here wis no warning and wants you to decide zee rest of your life. Who is he to demand zis? You have a whole life and zat doesn't disappear just because he shows up."

Gotta love Ravenna.

"Maybe that's why I feel a bit resentful," I said. "But then I feel guilty about feeling resentful because he's asking to *marry* me. After all these years."

"You and me, we have zee guilt about sings. I felt guilty when my husband cheated on me." She half-smiled regretfully at the memory of it. "Zat was ridiculous, of course. You feel guilty because someone wants to marry you. Zat's ridiculous. But zee feeling is real. Paul uses it against you, I sink."

I nodded.

"Zat's why he gets mad. He sinks if you feel guilty, zen you say yes."

It's amazing how insightful a person can be from outside of a situation.

"You still love him?" Ravenna asked.

"I think I'll always love Paul. He's an integral part of my life. Well, my past. Most people would think I'm crazy not to marry him, right?" Ravenna nodded. I continued, "Here's this handsome, intelligent, romantic, successful music producer who wants to marry me. He's willing to live wherever I want, support me, be with me until we're old and gray. And he speaks French!"

"Zis is important," Ravenna said jokingly.

My thoughts jumped from one subject to the next. "I don't

know what to feel. There's something about Daniel Perry that makes me angry about things I shouldn't be angry about."

"*Oui.* Some people are like zat."

"It almost pisses me off that he didn't lie to me about the famine benefit. I've been so wrong about so many things."

Ravenna laughed. "What will you tell Paul?"

"I don't know," I said. "He sounded pissed when we talked a little while ago. Like that's going to make me want to hitch my wagon to him forever."

Ravenna gave me a quizzical look. She didn't know the phrase *hitch one's wagon.*

"Marry him," I clarified.

"How long is Timothy in town?" she asked.

"I don't know, that's another thing!"

"Okay, okay," she patted my arm. "Instead of deciding what to do, decide how you feel."

"I can't!"

"Why not?"

"Because everything is happening at the same time," I said. "I don't look at Paul the way he looks at me, with all that pure reminiscence. Years have passed since we were together. He doesn't understand that, and I'm worried he's stuck in a different time. The worst part is, talking to Daniel Perry this morning got me thinking about those days, about how Paul was unhappy when I started my column."

"I remember," Ravenna said. "Zis is when we become friends."

"Exactly. And what if I marry Paul, like everyone always assumed we would, and somewhere down the line...I don't know. I'm afraid."

"You are always afraid," she said.

"What if I get a dream job in a new career, what will he do

then? Try to sabotage it? He says he's ready to be there for me, but he hasn't had any practice at it. Then again, nobody is perfect, right? In so many ways Paul is a wonderful guy."

Ravenna nodded and put out her cigarette.

"Timothy's not like that," I said wistfully. "He's so happy and positive, and he thinks my job is fascinating."

"And you sink his job is fascinating. Zat's good."

"It is fascinating to me. Thank goodness, because he talks about it all the time. And MIT this, and MIT that. I get it, you went to MIT! I swear, if they did a DNA test on Timothy, his double helix would have M's, I's, and T's coiled around each other."

Ravenna was lighting a new cigarette and laughed out smoke.

"Malcolm is like zis too, wis Harvard. But he is more calm."

"You really like him," I said.

"Yes, damn it. I like zat he's older, you know? He is wonderful in bed. But back to you."

I waited for Ravenna to ask the big question, but she didn't ask it.

"But what about Steven, you were going to say?"

She gave me a knowing smile.

"He sent me an e-mail at five a.m. this morning," I said.

"Oof, he's good."

"Ravenna, I can't stop thinking about him." My voice dropped to a whisper. "The truth is, when we were on that test drive, I could have kept going. If he had suggested we drive a thousand miles, I would have done it."

"You have not kissed yet?"

I shook my head.

"How is sex wis Timothy?"

"It's always been really good. He's short, but I've gotten used to it."

"He's not zat short," Ravenna laughed.

"In heels I'm taller than he is," I said.

"Wear flats," she said with a shrug.

I drank a hearty gulp. Beer in the morning, this was a new side of me.

"But you haven't slept wis him yet on zis visit?"

I shook my head again.

"But he is in your bed, no?"

"He just got to town yesterday and we were out all day, then out with you guys at night."

Ravenna looked at me with disbelief. "I've had sex five times since we saw you at zee museum yesterday." We both laughed hard. "So you have not slept wis any of zem yet?"

I shook my head again.

"Fok," she said.

"Don't get me wrong," I said. "Timothy and I came close this morning. Very close. But—"

"You have zee engagement ring sitting zer."

"Well, that too." I laughed because I hadn't thought of that point. "I was going to say he didn't call me for over a week. Or from his Scotland trip."

"But zis is not new. Timothy is like zis. Don't be hung up on it."

"Almost two weeks?"

"*Oui*, is a long time," she said. "But I don't sink he sinks zat way."

Ravenna and I shared a moment of introspection. I knew she was falling hard for Malcolm Werner, and she knew I was facing major romantic decisions.

"Who would have thought we'd end up here?" I said.

"We were young when we meet, no? Not so many years ago, but like another life."

"I feel the same. I swear, in the past few days I've looked at my life right now and thought, do things like this really happen to regular people? We watch movies where these things happen, and we spend our lives waiting for them to happen, but they never do. Or," I leaned forward to stress my point, "maybe they happen all the time but we're not programmed to notice it. What do you think?"

"I sink you've had enough beer," Ravenna said.

32

...

My tiny buzz had worn off by the time Ravenna and I finished lunch, which we didn't order but was presented to us, gratis, by the owner. He was a sixty-something Frenchman with a big thing for Ravenna, and a small thing for her columnist friend who just might get him some free press. Ultimately I took Ravenna's advice and switched to coffee and she switched to wine so, as usual, we balanced each other out.

I felt better as I pulled in my driveway, although I still sensed a lingering mystery with Daniel Perry. I had zero intention of writing the op-ed he suggested and, ironically enough, I was now completely turned off to writing my piece about truth. I had felt compelled to write it before the face-off, but once I got the confrontation out of my system, I didn't feel the need to explore it with my pen. Plus, I didn't know what I thought about truth anymore. Or "the big three." Both ideas had seemed so simple just a week ago. Like a child's matching game. Daniel Perry = bad. Third great love = the one you choose.

So Daniel Perry would now go easier on me? I'd wait and see about that. I didn't consider Daniel to be a man of his word, but now that he knew I wouldn't take his crap, perhaps my work atmosphere would change. It had felt amazing to threaten to quit. I smiled as I walked in my front door.

Quitting my job had never occurred to me before that morning, yet it was the most empowered I'd felt in ages. I hung my purse on the doorknob of the front hall closet and wondered if relationships weren't like careers. You planned them in your mind, and pictured a straight upward line to a bright future, but in reality you can't know how things will play out. Over the years different people appear on the scene, and the straight line to success—or happily ever after—sees dips and drops. Eventually you might have a light bulb moment and find yourself threatening to quit, just to see what happens.

I'd never done that in a job, or in a relationship. But Paul had. I plopped onto my sofa and recalled an evening years before when he was in a snit about something and said we should break up. I was heartbroken and left his place in tears and drove back to my apartment thinking I'd never hear from him again. A couple hours later he called to apologize, and to say he couldn't live without me, or something dramatic only Paul or a soap opera character would say.

Then I remembered another occasion. Then another. He'd done that quite a bit, threaten to "quit" us, then he'd say the right thing and we'd get back together. His heartfelt apologies were enough for me back then.

My cell phone rang. It was Anne.

"I have to tell you something," she said.

"Go for it," I said.

"Promise you won't get mad?"

"No."

"I'm going out with John tonight," she said.

"John Mayes?"

"Yeah."

"That's great!" I said. "Why would that make me mad? You already told me you kissed last night."

"I know, but we'd been drinking."

"Of course I'm not mad, Anne. I'm thrilled. I purposely invited him last night so you two could talk."

"That was a setup?" Anne asked in surprise.

"Yep."

"You're good," she said.

"I didn't want to tell you beforehand."

"Why?"

"Because things are iffy with you and Charlie and I didn't want it to seem like I'm trying to drive a wedge there, or discourage you from being with him."

"I wouldn't have thought that," Anne said. "But I appreciate it."

"Why would I be mad about you and John going out?"

"Well," Anne said hesitantly, "he's always liked you and, I don't know, maybe you were keeping him around as a backup."

I didn't respond.

"Just in case," she added.

"Anne, don't be silly. I've always liked John, but not romantically."

"He liked you, though. Maybe he still does."

"John's a really good guy," I said sincerely. "If he still liked me, he wouldn't date my best friend."

"Please, many guys would do that," Anne laughed.

"True, but not John. I've known him for years. He's a relationship guy, not a player." I got up from the sofa to make a cup of tea. I didn't realize I'd sighed, and that it was audible.

"Something wrong?"

"No," I said. "You just reminded me of something."

"What?"

"Remember when Paul called me a backup?"

"Wow, I forgot about that!" Anne said. She then heard my silence. "Amanda, don't think what you're thinking. That's not why he proposed."

"I wasn't thinking that. But now that you mention it."

"Okay," she said. "Then what were you thinking?"

"I was just remembering that he said it."

About a year after I had moved back East, Paul was still living in Los Angeles and our relationship was eking by. I was a harried new columnist trying to find my way in a new industry—new to me, anyway—and he was a grunt in the music business. Paul called me one night when he was in a car with some new friends. Our conversation lasted only a few minutes. We said goodbye but I didn't hang up right away; sometimes we did that to say an extra goodbye. Paul, on the other hand, meant to hang up but his phone didn't disconnect the call. I heard one of his friends ask, "Who was that?" Paul's explanation was muffled, as his phone was on the seat or in his lap, but I heard him say I was a girlfriend. The friend asked something else, and then I distinctly heard Paul say, "I love her, but she's a backup."

I became immediately incensed. Boiling. A volcano about to blow. I knew Paul didn't actually mean what he said but the sheer audacity and immaturity of describing me in such a dismissive way to a carful of meaningless guys showed me what Paul was made of. "A" girlfriend, as though I were one of several. A backup, as though I were sitting around, pining, hoping he'd give me a shot. I hung up, started pacing and waited for the line to clear, then I called him back. I told him what I'd heard. I waited for his excuse. He was pulling up to a bar and told the guys to go inside while he talked to me.

Paul apologized up and down, explaining that he didn't want the guys to know about his personal life. He told me I was over-reacting. I told him to take a running leap off a short pier. For me, that was it. I went on a date the very next day. To me, our relationship was over, but Paul continued to call, e-mail, write, and try to visit for many months. Until that moment on the phone with Anne, I'd forgotten about the "backup" fiasco.

"Amanda," she said, "Paul was really young back then. He was trying to be cool. He's a man now, grown up, successful. He was ready back then too, but it was a different time. He knew what he felt, but he didn't always know how to act."

"Yeah," I said. Anne was right. "Anyway, I talked to him a little while ago. He wants an answer, in person."

"Do you have one?"

"Anne, let me ask you a question. Did you think Paul and I would end up together one day?"

"Didn't everyone?"

"But did you? You're my best friend. Did you think Paul and I would eventually get married?"

"Honestly?"

"Honestly," I said.

"Yes, I did. Until you met Steven."

The water for my tea started to boil and I dropped a teabag into my favorite mug. Anne's response shot around my head like a pinball.

"Don't get me wrong," Anne continued, "I completely understood why you broke up with Paul. You were living on opposite coasts, and you were in different places in other ways. But I always thought you'd end up in the same place. Truthfully, I'd never seen a guy so openly want to marry someone. He pretty much shouted it from the rooftops. You don't find that every day. At least I don't!"

"He's unique that way," I said.

"Paul could land a wife in two seconds," Anne said. "He doesn't need a backup."

"That's true."

"He really is special," she said sweetly.

The Paul portion of the conversation concluded, for there was nothing more to say. After a few quiet moments, Anne said, "So you're fine with me going out with John? Really fine?"

"Totally fine," I said. "Super fine."

"I'm looking forward to it. So how is Timothy's big first day? When does he get back?"

"I'm not sure," I said. "I don't want to call and bother him. I'll text him and ask."

I shot Timothy a nice little text, then re-dunked my teabag.

"On to the important stuff," Anne said. "Have you slept together yet?"

"No," I laughed. "Ravenna asked me the same thing."

"Why not?"

"He just got here yesterday!"

"Hey," Anne said. "I wonder if John is good in bed."

"There's only one way to find out," I said.

After talking to Anne I carried my computer from my living room into my office to begin writing my next column. E-mails came in every few minutes, including one from an online dating site I had used a few years earlier. Have you found *the one* yet? the subject line read. Who the hell knows, I thought, then deleted it.

After a while I had to stretch my legs and think through my column. I walked into my bedroom and took off the clothes I'd worn to the paper that morning. I changed into a jean skirt, tank top, and flip-flops. I walked past my hand-painted dresser, the first real piece of furniture I ever bought, and casually slid Paul's lovely ring off it, and then onto my finger. I heard my cell phone *ping* from my office down the hall, obviously Timothy's response to my text message. I power-walked to my office and picked up my cell phone to see two texts: one from Ravenna and one from Paul. Nothing from Timothy. Ravenna wanted to know if I was doing all right. Paul's text merely said: Well?

I texted Ravenna to let her know I was fine. I texted Paul: Still thinking☺. He immediately texted back: You think too much. i love you. Thank goodness for emoticons; one little smiley can subdue a raging beast.

I sat at my desk and cranked through half of my next column. I kept the subject light: workplace romance. I'd been inspired by a letter from a reader, a woman screwing her boss. Those were her words, I noted in the first paragraph. Ah, sweet romance. It was a nice release to assess other people's problems. I hit the Save button just as I heard a knock at the front door. In the middle of a work-day, a loud knock at my door could only mean the delivery of a package, most likely from a publisher. I had amassed piles of books over the years from publishers who wanted me to interview and plug their authors in my column. I rarely did so, but it was fun to get free books. I skipped down the stairs and swung open the door expecting to see my friendly neighborhood delivery man. Instead I saw Timothy with a big smile on his face.

"Hey!" he said, hopping inside and wrapping his arms around my waist.

"Wow, this is a surprise! Are you already finished with your day?"

"Hell, no," he said. "I forgot some papers. We broke for lunch and I thought I'd stop back and get them. And see you," he said, kissing me with each word. Our mouths explored each other while Timothy closed the door without breaking from our kiss. His hands moved everywhere they could reach, running down the length of my miniskirt as his lips softly separated from mine.

"This is a very little skirt," he said.

Timothy picked me up and carried me into the living room, kissing me as he walked. I'd forgotten how strong he was. He wasn't a tall man but his confident hold made me feel petite.

Timothy set me down gently on the sofa and lay down on top of me, moving his body between my legs. I wrapped them around his waist. He reached down and pulled my skirt up from the bottom, kissing me deeply as we started to move in a slow rhythm. I could feel his hardness through his jeans, which he unbuttoned without hesitation. I slid them down, pulling his boxers along, just enough to expose him. When he felt my fingers dig into his skin, he began to press into me with insistence. He pushed hard against my panties, and then slid them aside with his fingers, not bothering to pull them off.

"I've been thinking about this all day," he said.

Timothy's fingers grazed against me and he grew harder every second. He moaned while he kissed me, and then grinded harder, desperate to feel me without going too far. In those moments I wanted him more than I ever had. We'd never had sex without condoms, but I just wanted to feel, not think. I tilted my hips toward him, and then he entered me, almost accidentally but with the full force of intention. Our mouths were still connected but our kissing ceased as sensation took over. He looked into my eyes with every thrust. He moaned with every breath as the wave of near-climax stiffened his entire body. I was already so close, urging him with my eyes to hold on a little bit longer.

Then, a moment later, I stopped moving. A few moments later, Timothy stopped too.

"We shouldn't do this, right?" he asked softly between kisses, still inside me, moving slowly.

"Probably not," I smiled.

The sun streamed in, shining a spotlight on our spontaneous afternoon tryst. I saw flecks of color in his light blue eyes that I hadn't noticed before. Then he said, "Your eyes are very green right now." I smiled as he gently removed himself and lay next to me. I didn't mention that I'd just taken notice of his eyes. There were many occasions when we thought the same thing at the same time. At some point it feels redundant to mention every one.

We lay still, wrapped up with each other, as our bodies calmed. He played with my hair and I ran my fingers across his face, smearing beads of sweat.

"Could I get a set of keys from you?" he eventually said.

"Keys? To my place?"

"Just for these couple days until we get everything set up at the museum," he said. "I don't have an office at the site. No one does."

"There isn't a work area?"

"It's just makeshift. A few tables and a bunch of chairs. Until this really gets rolling most of my work will be done from DC. Same for the Chicago guys. For now everyone is working from laptops. There'll be proper workspace once construction gets underway but the date keeps getting pushed back." He sighed and turned on his back, crossing his arms behind his head. "I can't carry all my stuff around all day. It just gets in the way. So would it be okay?"

"Sure. No problem." I'd never given my keys to a man before. Timothy turned his head, perhaps sensing hesitance in my voice.

"You sure?" he asked sweetly.

"Yes," I looked at him and smiled. "I've never given a guy keys to my place before."

"I'll guard them with my life," he said, leaning up to kiss me. "If you lived far from the university I'd figure out something else, but you're only a few minutes away, and it'd be easier if I can pop back here if I need to. I assumed you'd be at the paper, but if you'll be working from your office here I don't need them."

I wondered momentarily why Timothy couldn't keep stuff in his car, but he had two computers and so many papers and folders, his tiny car wouldn't have enough room.

"Really," I said. "It's fine. I have an extra set in the kitchen." I was proud of myself for agreeing without any substantial fear. It felt good to take this step, to entrust my keys to a man. For two days.

The sofa was so warm and soft. Our weight had sunken the cushions enough that they would need to be fluffed. I straightened my arms above me and felt a much-needed stretch across my back.

"What's that?" he asked.

"Just stretching," I said, turning toward him with a smile.

"No, this." He took my hand and looked at it like he'd found an interesting shell on the beach. I froze for a moment at the sight of Paul's ring on my finger. *Oh shit oh shit oh shit.*

"Is that Anne's ring?"

"Yes," I said.

"Why are you wearing it?"

"Uh, today has been a bit of a day so far. Like I said, I was going to take it to a jeweler downtown. Well, I had a huge blowout with my boss. I threatened to quit!" Timothy raised his eyebrows but didn't say anything. I continued, "Anyway, I put the ring on my finger so I wouldn't forget to take it in and, after everything that went down with my boss, I forgot."

"Oh, smart thinking," he said with his signature positivity. "Like putting a string around the finger." He grinned, kissed me, and arose from the couch, pulling up his jeans as he stood. "I really hate to do this, but I have to get back," he said. Timothy leaned down and hovered over my face. "There's nothing I'd like more than to stay right here with you."

"Do you want something quick to eat?" I wriggled to slide my skirt down to its proper length.

"I have you," he said as he kissed me.

"Really, can I get you something? I don't have much, but I'm resourceful."

"I'll just grab a soda when I get there," he said. "I'm too excited to eat."

"What time do you think you'll be done?" I walked toward the kitchen.

"I don't know," he said. "There's a mountain of stuff to do."

Timothy followed me and ran his hand around his jaw, rubbing his lunchtime shadow, which had already chafed my face.

"The guys from MIT, they're awesome. They're older, but we're cut from the same cloth," he said with satisfaction. "Actually, when I get back tonight, I'll probably have to work." He came up behind me and gripped my hips as I rummaged through a drawer of miscellanea to find an extra set of keys. "I've still got a couple projects going on aside from this one," he said into my neck.

"Right. Do what you need to do," I said, handing him the keys. "I guess I shouldn't wait up for you?"

"Please don't," he said. "I'd love to climb into bed with you already sleeping."

We kissed deeply, almost falling into things again, before laughing at our lack of discipline and pushing each other away.

"Don't read too much into this, but I've thought about that a lot."

"What?"

"Coming home late from work, and you're asleep, and I get into bed next to you."

"That's a great picture," I said.

We kissed, and then he ran out to his car, jumping all five of my front steps on his way.

33

. . .

"A man has keys to my place."

"Zis is good," Ravenna said. "A first step."

"A. Man. Has. Keys. To. My. Place," I repeated. "I actually gave my house keys to a man, while I was wearing an engagement ring from another man."

Ravenna handed me a beer. "Forget zee ring," she waved dismissively. "Have you slept wis him yet?"

"Sort of," I said.

"What does zat mean?"

"We started, but we didn't have condoms. It was stupid. I just didn't want to think anymore, you know? And we have such great chemistry."

"Zat's zee best," Ravenna said.

"Yes, but hear me out," I said, hopping up onto the kitchen counter. Ravenna sat on a footstool, because I insist on only the best for my friends. "Timothy and I have great chemistry, like really great, and we like the same funny movies, and we laugh a lot, and even though his taste in music needs some work, it's acceptable." I took a swig of my beer.

"*Oui.*"

"We're the same age. Almost the same height," I added jokingly with a roll of my eyes. "We both went to grad school, so we both understand that world. We're both from the East Coast. He's a good dresser for an engineer. And—"

"I thought you say he is an architect," Ravenna said between swallowing wine and inhaling a cigarette.

"He is, but he works mainly as a structural engineer."

Ravenna looked at me with confusion.

"He is an engineer first and an architect second," I said. "That's how he explains it. Basically, he doesn't spend his days designing new buildings, even though he can and ultimately will. He's insanely ambitious."

"You've said zis before. But something is bothering you."

"He wants to be a rock star," I said.

"He sings too?" Ravenna was astonished.

"No," I laughed. "I mean a rock star in his field. He wants to be like I.M. Pei." Ravenna nodded in acknowledgement and we both drank a little bit. "Timothy started as an engineer but he decided that it wasn't enough for him. He was creative enough that he also wanted to design, though I don't know if he's great at it. He is a brilliant engineer, so say his colleagues. I've met some of them over the past few months. Of course, they all call each other brilliant. Anyway, he didn't want to work only with architects, supporting their plans and designs. He wanted to do it all."

"Malcolm said zis about him, zat Timothy is a whippersnapper. What is zat?"

"Malcolm said that?"

Ravenna nodded deeply. "I sink it is a compliment."

"Um, it sort of implies that Timothy is maybe a little overeager." I thought about that, let it roll around in my mind. "It's interesting Malcolm sees that already. They've known each other only a few days, including their brief time in Edinburgh."

"Malcolm is wise. Is very attractive. But tell me about Timothy and zee architecture stuff." As an artist Ravenna had always appreciated and loved architecture.

"Here's the deal," I said. "Most architects are not engineers. They design a structure, let's say a house or office building, but an engineer has to make sure it can be built and figure out exactly how to build it."

"You know a lot about zis," Ravenna said.

"You would too, after dating an MIT architect for months." I stressed *MIT* with air quotes. "Essentially Timothy is an architect who works from an engineer's perspective."

"I see," Ravenna said.

"I think he looks at everything from an engineer's perspective. I've dated them before, I know the signs. But..." I hesitated for a moment, not wanting to make Timothy look bad to my friend, then decided *the hell with it*. "He thinks a lot of architects are not very bright. He says most of them are fools who must be tolerated."

"Oof," Ravenna said. "Zat's harsh."

"Isn't it? But it makes sense why he became one. There's a ton of ego there. In ten years I bet he will lead projects like this museum thing. Actual rock stars will want him designing their houses. That's what he wants and he'll probably do it." I drank most of my beer and then tilted my head back to look at the ceiling.

"You're worried about something, *mon amie*."

"I'm worried that's all he wants. He says beautiful, romantic things, like picturing us together in the future, and imagining coming home from work to find me there. But absolutely everything he talks about circles back to his work. It's his whole life."

"Do you love him?" Ravenna asked me.

Before I could respond, both our phones rang. Ravenna flipped open her phone and mouthed *Malcolm* to me, and then walked to the living room to talk to him. I said, "Paul," and answered as I hopped off the kitchen counter.

"Hi there," I said sweetly.

"Whatcha doin'?" Paul said cutely.

"Hanging with Ravenna, talking about boys," I said.

"You wearing my ring?"

"I sure am." I extended my arm and looked at the ring on my hand. "It feels good."

"I miss you," he said.

"I miss you too."

"Want to come to the city tomorrow?" Paul asked.

It's funny how New Yorkers refer to Manhattan as "the" city, like it's the only one in the world. Or the country. Or even the state of New York.

"I'm sorry, Paul, I can't tomorrow. I have work."

"Work on the train," he said.

"No, I mean I have meetings at the paper tomorrow and Wednesday."

"Blow them off," Paul said, as though I were referring to mani and pedi appointments.

"Paul," I said.

"We need to talk, Amanda."

"I know," I said.

"I want your answer," he said plainly. "And I want it to be yes," he added sweetly. I felt a little rush of excitement run through me.

"I could be Mrs. Paul Smith," I said as the reality of my potential future hit me.

"Say that again," Paul said. "No, say, 'I am *going* to be Mrs. Paul Smith.' Go on, say it."

"I am going...to the living room to talk to Ravenna."

"If you don't come here, I'll come to you," Paul said.

"No, don't," I said with alarm.

"Why not?"

"Because I'm so busy the next couple days. I want us to have time. And, well, I still need a little more time."

I heard him sigh. "How about this weekend?"

I couldn't say no. By then Paul would have waited over a week and it wasn't fair to put him off any longer. I didn't know if there existed an official rule about how long you're allowed to make a man wait for an answer to a proposal, but anything more than a week felt unfair. Plus, I assumed Timothy would be gone by week's end. Nothing in the world, not even great sex, could keep him away from his office for very long.

"This weekend," I said.

Paul and I hung up just as Ravenna and Malcolm did the same. I noticed I was out of wine and couldn't offer Ravenna a refill, so I grabbed two beers from the fridge and we walked out to my backyard to talk about our respective conversations. Malcolm had convinced Ravenna to stay the week, which made me incredibly happy. She told me not to worry about Paul's impatience, that I should focus on Timothy and wait to decide anything until after he left.

"I was sinking about you and Timothy while I talked to Malcolm," she said.

Ravenna and I shared a unique habit—the ability to talk sincerely to a lover while thinking about something completely unrelated.

"I sink maybe Timothy is still young for his age," she said carefully.

"I'll be honest, I've thought that too," I agreed. "Sometimes I feel like he's always trying to impress me. I'm already impressed, and I've told him that, but he's always giving me his résumé."

"I really listen to him last night at zee restaurant," she said. "He talked about his accomplishments and always he was looking at you. Kissing your hand. Smiling at you."

"But did you know he went to MIT?" I said. "If you didn't know that, you really should. Did you know? Can I tell you now? He went to MIT. He is so smart. He's like the smartest guy in the world." Ravenna laughed. She knew I was innocently teasing.

"Zis is what I was sinking," she handed me a cigarette. "I know what bothers you."

"Let me hear it," I said.

"You fear zat he has not enough interests outside of work."

I nodded.

"But zis is not zee real problem." Ravenna shook her head *no* with a self-satisfied frown.

"Okay," I said.

"Timothy is a very smart man. But…"

I waited. And waited.

"But what?" I finally said.

"He is not smart enough for you."

"What?"

"You sink I'm crazy," she said.

"Crazy doesn't touch how ridiculous that is."

"I feel it here," Ravenna placed a hand on her stomach.

"Not smart enough for me? You are crazy," I laughed. "A bat-shit-crazy Frenchwoman."

"No." She sucked her teeth a few times. "I am right. Timothy is a wonderful man, I am sure. And he can make bridges and buildings and many sings. And you may have a beautiful romance for zee rest of your lives. But I know zis is true."

"Ravenna, I love you," I said gently, "but that doesn't make sense. I may joke about his obsession with MIT, but not just anyone graduates from there."

"*Mon amie*, you are zee smartest person I know. Timothy knows it. Zat is why he is always trying to impress you."

"First of all, you must know a lot of idiots," I said and Ravenna nodded in agreement. "Secondly, I could never build a bridge. I couldn't even get into a place like MIT, much more graduate from it."

She tsk-tsk'd me. "Zis is not zee point. Everyone has strengths. For Timothy, it is zat kind of stuff. Maybe smart is not zee right word." Ravenna paused and took a slow drag on her cigarette while she searched for a way to express her thought. "You sink in many ways. He sinks in one."

I was about to respond but instead I thought about her words.

She continued, "He misses you but does not call you. He sleeps in his office. He does not see his friends very much. He does not speak to his parents. Okay, maybe zey have issues, but I sink he doesn't have room up here." She pointed to her head. "And you say he talks about school all zee time? Zat was years ago. He works and nothing else. Zis is my sense."

I was listening while staring at a moth that had landed on a leaf. It twitched its wings.

"I hope you are not mad at me," Ravenna said with a worried expression.

"Not at all. I just really want you to be wrong."

"Why? Zis is not bad about him."

"It's not great," I said. "But it's not about him."

"What do you mean?"

"Well, if a rock star architect isn't good enough for me—"

"Is not about good enough," Ravenna said. "You and Timothy are new, zat is all. You are used to men wis many interests. You are worried zat Timothy is boring."

"He's not boring! He's really fun, and so positive and upbeat all the time. It's very refreshing."

"No, no, I don't mean boring. He might be, how you say, limited?" I looked at Ravenna and waited for her to finish. "You love what he does, you sink his work is fascinating, but zer must be more, no? His happiness is wonderful and refreshing, but sometimes a man needs to get strong or angry and say *fok zis*! Or *fok zat*!"

I laughed briefly as I walked in a slow circle on the grass.

"*Mon amie*, you loved Paul wis all your heart and he was emotional and musical and wrote poetry and all zat crap. You loved Steven and he was extremely smart but also a very complete person. He did not hop around like a chicken wis no head. I sink you worry zat Timothy is not complete enough."

"That's different than him not being smart enough. What was that about?"

"It was a wrong word," Ravenna said, lighting another cigarette.

"Go ahead," I said. "Don't stop now."

"MIT, MIT, MIT, is enough already!" Ravenna shouted. "Zis is not enough for you. But it might be enough for him. Do you see?"

I nodded.

"It has only been a few months," Ravenna said. "In time you will learn everysing about him. You will see him completely. Give it a chance."

I stopped circling. Ravenna and I looked at each other. I was so lucky to have her as my friend. She gave words to feelings I couldn't articulate. She knew I over-thought some things and worried when I shouldn't. She encouraged me to get out of my head and just *feel*.

I told her all of this, in not so many words, and she said, "Zis is what friends do." Again, as if on cue, both our phones pinged with incoming text messages.

"Malcolm," she said, smiling as she read it.

"Steven," I said, having to catch my breath.

"Well," Ravenna said, "what does he say?"

"It says, 'I want a Porsche.'" I laughed.

"It does not," Ravenna said, reaching for my phone. "Oh, it does," she laughed.

I texted him back: You already have a Porsche. Less than thirty seconds later he sent another one.

"He wants to know when he can see me," I said.

"Oof, not zis weekend," she laughed. "Paul would go crazy if he sees Steven again."

"Now he is not boring," I said, holding up my phone, indicating Steven.

"*Oui.* Zis is zee problem," Ravenna said.

I texted Steven to call me tomorrow. Ravenna thought that was a good idea. At that moment in time my thoughts and feelings were so up in the air, if Ravenna thought something was a good idea, I did too.

34

· · ·

Tuesday morning came softly. My eyes adjusted to the sun streaming in through the window as I became aware that I was pinned down by Timothy's arm and leg, and he was snoring. I had stayed up fairly late, working and talking to Anne about her date with John Mayes, but eventually I'd nodded off over my computer. Some time after getting in bed I heard Timothy's keys in the front door, but I was so tired it could have been ten minutes or two hours later.

Over the months I had learned that Timothy shifted between operating at full speed and no speed. When he was raring to go, nothing could stop him. When he was down for the count, he was fully out. I looked at him lying next to me in bed. His mouth was slightly open and his face was half-buried in the pillow. He was comatose—the antithesis to the guy who flew over my front steps and sped away.

I kissed his cheek and he smiled as a reflex but did not open his eyes or move, other than to tighten his arm and leg around me and pull me closer to him. I knew his cell phone alarm would go off any minute. I tried to reach over him to the bedside table to turn it off rather than hear its annoying buzz. He wouldn't let me move, which made me laugh.

"What's so funny," he mumbled almost incoherently. It sounded like *wa so fuh-ee*.

"You're so asleep," I whispered. "It's cute."

"You're cute," he said somewhat clearly. Then, "What time is it?"

"Almost seven," I said.

He groaned and mashed his face further into the fluffy down.

"What time did you get in?" I asked softly.

"One. But I worked until three."

"Let me turn off the alarm," I said and tried to escape his hold on me.

"I have to get up anyway," he said, and then moaned and turned, reaching almost behind him to slide his phone off the table and turn off the alarm. He did all of this without opening his eyes.

"You don't get started until nine," I said. "The university is so close. You can sleep for another hour if you want." I had frequently seen Timothy sleep for twelve hours straight.

"Gotta get up. Don't want to. Have to." He squeezed me and kissed me, then finally opened his eyes and looked at me. "You look fucking great in the morning," he said in a sleepy voice. He was lying, of course, but I was flattered by the compliment, and unaccustomed to his use of profanity.

"What?" he said, waking up more fully and noticing my widened eyes.

"You said fuck." I was reminded of Ravenna's comments about him.

He laughed sleepily, "So?"

"I've never heard you say that before," I said.

"I meant it as a good thing. Sorry." He smiled sweetly.

"I'm not," I said.

Timothy and I finally made it out of bed a half hour later. The sex had been slow but intense, and long overdue. We showered together, and then he primped in the mirror longer than I ever would. We walked downstairs with our arms wrapped around each other, he grabbed a Gatorade from the fridge, kissed me goodbye, and then he left for work.

• • •

I parked outside the newspaper and fed eleven quarters into the meter. I didn't look at exactly how much time that allowed because deducing such tiny numeric increments required Einsteinian mathematical abilities. Freelancers were not allowed to park in the newspaper lots. Freelancers did not get a discount in neighboring lots. Freelancers were not even invited to the annual Christmas party. On the bright side, as Leona Vargas had once said to me with her usual patronizing tone, in front of Daniel Perry, free-lancers got "the luck of being in print." I didn't point out to Ms. Congeniality that being published wasn't a matter of chance, like winning the lottery; it had something to do with talent.

I was happy and relaxed for the first time in days, not only from waking up in such a sexy way, but also from talking with Ravenna. She had given me perspective, de-stressed me, and reminded me to enjoy myself and my time with Timothy. I stood on the side-walk and fished around for my newspaper ID, which had a habit of diving into my handbag's equivalent of the Mariana Trench.

My fingers explored the innards of my purse as I walked into the building and I thought how great it was that Anne and John had spent a nice evening together. Who knew what the future would bring for them? Even if things didn't work out, they were mature enough to not put me in the middle of it.

The newsroom was buzzing that morning. I'd been online before leaving the house and looked at the paper's homepage but I didn't recall any big news that would cause a stir. I walked past Mia's desk and asked what was going on. She said the paper's own-ers were in the building and there was talk of selling. Such rumors swirled every year and put everyone on edge. John Mayes saw me from his desk and waved as I slung my bag over my chair. I ges-tured that I'd stop by his desk in a moment, after checking my mailbox.

I had to walk past the glass cage to get to the wall of mailbox cubbies. I saw Daniel out of the corner of my eye and continued walking as though I hadn't. He motioned for me to come in by waving his arm in a spastic circle. For the first time in years, I didn't feel a sense of dread.

"Good morning," I said pleasantly. I was in a post-sex floaty state and I didn't care if my afterglow was apparent.

"Morgan," he said.

I thought briefly of Timothy's orgasm face and felt my stomach tighten and a tingle travel through me.

"I hear the owners are here," I said. I could feel myself smiling, maybe even blushing.

"Yes." Daniel didn't say anything further and I suddenly worried why he'd arm-summoned me to his office. He rifled through papers on his desk, then sat still and did nothing.

"Do you think they'll sell this time?" I asked, still standing, trying to make conversation.

"Probably not," he said.

He adeptly threaded his chubby pen through his fingers and stared at me.

"That's good," I said.

"Everything fine here?" he finally asked. He tilted his pen back and forth like a metronome to indicate *between us*.

"Oh. Yes. Sure. Everything's fine, Daniel."

Could he sense my sex vibe? Most men could sense it—or at least respond to it—without being consciously aware of it. Daniel looked at me as though he hadn't seen me in a long time.

"How's the piece coming?" he asked.

"It isn't," I said with a chipper tone.

"I was thinking," he said.

"Yes?"

"You should write a political piece here and there."

My floaty-ness disappeared. It was the last thing on earth I expected him to say. I looked at him with confusion. I tried to read his expression, but fortunately I didn't know him well enough to know his faces. Normally his horns were a dead giveaway.

"Let's be frank," he said, "the entire editorial board combined doesn't have your political background and your connections."

I raised an eyebrow, curious that he'd brought up my background again.

"Senator Morgan, right?" he said.

"No relation," I said.

"Uh huh. So, you interested?"

"Um, no, I don't think so. I've established myself in a certain way in the paper and I wouldn't want to confuse my readers." It was a lame excuse but I was caught off guard.

"Confuse your readers?" Daniel's tone was pitying, both to my excuse and my readers' brains.

"Yes," I said. "It's no different than a political reporter suddenly writing relationship and dating articles."

Daniel Perry continued to stare at me while he fondled his huge Mont Blanc pen. Come to think of it, Daniel had a reputation for being cheap and probably wouldn't buy a Mont Blanc. It was more likely a freebie from a conference. He seesawed it in his fingers as he stared at me. I was uncomfortable and didn't know which direction to go with my explanation. Daniel Perry was stone, as usual.

"The thing is, Daniel, I did write a few pieces over the years, but honestly the money isn't worth it."

Aha! Hit 'em where it hurts. Bring up money and newspaper editors scamper away.

"What would make it worth it?" Daniel asked, still treating his pen like a joystick.

Whoa, this was unexpected. I'd never thought about writing political pieces for the paper.

"Give me a number," Daniel said as though he were trying to keep his annoyance in check.

"It's probably not the best idea," I said.

"Look," Daniel leaned forward, putting his elbows on his desk. "The paper is drowning. Last year we cut twelve pages and we're about to cut more. For Christ's sake, so many people have left, you can now fit everyone in the main newsroom. We're still turning a profit, which sets us apart, but it's immaterial because every dime will be going into new presses, and that's if we can convince the owners not to sell. The website needs a complete overhaul and we can't do that in-house. Pulling stories from the wire is fine but—"

"Readers can get most of it for free on the web," I said.

"Right," he said. "We need something new. Something that gets attention. A surprise." He said *surprise* mockingly, with a down-turned mouth. "This paper had two Pulitzer winners but that was a long time ago. We're a few hours from New York and a few from DC. We're stuck in the middle, and the middleman gets the shaft."

"The paper should charge for online content," I said in an *I've said it a million times* tone.

"That won't do it," he said.

"It would help offset the costs of redoing the site."

Daniel waved me off.

I could imagine what the paper's sale and ultimate closure would do to Daniel's ego. He wouldn't care about the fate of hundreds of employees who would be ruined.

"Give me a number," he sighed and leaned back from his desk, into his chair.

I couldn't digest that Daniel Perry thought I could make any difference to the paper's future. Then it occurred to me that he'd probably had this kind of impromptu meeting with many other people, and now he was desperate and scraping the bottom. I had good reasons for not wanting to delve into the political reporting realm but I didn't want to share them with Daniel, so I decided to lie with the truth.

"The editors have always said the freelance budget is next to nothing. For magazine pieces I get paid ten times what I get here. I'm sorry, Daniel, it's just not worth it."

He looked at me skeptically and said, "You don't write political stuff for magazines."

He stared at me. It was discomfiting.

"I meant lifestyle pieces," I said.

"A number, Morgan."

"Three dollars a word," I said with a *what-the-hell* gesture.

"One," he said.

"One-fifty."

"Done," he said.

Wait, what just happened? Daniel Perry had offered me work? Well-paid work? At least in the newspaper realm. At that rate, one op-ed would pay my utilities for two months.

"Get me a draft by Thursday. Six to eight hundred words. Eh, closer to six."

"A draft," I said.

"Yes," he said, and then started typing something on his computer.

"Of?"

"What we talked about yesterday," he said. "Why an exclusive interview isn't always the real scoop."

I half-laughed. "Like the story last month about the possible investigation of the FCC chairman."

Daniel's eyes left his computer and focused on me over his

imaginary bifocals.

"What about it?"

"You know," I said. "How there might be a conflict of interest because he used to be on the board of Station Industries."

"Yeah? And?"

"Total duck hunt," I said.

Daniel jerked his head back to stare at me with surprise. It caused his chin to double.

"He had an affair with the daughter of Station's president," I said. "He's just trying to avoid a messy public divorce."

Daniel leaned forward and said, "You know this for a fact?"

"Of course," I said.

"How?"

"I'm a wizard," I said.

"Can you prove it?"

"Can I or will I?"

Daniel sat back, squishing the tufted leather seat.

"Get me that draft," he said.

"Next week, if that's okay," I said.

"Fine. Middle of next week. No later." He looked at his computer. "You can go."

I left Daniel's office in a daze. When the glass door closed behind me, I didn't hear the usual clang or feel its immense heaviness. Something had shifted—my instincts said for the better and I hoped they were right. I walked to the wall of mailboxes and pulled a thick stack out of my cubby. Then I headed to John Mayes's desk to get the dish on his date with Anne.

35

...

I drove home from the paper and felt worlds away from my morning sex with Timothy. Galaxies. Universes. I drove more slowly than usual and thought about many things, including Daniel Perry. What a one-eighty he'd done!

I had already texted Anne and Ravenna to brief them on my new work status, and I thanked Ravenna for her words of insight the evening before. Naturally I reported to both of them that Timothy and I had finally slept together. Not sort of, not kind of, but full-on slept together.

In the normal course of all our dating lives sex wouldn't be such a reportable event, but in recent weeks I'd worried that things with Timothy might be on the outs. When a guy doesn't call you for a week or two, or only e-mails and texts here and there, that's what you're bound to think. Anne and Ravenna hadn't been as pessimistic because they accepted Timothy's workaholic ways as "nothing personal." I tried to do the same but it was difficult. Then with Paul's reemergence—and proposal—during Timothy's absence, I needed sex with Timothy to bring me back to earth.

I was ecstatic to have the afternoon to myself and forgave myself for lying to Paul about having meetings at the paper. I idled at a stoplight a few blocks from my street and had another light bulb moment. I finally knew why I hadn't yet been able to give Paul an answer, and my ringing cell phone was like a bell signaling my epiphany. It rang through my car speakers, thanks to the hands-free setup. I hit Answer without even looking. I knew it'd be Paul. I just knew.

"Hello?" I said loudly since my windows were open.

"Want to play hooky?" Steven said.

Everything in my world stopped.

"You there?" he said.

"Yes. I'm here." My arms felt a little shaky and my suddenly clammy hands gripped the steering wheel. A loud honk came from behind me. The light had turned green and I was holding up a line of cars. I waved briefly as an apology to the driver behind me and then pressed my foot to the gas. The tires shrieked as I took a hard turn.

"I hear wind," Steven said. "Where are you?"

"Driving," I said.

"Thought you'd be working," he said.

"I was."

"Driving where?" he asked.

"Just driving."

"I'm on speaker, aren't I?"

"Yep."

"Is someone with you?"

"No."

"Where are you?"

"Near my place," I said.

"Me too," he said.

Steven was in my neighborhood?

"Want to meet for coffee?" he asked.

My head swirled. *Should I see Steven right now? I want to see Steven right now. I had sex with Timothy just hours ago. Good sex. Not as good as it used to be with Steven. If I meet him for coffee, am I a slut? I can't touch him. If I kissed him, then I'd be a slut. We're not going to kiss. It's just coffee. The last time you met him for coffee you ended up on a three-day-long date. The date to end all dates. Don't meet him right now. Go home and work.*

"Sure, we can have coffee," I said.

"Café Mimi, ten minutes?"

"I'm just about home," I said, turning into my driveway. "I need a few minutes, then I'll walk up there." I parked my car, pulled my bag over my shoulder, and got out. "If you get there first, try to get a table outside."

"Want to walk there together?" Steven said as I hurried up my front walk and saw him outside my front door, sitting on the low brick wall, holding his phone to his ear.

Just the sight of Steven made my pulse quicken. I should have been angry; he could run into Timothy, after all. But I wasn't angry. I was excited. The danger of his presence increased the excitement. I'd heard storm chasers got the same rush.

"I need to change," I said. My body temperature had already risen several degrees.

Steven nodded once and remained seated.

"Be just a minute," I said.

I walked calmly inside, closed the door behind me, dropped my bag on the floor, and then raced like an amphetamine addict upstairs to put on a gauzy sundress and check my face in the mirror. My skin was still a bit chafed from Timothy's early morning scruff but there was nothing I could do. I didn't look my best but if Steven didn't like it, tough.

I exited my place casually, as though I had nothing better to do than check the weather. Steven gestured with his arm for me to walk down the steps ahead of him. We didn't speak as we made our way down my front walk. As we crossed the street, we walked past his parked car.

"Did you get it?" I asked, referring to the Porsche we test-drove.

"Not yet," he said.

"So you are getting it, then?"

"I don't know." Steven ducked his head under a low tree branch thick with white flowers. "It's a lot of money."

"Just think if you hadn't given God-knows-how-much to that benefit last week," I said.

"Two mutually exclusive expenses," he said.

"Perhaps. But that was a lot of money to spend just to see me for a few minutes. You'll have the car for years."

"Not necessarily," Steven said, looking at me briefly. "I could get sick of the car."

We made the three-block walk to the quaint, French-inspired coffeehouse without rushing. We inquired about each others' families and commented on charming and not-so-charming gardens and facades of houses and small apartment buildings in my neighborhood.

"I should have stayed here," Steven said.

"You don't like your place?"

"I like my place, not my neighborhood."

Steven had lived in my neighborhood when he first moved back from Manhattan. Then he decided to buy a huge, modern loft—a full floor—in one of the city's up-and-coming industrial neighborhoods. But the neighborhood never came up.

Back when we were together, and I spent nights at his place, he worried about my car sitting on the street overnight. He always insisted on parking it in his indoor spot and risking his own car to the perils of the night. It was a hell of a sacrifice for a Porsche owner to make for a six-year-old Saab with fabric seats and nicked rims.

We arrived at Café Mimi and I grabbed the only free table on the sidewalk while Steven went inside to get our coffees. He walked out a few minutes later, laughing and patting a man heartily on the back. He set down our drinks, and then pulled out a dozen sugar packets from his pocket and slid them to my side of the table.

"Who was that?" I asked.

"A client," he said.

Steven knew people wherever he went. I ripped open four sugars and poured them into my latte.

"Did you remember to get me decaf?"

Steven nodded as though I had asked the silliest question in the world.

"You're not wearing the ring," he said, gazing out to the street. His eyes squinted as though he were trying to read a distant sign.

"It's in my purse," I said.

"No, it isn't." Steven took a sip of his black coffee.

I reached down, grabbed my purse from beneath my chair, set it on my lap, and unzipped it.

"Don't bother," Steven said.

"Sure you don't want to see it? It's pretty."

Steven smirked. I zipped my purse and put it back on the ground.

"Is Mr. California history?" he said, undeterred.

I shook my head with mock frustration. Steven was baiting me by saying "Mr. California" but I wasn't about to bite. I wanted to laugh but I wouldn't give him the satisfaction.

"Mr. DC will be glad to hear it," he said, still not looking at me, at least not when I was looking at him.

I wasn't sure what to say, how much to share. Steven was the only man I had ever really trusted. I never fully poured my heart out to him, even though he'd wanted me to, but I knew no matter what I told him, he wouldn't ever use it against me. Not then. Not now. In truth, Steven knew more about me after only a few months than Paul did after years, the kinds of things about which Timothy didn't even inquire.

"Though I must say," Steven added, "I question the grain of a man who drives a Z3."

Uh-oh. Steven mentioned Timothy's car. His mentioning Timothy at all was out of the blue.

"How do you know what he drives?"

"I was on my way to an early meeting this morning and came down your street, saw it parked in the driveway," he said.

"Aren't we presumptuous," I said. "You see a car in my drive-way and automatically assume it belongs to someone I'm dating."

"It's his," Steven said. I didn't confirm his correct assumption. "Good lord." He faked a shiver.

"It's a BMW," I said. "I shouldn't have to tell you it's one of the greatest cars in the world."

"One of the greatest car *companies*," he said.

"Do enlighten me. What's wrong with a Z3?" I would never admit to Steven that I wasn't crazy about Timothy's car. I loved BMWs but Timothy's little roadster didn't do it for me.

"Let's just say I'd expect more from an MIT graduate," Steven said, finally turning to me.

"What does that mean?"

"He came out of MIT, chances are he's making decent bank. He probably didn't get laid in all those years so he'd want a good car to make up for lost time. Especially if he's ugly."

"Not every man chooses a car just to get laid," I said. "I can't believe you're knocking a BMW."

Steven tilted his head back and sniffed the air. "I can smell the estrogen from here."

"It's a chick's car, that's what you're saying?" I quelled a laugh. "That car is hot."

"It is hot, with a chick driving it," he said.

A man with two dogs walked past our table. Steven and I patted each of them. After they walked on I told him it was time for me to get going. If I spent any more time with him my brain would be mush for the day. I told him I would be writing some political pieces in the near future and I wanted to get started on the op-ed for Daniel.

"Good," Steven said. "It's about time they utilized your talents."

I glared at him.

"Oh sorry, Amanda, I didn't mean anything about your column," he said.

I knew he didn't mean it as an insult but it was fun to see him squirm.

"It's just high time they use you for more," he said. "If anyone should be writing political pieces, it's you. They've got a decent editorial board, but they could use a little snap."

Steven rarely complimented people, but when he did, it was genuine. From our earliest dating days he had been immensely supportive of my work. Shockingly so. It was the main reason I came to trust him.

"Thanks," I said. "I don't know if I'll pull it off, but the very fact that Daniel Perry," I said his name with disdain, "wants me to do more for the paper is like an olive branch I feel compelled to accept. Plus, it'll feel good to write new material."

"Hey," Steven said, leaning on his elbows on the table, "I'm sorry I got you in hot water with him."

"You couldn't know," I said.

"I had no idea Emily Richmond would call him at home." Steven repositioned himself in his chair. "I didn't know things were so bad with him. I should have remembered that," he said mostly to himself.

"I didn't talk about it much back then. As bad as it was, it got much worse over the past year."

"Well, I'm sorry, for what it's worth," he said.

Steven's apology was worth a lot, because it was sincere.

After cleaning up our table and tossing out my many ripped sugar packets, Steven and I walked slowly back to my place. Our gaits fell in and out of rhythm. There was a moment Steven's fingers grazed mine but he didn't take my hand. I felt electrified from the brief contact.

"I didn't say no," I said. "To Mr. California."

Steven's pursed his mouth and squinted his eyes.

"It's Mr. New York now, remember," he said.

"And Mr. DC isn't ugly," I said.

"Of course he's not."

"He's handsome," I said.

"Of course he is." Steven sighed loudly. "Little and handsome."

I laughed and looked at him.

"He's gotta be little with that car," he said. "Gotta be."

"He's not six-three like some fucking egotists, but he's not little," I said.

I wanted to laugh again but I held it in. Steven and I walked another half block without speaking. Occasionally his arm or hand accidentally touched mine.

"I want to hold your hand," he finally said.

I slid my hand against his and he gently inched his fingers until they were wrapped around my hand. His warm skin sent a shockwave through me. Though he'd touched my hand briefly a few days earlier, we hadn't truly held hands since our last date more than a year ago.

Our paces finally fell into a rhythm despite his legs being so much longer than mine. As we neared my street I had an inexplicable urge to cry. We turned onto my block and walked past his car. I wanted us to jump in and drive away but I pushed the thought away. Steven squeezed my hand as we waited to cross the street. He walked me to my front door and, once there, finally released his hold.

"Thanks for coming to meet me," he said, as though we were finishing a business meeting.

"I had time to kill," I said.

I unlocked my door, then turned to look at him. He was leaning on the doorframe, positioned almost above me.

"I want to kiss you," he said, looking down at the ground.

I tilted my head and placed my face under his. Before our skin touched I could feel his energy. I brushed my cheek across his mouth. His lips were like silk as they moved across my skin. The moment our lips met we exploded, and in an instant we were devouring each other. Our sudden fury forced me to step up and inside my doorway, almost tripping backward, and he caught me as the screen door slammed against him.

We couldn't kiss hard enough, as though we'd been starving and suddenly there was food. My purse dropped to the floor and I heard the smack of my cell phone against the cold tile. We were walking, me backward, Steven forward. His hands gripped my face, my shoulders, my hips. I pulled his hair, dug my nails into his arms, bit his lips. I ripped open his Oxford shirt and ran my hands over his chest and around his back. The moment he felt my hands on his body's skin, his intensity increased. In seconds we were against the far wall of my hallway and, with nowhere further to go, he picked me up and my legs automatically wrapped around him.

The hem of my sundress was pushed up to my waist and Steven's hands found their way up the sides of my thighs. He grabbed my hips and pressed into me. I could feel the texture of his jeans and his cold belt buckle and his tensed stomach and overall force against every part of me. For a good five minutes we had sex with our clothes on. Amazing sex. Hot sex. Sex with abandon. All without actually having sex.

Eventually I stopped pulling at him and let my mouth relax. In turn he lessened his grip and pulled his face away just enough to stare at me. His hair was wild. I'd pulled it every which way. His forehead was slick with sweat. His breath was still coming quick but he was getting it under control. He lowered me slowly without removing his gaze. Once I was standing on my own, Steven leaned against the wall and placed his arms on either side of me.

"Well," he finally said. "That was—"

"Yeah," I said, running my hands through my hair.

"I guess I should go?"

"He has keys," I said.

Steven grinned briefly, then leaned down and softly pressed his lips to mine, holding them like that, as though he were placing his imprint on me. He rested his forehead against mine and remained there for a few moments.

"Okay then," he finally said, and stepped away from me.

I stood in my front window and watched Steven walk down my front walk, wait for a few cars to pass, cross the street, and get in his car. He didn't look back at my place as he pulled away.

36

• • •

"It was a mad make-out. Off the charts. Out of control," I said. Anne, Ravenna, and I sat on a blanket on the unmown grass in my backyard. I spoke quietly but with unabashed enthusiasm, as though I were eighty years old recalling an affair decades earlier. We had already talked about Anne and John Mayes's date, and Ravenna and Malcolm's relationship progression. Turns out John Mayes was a surprisingly good kisser, and Malcolm already wanted Ravenna to move here and live with him.

"I'm a slut," I said, despite my inability to stop smiling. "A complete and total slut."

"Look at her," Anne said. "That smile is plastered on her face."

"Wis zat kind of day I'd be smiling too," Ravenna said.

"What does this mean?" Anne asked me.

"I don't know." I shook my head in amazement. "I'm not even sure I care."

"I just remembered Timothy has your house keys now," Anne said.

"I know! He could have walked in at any minute!"

"I knew zis would happen," Ravenna said. "Steven is like a force of nature."

"Exactly," I said.

After Steven left that afternoon I pardoned myself from the crime of "cheating" on Timothy. I then took a long shower and spent the rest of the afternoon writing. I dived into the op-ed like it was a cool swimming hole on a hot day. In three hours the piece was nearly finished. I then got started on a new column, purposely choosing a subject that related in no way to my current love life. Ultimately I chose "bad roommates" over "office etiquette" because *office* reminded me of Daniel Perry, which reminded me that he had asked about whether I had accepted Paul's proposal, which reminded me that I gave Timothy keys to my place only hours before making out with Steven, which made me feel guilty despite my pardoning myself. By the time Anne and Ravenna stopped by, I was ninety-percent done with my work for the entire week.

Anne toyed with a leafy vine on the wooden fence near her.

"What is this called?" she asked.

I turned to look. "Poison ivy."

Anne panicked and snapped her fingers away, and then realized I was kidding.

"Really," Anne said. "These flowers and leaves are pretty."

"They are," I said. "I can't remember what it is, though."

"Zat is chlamydia," Ravenna said.

Anne looked at me and we busted out laughing.

"It's not chlamydia," Anne said.

"No?" Ravenna asked, sincerely curious and unaware what was so funny.

"No," I managed to say through my laughing. "Clematis, maybe."

"Oh yes, clematis," Ravenna said. "What does chlamydia look like?"

"You don't want to know," Anne said.

Ravenna nodded and let the point go.

The three of us leaned back on our elbows and looked at the bright early evening sky, each of us musing about our men, I assumed. In my case, definitely. It was impossible to push Steven from my mind.

"That cloud looks like a dog," Anne said, her head craned back as far as it would go.

"Zat one looks like a naked man," Ravenna said. "A fat man," she added.

"That one looks like you, Anne," I joked, but she looked anyway.

The back screen door screeched and we all turned as Timothy walked outside.

"There you are!" he called out to me and walked toward us.

"Hi!" I awkwardly sat up from my reclined cloud-gazing position. "I didn't expect you so early."

"Ladies, great to see you," he said to Anne and Ravenna. He knelt to kiss me.

My friends smiled at him. They were unable to resist Timothy's beaming positivity. It was like a drug that permeated everything in its immediate vicinity.

"We should go?" Ravenna said, nodding to Anne.

"Please don't leave on my account," Timothy said. "I can only stay for a few minutes."

"Why?" I wrapped an arm around his leg.

"Just stopped back to get some papers. This'll be another late night. On the flip side, I think I'll be here until Thursday."

"That's great! I feel like I've barely seen you," I said.

Despite our great wake-up sex, my comment wasn't far from the truth. I could probably count how many waking hours Timothy and I had spent together in the past month.

"I know," he said. "It's been crazy. But I'm glad to see your friends are keeping you company." He smiled. They smiled. There was smiling all around.

"You're not wearing the ring," Timothy said as he played with my hair. "Finally remember to take it in?"

"Uh, yes," I said. "Yes, I did."

"So it'll be all shipshape for you," Timothy said to Anne. "It's really nice, by the way."

Anne looked at him blankly.

"Your grandmother's ring," I said to her. "Her engagement ring?"

"Right right right," Anne said. "The engagement ring."

"Well, ladies," Timothy said, then kissed my cheek and stood up. "I'm off. Have fun!"

We waited a minute and listened for the sound of the front door slamming. Anne stood up and walked to the backyard gate to peer down the narrow path leading to the front steps, to make sure Timothy was gone. She came back a moment later, stood above me, and said, "My grandmother's engagement ring?"

"I'm sorry," I said.

"That's one of your worst lies ever."

I dropped my head in shame.

"It's the only thing that came to mind," I said.

Ravenna laughed.

"I'm going to tell my grandmother," Anne said.

"Don't tell Nana. She'll hate me," I said. I'd known Anne's grandmother for years.

"You're not actually a family member, so you're safe," Anne said.

Anne reclaimed her spot on the blanket.

"Amanda," Ravenna said, as though she'd just discovered a new element for the periodic table, "I sink Timothy is zee nicest man on the planet."

"I know." I buried my face in my hands.

"Well, maybe not zee nicest," she reconsidered. I split my fingers to eye her through the slit. "But zee happiest. He smiles more zan anyone I know. Does he wake up like zat?"

"Pretty much," I laughed.

"Zis is very unique. And he has a cute butt."

"That he does," I said.

Anne and Ravenna nodded in agreement.

"I feel weird," I said, not knowing where my thoughts were heading.

"Uh-oh," Anne said, and Ravenna shot her a knowing look. "You were going to say 'bored.'"

"No, I wasn't."

"Yes, *mon amie*," Ravenna nodded, agreeing with Anne.

"I had sex with two men today," I said. "One time with clothes on, but still, you can't be bored after that kind of day."

"*I* could never be bored after that day," Anne said. "I'd be clicking my heels and jumping for joy. But you? You could be bored. It's a gift."

"I wasn't going to say bored, I swear." I meant it, although I couldn't blame them for assuming it because they'd heard it from me before.

"Zen what?" Ravenna said.

"I feel guilty," I said.

"Guilt is bad," Ravenna offered in a disappointing tone.

"Guilty about what?" Anne asked.

"About what excites me the most," I said.

Their expressions said they expected me to say something different.

"I have a wonderful man who wants to marry me. And a fantastic boyfriend staying with me." I hesitated to finish my admission.

"Yes?" my friends said in unison.

"Then I have an asshole boss who's suddenly taken a shine to me and a probably-still-an-asshole ex practically screwing me against the wall. Guess which ones excite me the most? The asshole boss and the wall-screwer! That makes me feel guilty."

There was silence as my friends searched for consoling words.

"Wait," Anne finally said. "You're excited by your boss?"

"*Blaaacgh*, not excited like that," I said. "I had a great time writing that op-ed today. I flew through it. I haven't enjoyed writing like that in a long time. It was new and fresh and motivating."

"But that's great," Anne said.

"Daniel Perry is one of the biggest pricks on the planet," I said, "but obviously something has changed. Not his prickness, I'm sure, that's probably in his DNA, but something is different."

"Zis is all good," Ravenna said.

"It really is," Anne agreed. "You're looking at this wrong. You should enjoy your work."

"Do not feel guilty about Steven," Ravenna said with a *tsk-tsk*. "You loved him very much. Zis may not be anymore but of course you screw him against zee wall."

"I would," Anne said.

Ravenna nodded deeply in agreement.

"It's not fair to Timothy," I said. "Or Paul."

"Why?" Ravenna was at a loss to understand. "Paul asked you to marry him. Zis does not mean you become celibate."

"True," I said. It was reasonable logic.

"Timothy is kind of her boyfriend, though," Anne said. "And he is staying with her." Ravenna and I looked at her. "I'm just saying," she added.

"So what!" Ravenna became almost angry. "I would not be celibate for a man who doesn't call for two weeks." Ravenna waved a chastising finger. "Timothy is a man she is seeing, zat is all."

"We're more than that," I said.

"What is more?" Ravenna asked.

"I agree with Amanda," Anne said. "They've been dating for months. They travel to see each other, they e-mail, text, talk on the phone. They're sleeping together. That's a real relationship."

"Zen you must talk to him and decide what you are. Until zen, you are a free woman. You can screw Daniel Perry against zee wall if you wish."

"Don't make me sick," I said.

"Ravenna has a point," Anne said. "Technically you are free and clear but—"

Ravenna scoffed.

"With Timothy actually staying with her for the week? I don't know." Anne threw her hands up to say *I give up.*

"Don't tell her zis! Timothy gave one day's notice about his visit." Ravenna was actually getting pissed. "Amanda likes him very much, or loves him, but zis is not zee point. She is allowed to date."

"True," Anne conceded, "but some relationships don't need a big conversation. Right, Ms. Relationship Columnist?" Anne looked to me for confirmation but I was Switzerland. "At a certain point the relationship is implied."

Ravenna shook her head firmly. "Zat is dangerous. Look what happened wis you and Charlie. Was zat relationship implied?"

Something had struck a nerve in Ravenna. I stayed quiet and let the two of them duke it out.

"Good point," Anne said, chagrined.

"Amanda can marry Paul if she wishes," Ravenna continued, "zen all of zis will just be stories from zee past. Stories of passion and sex and house keys. Good stories, zat's what life is about."

"You know what, you're right," Anne said. "Fuck all the guilt."

"*Oui*! Fok it!"

We all laughed; Anne and me at Ravenna's pronunciation of "fuck" and Ravenna as a release, I suspected.

"Let me ask you," I said to Ravenna, "considering how quickly things are moving along with you and Malcolm, could you go out with someone else right now?"

"Of course," she said without hesitation.

"What if he went out with someone else?"

"Zen he would be an idiot. Because he will never get another woman like me. And I don't want to sleep wis an idiot."

"Well, that settles that," I said.

"Amanda writes zis stuff in her column and it is zee truth," Ravenna said, lighting a cigarette. "Do not let a man sink he can just walk away and come back. If he sinks zat, he will walk away. It is zer nature."

"I never wrote that," I said. "Not all men are roamers."

Ravenna waved me off. I wondered what bee had gotten into her bonnet. I knew she was scarred from her short marriage years ago but she had never seemed truly bitter. But perhaps she was. Perhaps it was one of her secrets.

"I just got an idea," I said. "I should have a party tomorrow."

"*Oui*, zat's a good idea."

"Totally," Anne said.

"You're leaving at the end of the week," I said to Ravenna. "Timothy is leaving Thursday. Tomorrow night is the last night we'll all be able to hang out together."

"A Wednesday evening party," Anne said. "I like it."

"I'll invite Mia and Terry," I said.

"Terry?" Ravenna asked.

"He's the society writer," I reminded her.

"Oh yes, he is funny," she said.

"Mia's really nice too," Anne said. "But will Timothy even be able to make it? And would he want that? He'll probably want to spend his last night with you."

"Let's do it early, totally casual," I said. "I'll use my womanly wiles to convince him to break away for an hour or so. He really likes you guys. I know he wouldn't want to miss it."

"Zis is a good idea."

"Bring Malcolm," I said to Ravenna. "Then Timothy will have no excuse. And you bring John," I said to Anne.

"Will you ask him?" she asked.

"Sure," I said. It was cute to see Anne hesitant to ask John to a party, even one hosted by me.

We hung out for another hour, until Ravenna left to see Malcolm and Anne left to get a pedicure. I spent the rest of the evening writing. Not the op-ed for Daniel. Not my column. Just writing for me. I went to bed alone that night but I looked forward to waking up with Timothy, pinned down by his arms and legs. I rarely recalled my dreams, but that night I dreamt about a Porsche filled with house keys.

37

$\cdot\;\cdot\;\cdot$

I woke up exactly as I'd hoped—intertwined with Timothy, the fluffy white comforter half-hanging on the floor, and the sun shining in. I didn't know what time he came home or crawled in bed. His soft snoring indicated *pretty late*.

Despite Ravenna's impassioned rant about forgetting all guilt and doing whatever I pleased with whomever I pleased, I had lingering guilt about my make-out with Steven. It was wrong and I knew it. For all I knew Timothy had dated other women since we met. He had said more than once that he wasn't dating anyone else, but a woman can't rely on those comments; I had learned that lesson with more than one man. What would my answer be if Timothy woke up and asked me to fully commit to him? A week earlier I would have said yes without hesitation.

Was Anne right, were some relationships simply implied? It was dangerous to assume such a thing, but it could be equally dangerous to have "the talk." Look at Anne and Charlie! I'd explored the topic countless times in my column and still, as I felt Timothy's breath against my cheek, I didn't have a definitive answer. To top it off, I wasn't even sure if I wanted sex again that morning, and that too made me feel guilty.

I'd spent the previous afternoon enveloped by work. In the moments I wasn't, my mind drifted to Steven. My eyes would glance at the wall where he'd held me hostage, and then I'd refocus on my computer screen. Minutes later the memory would return, and I could feel the texture of his white shirt tangled in my fingers and hear the snapping sound of buttons flying off. I could smell his skin and feel the sharpness of his teeth against me. I'd write a paragraph about the bubble in which politicians actually lived as opposed to the casual, hardworking everyman life they claimed in campaign ads, then I'd feel Steven's belt buckle digging into my thigh.

It was a one-time explosion, I thought, as I felt Timothy breathing against my side. Yesterday's passion with Steven was like getting caught in a wild thunderstorm. But it had moved on and the sky was now clear. My relationship with Steven was over, done, finito. Yesterday had merely been the result of a year's worth of buildup. I hadn't heard from him since he drove away. No text. No e-mail. No phone call.

In the past week I had wondered: What if I hadn't run into Steven at the benefit? What if I'd walked in, stayed two minutes, and then left? What if I'd stood up to Daniel Perry sooner, and refused to put myself in the line of fire of Mrs. Richmond, newspaper ad sales be damned? Would Steven have given up? For a long time he'd had my phone number and not used it. For even longer he'd lived ten minutes away and didn't try to see me.

Timothy was right next to me, sound asleep. He was a workaholic and we lived in different cities, but he used my number all the time, and he came to see me, and invited me to see him, and talked about our future. Maybe he didn't pin me against the wall and I didn't want to bite off his buttons, but we had great chemistry. If properly motivated I might gnaw on his buttons; that should mean something.

Steven had only asked for a chance, whatever that means. At least I knew I would see Timothy again after he left tomorrow.

I knew during our goodbye he would sweetly demand for us to see each other as soon as possible. I also knew that weeks would elapse and we would talk on the phone, exchange lots of e-mails and texts, and wait for his schedule to open up. And it would, perhaps not in the timeframe I wanted, but eventually it would open, and he would fill it with me.

As it turned out, Timothy didn't try to sleep with me that morning. We snuggled under the covers and kissed until he jumped out of bed, showered, dressed, downed a Gatorade, and ran out the door. I had just enough time to tell him about my party that evening. He said he would absolutely be there and couldn't wait.

• • •

In less than two hours I finished both my column and the op-ed. I e-mailed the first to Mia and the second to Daniel Perry. Then I called John Mayes and invited him to my party. He didn't ask if Anne would be there but I could tell he wanted to. For the next hour or so Paul and I exchanged texts, mostly saying *I miss you* and *Can't wait to see you this weekend*. I meant the words, though I was relieved to have more time before seeing him. The make-out with Steven had set my brain on tilt and I needed to right it again.

Near lunchtime my phone rang.

"I like this," Daniel Perry said without saying hello.

"Oh," I said. "Thank you."

Daniel Perry likes something I wrote?

"Thought you needed until next week," he said.

"Some time opened up," I said.

"It's been twenty-four hours since I asked for this."

"Would you like me to work on it some more?" It would not be an unreasonable request since I had not edited meticulously.

"No," he said. "In fact it's quite polished."

"Thank you, Daniel."

Silence fell on the line for a good five seconds.

"A piece like this would usually take some time. A few days at least." Daniel was fishing but he wasn't going to catch anything.

"Well," I laughed, "I'm speedy when I set my mind to it."

"Uh huh," he said. Then, "You sure about the congressman? The committee won't screw around. We can't afford to have this come back and bite us in the ass."

"Yes," I said.

"You're *sure*," he repeated.

"Daniel, I'm not saying anything that hasn't been floated before."

"True," he said.

I imagined Daniel tilting his head from side to side, thinking, with his fat pen in his mouth.

"It's really about holes in the interview process," I said. "And press conferences. What information is disseminated, and how. It's about reading between the lines." I paused for a moment, then said, "Just like you asked for."

Good on me! Remind Daniel this was *his* idea. If he had second thoughts, he could blame only himself.

"Besides," I added, "it's a one-off. It'll be lining birdcages next week."

If Daniel and I had been conversing in the glass cage rather than on the phone, he would have been looking at me above his imaginary bifocals.

"Okay," he finally said.

"Should I add this to my regular invoice?" I asked.

"No, make a separate one and give it to John," he said.

"Sure. John who?"

"John Mayes. Remember him? Tall guy, brown hair, dateless."

I laughed and then wished I hadn't. I didn't want Daniel Perry to think he was funny.

"Why am I sending this to John?" I asked.

"He's moving to Editorial," Daniel said.

"What? When did this happen?"

"It's been in the works for a while. He's a good reporter, strong writer."

"I agree," I said.

"That piece about men in the dating world? Jesus." That was Daniel Perry-ese for *it sucked.*

"I haven't read it yet. He interviewed me for it."

"I know," Daniel said. "It's not his milieu."

I was pretty sure I had just been insulted, but I let it go.

"John would be great in Editorial," I said, digesting the news but incredulous that John hadn't shared this development with me. "I just talked to him a little while ago. I'm surprised he didn't mention it to me."

"Anyway," Daniel said. "What was the final number? A dollar a word?"

"One-fifty," I said.

"Right. One-fifty."

Silence again. One second. Two. Three.

"Fine, get the invoice to me," Daniel said.

"I shouldn't send it to Editorial?"

"Yes, right. Editorial."

"No problem," I said.

"Good." And with that, Daniel hung up.

I immediately called John even though we'd talked less than an hour before.

"John Mayes," he answered.

"Hello there, may I please speak to the newest member of the editorial board?"

"Amanda?"

"I can't believe you didn't you tell me!"

"Oh," John said. "It's no big deal."

"It's a huge deal. Congratulations."

"Bit of a pay raise, better title," he said.

"I'll say. Being on the board is major, John. Even Daniel Perry is in your corner. That's something."

"It's not *The Washington Post*, Amanda." John's lack of enthusiasm surprised me.

"So what? It's very prestigious," I said.

"To be honest," John's voice dropped to a whisper, "I'd rather be in the DC bureau. It's a tiny office but it's closer to the action. That's what I asked for but they said no."

"I never knew you were so interested in politics," I said.

"I never knew you were either," he volleyed back with attitude.

"Um, I'm not." I tried to figure out where the conversation was heading. "Not from a reporter's perspective, anyway. You know me, John, I'm just a columnist."

"How do you know Daniel is in my corner?"

"I just talked to him and he said what a good writer and reporter you are. It's rare for him to compliment anyone, John."

"Since when do you and Daniel Perry chat on the phone?" John's attitude was obvious now.

"Since never," I said. "I e-mailed him an op-ed—"

"That he asked you to write, or that you chose to write?"

"Both," I said sharply. "He asked me to write it and I chose to say yes. What's the problem?"

"Nothing," John said with a sigh. "I read the piece. It's good. Very you."

"Thanks, I think. John, what's going on?"

"Sorry. It's just..."

"What?"

"Be careful," he said.

"Careful with what?"

"With Daniel," he said.

"John, what in the world are you talking about?"

"I'm talking about nothing, Amanda. He's just a prick."

"Excuse me," I laughed. "Nobody knows Daniel Perry's prick-ness more than I, my friend."

"Yeah. So can I bring anything tonight?" John regained his regular, friendly tone.

"Nothing is required other than your presence. See you later, then?"

"Absolutely," John said. "I should be there at about six. And Amanda?"

"Yes?"

"I'm sorry," he said.

38

. . .

My strange conversation with John Mayes was on my mind as I wandered through the grocery store. I had never before heard John give attitude, and off-putting as it was, my interest was piqued. There had been occasions when John could have used some attitude, but he always maintained a calm, gentlemanly air—never sinking, never using profanity, never displaying frustration or anger. He was like Timothy in that way, but less hyperkinetic. I didn't view Timothy as a happiness poseur, but he did seem impossibly cheerful no matter the circumstance. John never seemed to put on an act. Then again, maybe he did. I didn't actually know John all that well. Something about my newfound accord with Daniel Perry had tripped something in John, and I couldn't guess what it might be.

I didn't buy much at the store. A selection of cheeses, breads and crackers, several boxes of frozen hors d'oeuvres, vegetables, and all the ingredients for my homemade dip. People enjoyed grazing like cows in a meadow. At least I did. Plus hell would freeze over before I cooked a full meal for six people.

By the time I got home, my car loaded up with food and drink, I had just enough time to shower and prep the food. I did that, then quickly set up the grill and prettied the backyard. It didn't take much effort since it would be a casual evening. I arranged lanterns outside and placed small drops of mosquito repellant near the seating. Not enough to smell it, just enough to keep the little bastards at bay. As six o'clock neared I found myself excited at the prospect of enjoying an entire evening with Timothy. The past week-plus had been a whirlwind of drama and I was relieved to be rid of it for one night.

. . .

Ravenna and Malcolm were the first to show up.

"For you, my dear," Malcolm said as he entered, presenting two bottles of probably exquisite wine.

"Bordeaux," I said. "My favorite."

"I considered a crisp Australian white, it being summer and all, but Ravenna says you prefer red and French."

"Ravenna speaks the truth," I said. "And this reminds me of Ravenna."

"She's not from that region," Malcolm said with a concerned tone.

"I know," I said. "But everything French reminds me of Ravenna."

"Me too," he said with a smile. "Doesn't even have to be French."

"Do not listen to him. He talks nonsense," Ravenna said.

They offered to help with anything and everything. Malcolm offered to bartend, to which I replied, "You're hired."

They carried food dishes and makeshift ice buckets outside. I had decided long ago that traditional wine buckets were of no use when entertaining more than three people; chilling one or two bottles at a time wasn't practical. I used colorful stone and clay planters that were different enough to be interesting but not strange enough to make me seem eccentric. I knew Anne would bring something, and John might too, plus I'd bought enough alcohol to inebriate the neighborhood. Some of the booze would stay in the kitchen, but it would be handy to keep a bottle each of white and red, gin, rum, and vodka chilled outside.

I walked past the front hall as Mia and Terry appeared on the other side of the screen door. They were about to ring the bell when they noticed me.

"Hi there," I said, opening the door and moving aside for them to step in. "What's all that?"

Mia carefully handed me a big shopping bag. I could tell the moment I took it in my arms that it contained a cold pitcher.

"It's sangria," she said. "Throw it in the fridge for ten minutes."

"I love sangria!"

"Sorry about the glass pitcher," she laughed. "I didn't have a plastic one and I always mix it right in the pitcher."

"Hers is the best, honey," Terry said. "And this is my best." He handed me a basket filled with beautiful summer fruit. "I didn't make it, but believe me, you're better off. I got a ton this weekend at the farmers' market."

"This is wonderful, thank you both so much," I said.

Mia and Terry walked to the kitchen with me and I placed the heavy glass pitcher in the refrigerator.

"Go ahead out back," I said. "My friends Ravenna and Malcolm are already out there with food and whatnot."

"Any chance the whatnot is booze?" Terry asked.

"Uh-oh, it's already starting," Mia said.

"One hundred percent chance," I said. "And plenty of it. Malcolm is an ace bartender and wine connoisseur so you'll have a lot to talk about." Terry was an entertaining and partying pro. He and Malcolm would have a great time concocting drinks together.

"Don't let him get drunk too fast," Mia said to me, elbowing Terry. "That's when the dirty stories fly."

Within moments of Mia and Terry walking out to the backyard, Anne arrived toting two bags filled with bottles upon bottles of alcohol.

"Jeez," I said, hoisting one from her. "Who's turning twenty-one?"

"I am," Anne said, straining as she carried the other bag into the kitchen and set it on the counter with a grunt. "I've decided to reverse time and grow younger rather than older."

"Excellent plan," I said.

"I'm thirty-seven," she said. "My eggs are drying up."

"They are not," I laughed.

"They're talking about it." Anne opened the fridge and found no space to shove in anything more. "So is Timothy here?" she asked.

"That's not what you want to ask me," I said.

Anne looked at me with ultra-dramatic ignorance. "What do you mean?"

"You want to know if John is coming." Anne smirked at me. "He is," I assured her.

That was the only update about John I planned to give Anne. I would not share his dose of afternoon attitude. Anne knew everything about my pained working relationship with Daniel Perry and she also knew about my friendship with John Mayes, but something about the two had collided that afternoon and I thought it best to keep quiet about it.

A knock at the door turned both our heads. I looked at the clock. It read six on the dot.

"John's ears must have been burning," I said.

I dangled sideways from the kitchen wall to see John standing outside the front screen door. "Come on in, John," I yelled. "We're in the kitchen."

I shot Anne a big, knowing smile and heard the screen door creak open.

"I forgot to tell you," Anne whispered, "I talked to Charlie today."

I didn't have time to respond before John stepped into the kitchen holding a bakery box.

"Hi, Anne. Amanda." He nodded with a smile.

"Hey there," we said together. "What's this?" I asked.

"Cheesecake," he said, almost as a question.

"Thank you! John, you didn't have to bring anything. Good choice, though. Anne loves cheesecake."

"Oh, good," he smiled at her. "You don't like cheesecake?" he asked me, obviously worried he brought something I didn't like.

"I love it," I said. "In fact I might skip dinner altogether and just eat this."

"I'll believe that when I see it. The two of you together probably weigh the same as this cheesecake."

"Did you hear that, Amanda?" Anne said. "John's trying to say we're skinny."

"That's because John wants free drinks," I said. "But he has to pay a cover just like everyone else."

John looked pleased. Anne looked pleased. Their budding romance was palpable.

"Mia and Terry are already here," I said. "They're in the back with Malcolm and Ravenna. Malcolm's bartending, which means we'll all be drunk by seven."

"Ladies," John said, gesturing for us to accompany him.

"I'm going to help Amanda for a few minutes," Anne said.

"Yes," I said, "Anne brought enough booze for the entire city. I don't have enough room so we might have to drink it. If we're not outside in five minutes, assume the worst."

John laughed, waved me off as if to say *you're silly*, then walked out of the kitchen.

Anne said quietly, "So I finally talked to Charlie this afternoon."

"And?"

"And I'm going to give him another chance," she said.

"What?" I had been sure Anne was going to tell me Charlie wasn't reliable enough for her to count on, but that she wished him well in his move to Manhattan.

"Why are you looking at me like that?" Anne asked.

"What about John? I thought things were starting with you two."

"John's a really nice guy," Anne said sincerely. "Handsome, very smart, good kisser."

"And?"

"And I'm just not ready to say goodbye to Charlie yet," she said.

"But—"

"But he's moving away? I know, but it's only New York. We'll try it for a little while."

"I was going to say, 'but he disappeared for a month.'"

"Steven disappeared for a year," Anne shot back. "That didn't stop you from hooking up with him right after sleeping with Timothy."

Anne's retort stung. In a matter of hours I'd gotten attitude from both John and Anne, two people who never got snippy, and now both had done so with me.

"I'm sorry," Anne said with a sigh. "I shouldn't have said that."

And now both of them had apologized, but I didn't hurt any less. I felt a lump in my throat. Guilt? Impending tears?

"I just don't want to be judged about Charlie," Anne said.

"I wasn't judging you," I said.

"Yes, you were," she said.

"The last time I heard about Charlie, you couldn't care less about him. I was impressed."

"And now you're not," she said conclusively.

"That's not what I mean."

"Look," Anne said, "I know John is your friend. I'm not going to stop dating him. He's a great guy."

I stared at Anne with utter bafflement. She stared back and held her ground. I huffed and then grabbed a tea towel and began wiping the counter and pushing items to different places and stowing things in cupboards—anything to avoid eye contact. Neither of us had heard Ravenna come inside and we were surprised when her voice broke the silence.

"Okay, what can I do? What can I bring out?" She crunched on a carrot. "Oh my God, zis dip is good."

"Thanks," I said to the cupboard door. Anne just looked at her.

"What is going on in here?" Ravenna asked.

"Nothing," I said.

"Nothing," Anne said.

Ravenna's eyes darted from Anne to me. "Did I miss something?"

"It's nothing," Anne said with a clipped tone.

"Zis is not nothing. It is very tense in here. What's going on?" Ravenna lit a cigarette.

"Can I have one of those?" I said.

Ravenna furrowed her brow as she tried to get a handle on what she'd walked into. She handed me a cigarette and gave me a light. Anne rolled her eyes.

"What?" I said sharply.

Ravenna was startled by my tone toward Anne.

"I don't care if you smoke," Anne said. "I just haven't seen you smoke inside your house in forever."

"Well, now I am," I snapped. I took a long drag and exhaled a smooth, defiant stream. "I'm sure you'll remind me of it when I'm sixty and coughing."

Ravenna said, "What zee hell is going on?"

"Anne's getting back together with Charlie," I said in a chipper, cheerleader tone.

"Oh, zat's news. Good for you," Ravenna said to her. "No more John?"

"Oh no, she's still going to date John," I said.

"So what's zee problem?" Ravenna asked both of us.

Anne said nothing. I hopped up to sit on the counter and said, "The problem is—"

"The problem is," Anne interrupted me, "Amanda thinks I'm a doormat for giving Charlie another go."

"I do not!"

"And you don't want me to dump John," she said.

"I don't want you to play John. There's a difference," I said.

"So you care more about John's feelings than mine?"

"Please spare me the dramatics," I said.

Anne looked at Ravenna, then at the floor, then out into space.

"I can't believe you threw Steven back in my face," I said.

"I'm sorry," Anne pleaded, "but I still have feelings for Charlie, I can't help that."

"Just yesterday you told me it was wrong that I hooked up with Steven. Now you're telling me not to judge you? John is a really nice guy. One of the good ones."

"So is Timothy," Anne said snottily.

I scowled at her, the first time in the history of our long friendship.

"You barely know Timothy," I said.

"And how well do you really know John?"

"What the hell is your problem?" I practically yelled. I'd never before raised my voice in anger at Anne.

"Mmm mmm mmm," Ravenna said, touching each of us on the arm while a cigarette hung from her lips. "I sink I see what's going on." Ravenna looked back toward the living room to make sure neither Malcolm nor John had come inside during our heated exchange.

"Okay," Ravenna began, "Anne is going to date Charlie. Zis is fine." Anne nodded with satisfaction. "Amanda, you don't want her to hurt John." I nodded to say *correct*. "Bos of you have unresolved feelings for men and zis is ok. But, Anne," Ravenna leaned her head downward in a very teacher-like manner, "you judge Amanda for kissing Steven. You are allowed to your opinion, but—"

"He's going to hurt her again!" Anne yelled.

Silence fell upon the kitchen in the wake of Anne's proclamation.

"Amanda," Anne said, "I didn't mean to come down on you about Steven. You know I have your back no matter what. If you killed someone, I'd help you hide the body."

I remained seated on the counter, staring down at the floor. Ravenna lit another cigarette from her current one. I had forgotten about mine entirely. It sat between my fingers with an inch of ash at the end.

"The truth is, I'm worried about you," Anne said to me. "We've been best friends for almost twenty years and I have never seen you as hurt as after Steven broke up with you. Right?" She looked to Ravenna for support.

"*Oui*," Ravenna quietly agreed.

"I thought you were going to get married. We all did, right?"

Ravenna barely nodded, trying not to take sides.

"After that," Anne said, shaking her head slowly, trying to control her anger, "I swear I wanted to kill him. Seriously, I thought about calling my cousins."

Ravenna cocked her head at Anne's threat.

"Italians get things done," Anne said. "Mikey and Joe, they're no joke."

Ravenna laughed a little but I couldn't.

Anne continued, "But somehow you got through it. I don't know how, but you did. Then Timothy came along and he's such a great guy. So sweet and happy, and he's an architect! You always wanted to date an architect."

I remained quiet. Anne looked at Ravenna for the green light to continue.

"Amanda, I always ask for your advice before anyone else's. Hell, even my own. I wouldn't ask your opinion about everything if I didn't trust your judgment. Who knows, maybe I'm making a mistake with Charlie, but that's not the point."

"What is the point?" I asked softly.

Anne took a step toward me. "It's no big deal if I date Charlie again. He'll live there, I'll live here, and John and I can still date and see what comes of it. If you get back together with Steven there's no casual, middle ground. It's a huge risk. You'll be turning down marrying Paul, who loves you so much, and being with Timothy. Two wonderful men and they both want futures with you." Anne opened her mouth to say more, but then stopped herself.

"What?" Ravenna said.

Anne took a deep breath. "All signs point to this being the big three and I don't want you to choose the wrong one, and then have him walk out on you."

What could I say? Anne's point was valid. Scary but valid.

"You're the strongest person I know," she said gently, which made me scoff. "But could you survive that again?"

I did my best to hold back tears.

"Amanda, I just want you to be happy," Anne said.

I had never realized Anne took my theory of the big three so seriously. She looked at me with kind, apologetic eyes.

"I'm actually glad Steven came back," she said.

I looked at her like she was crazy.

"Because now you know he didn't forget about you! That's what you thought back then, that he walked away and didn't give you another thought. Honestly, Steven was my favorite. No offense to Paul or Timothy."

"Anne," I said, "you're assuming Timothy wants a future with me."

"Nobody does long distance if zey are not really into it," Ravenna said.

"Which one would you choose?" I asked both of them.

"Don't ask me, I'm an idiot with men," Anne laughed. "Leave something like that up to me, I'd probably choose Steven!"

They laughed. I almost did.

"Zee important sing is," Ravenna said with a calm voice, "no matter who you choose, we will support you. *Oui?*" she said to Anne.

"Right," Anne said. "No matter what."

"Paul speaks French, zat's all I'm going to say," Ravenna joked. But I knew, deep down, her first choice wouldn't be Paul.

"But he lives in New York," Anne said.

"So? I live in New York," Ravenna said.

"Yeah, but Amanda isn't dating you," Anne responded.

"Steven is very, very smart," Ravenna said. "And he likes zee cars. Amanda likes zee cars."

"Timothy's really smart too," Anne said. "He went to MIT."

Finally we all laughed together.

"Where is he, by the way?" I said, checking the time.

"Zat is always zee big question wis him, no?" Ravenna smiled.

"Are we okay?" Anne asked me.

"Yes." I slid off the counter and hugged Anne. "We're okay."

"I'm not going to hurt John," she said while we hugged. "I promise."

Ravenna put out her cigarette with tap water from the sink, tossed the butt in the trash can, and said, "Can we get drunk now?"

39

• • •

Anne, Ravenna, and I walked from my kitchen at the front of the house, back through the living room, and out the terrace doors to the backyard. They each carried two bottles of alcohol and I carried Mia's pitcher of sangria. I was the last to exit, and as I used my foot to keep the screen door from slamming, I heard Anne say, "Hey, Timothy. When did you get here?"

He jumped up the few steps leading from the yard to the small terrace and took the pitcher from me, kissing me quickly as he did so.

"About ten minutes ago," he said with a smile.

"I'm so glad you're here," I said. "Why didn't you come through the house?"

"I was going to, but I heard laughter coming from here so I came through the back gate."

Timothy and I made our way down to the group and he set the sangria pitcher on a wooden table, one of several I'd placed around the yard. The table teetered with the pitcher on it but Timothy didn't notice. The battered set of three wood tables of different heights had moved with me to my last few places of residence. They were worn, faded, and rickety but I couldn't part with them. To their credit, none of them had wounded my legs, unlike my sturdy coffee table, which I'd finally decided to replace. I picked up the sangria pitcher from the wobbly table and placed it on the main serving table, which was just a collapsible card table with gingham cloth draped over it, but "serving table" sounds more impressive. The weight of the pitcher could have killed the small wood table and that would break my heart.

Mia and Terry welcomed Timothy back to the conversation after his one-minute absence.

"Amanda," Terry said, "I was just telling your Timothy about that crazy party at the university museum last month." He leaned toward Timothy. "Amanda wouldn't go, of course."

"But I heard all about it," I said. "More than I wanted to."

Mia piped in, "Why is it that Terry's party stories are always raunchy? Terry, do you ever just attend a party?"

Malcolm interjected as he handed Ravenna a mojito, "I rather like Terry's MO. He doesn't merely attend a function, he conquers it."

Terry bowed in thanks, then said, "Amanda, I had no idea you knew the great Malcolm Werner."

"Terry and I go back a ways," Malcolm said. "He covers every event, gala, fundraiser, garden party, gallery opening, you name it. Why do you never accompany him, Amanda? You'd be marvelous at those functions."

Terry stepped to me and put his arm around my shoulder. "Amanda doesn't like limelight. I find it flatters my complexion."

"It's great to finally meet you all," Timothy said. "Heard about your flu, Terry. That's rough."

"Don't even try to make it seem like Amanda felt bad for me," Terry joked. "She was pissed that she had to attend that gala. What was the name again?"

"Famine something," I said, recalling the drama surrounding that night.

"Right, right, the famine one," Terry said.

"I don't believe I was there," Malcolm said.

"Well, you missed all the excitement," Terry said.

"There was excitement?" Timothy asked as he sipped his drink.

"Oh yeah," Terry said. "Amanda was making out—"

I faked a cough and "accidentally" elbowed Terry in his rib. Timothy stopped sipping his drink.

"Like a bandit," Terry said. "Like a bandit, girl!" Terry shook my shoulder and smiled big, hoping his cover didn't faze Timothy.

"Oh yes? How so?" Malcolm asked me. His voice boomed but not in a grating way. He must have fancied himself as the lord of the manor, even when it wasn't his manor.

"I'd like to know too," Timothy said, truly interested, apparently unaware of Terry's flub.

Anne, Ravenna, and Mia looked at me with anxious smiles. The news that I'd made out with Paul in front of Percy Hall, with all the socialites' eyes upon me, had spread like wildfire. It was one moment I was grateful Timothy and I lived in different cities.

"Don't listen to Terry," I joked. "He just means I ended up with lots of juicy gossip. None of which I included in my coverage of the benefit, of course."

"That she did, that she did," Terry said.

Mia shot him a look that said *someone's in trouble*!

"Do tell," Malcolm said.

I was about to create a fiction about Emily Richmond and her cohorts when Timothy's cell phone rang.

"Sorry, everyone," he said, pulling it from his back pocket and looking at the caller's name. "It's work. I have to take this," he said to me.

"Sure, go ahead," I said.

Timothy turned to answer the call and we suspended conversation as he responded to the caller with various strained responses such as, "You're kidding me," and, "Can't it wait?" and, "Shit, not again."

I wasn't surprised when he turned to me and whispered, "This might take a while."

"If that's the Chicago folks," Malcolm yelled, "tell them to take the night off for once."

Timothy gave Malcolm a thumbs-up and headed up the steps to go inside. My disappointment at Timothy's work intruding on the fun must have been apparent because Ravenna softly patted me on the back.

"Oh well," I said, grabbing the handle on the sangria pitcher, "more for us!"

Anne mouthed the words *I'm sorry*, to which I shrugged and motioned *what can you do?* A moment later the conversation got rolling again.

Terry sidled up to me.

"I am so sorry," he laughed. "I can't believe how stupid I was!"

"It's fine. He didn't catch on," I said.

"What were you going to say? About how you made out like a bandit? I was shitting!"

"I would have come up with something," I said with a lame laugh.

"Well, I'm set to get drunk, if I'm not half there already," Terry said. He walked to join Malcolm, Anne, Mia, John, and Ravenna.

I poured myself a glass of sangria, tasted it, and raised my glass to Mia who was already enjoying it.

"This is, hands down, the best sangria I've ever tasted," I said and meant it.

"You don't want to know what's in it!" Terry shouted.

"Shut up," Mia joked.

John Mayes slid out of the group and walked towards me. He smiled stiffly, as though he was unsure what to say.

"Mia makes great sangria, doesn't she?" he finally said.

"Wow, she really does," I said. "It would be good with your cheesecake."

A few quiet moments ensued, for what reason I wasn't sure. John rocked back and forth on his heels. I noticed the earliest beginnings of sunset.

"So that's the architect?" John asked.

"Yes," I said.

"Seems like a good guy."

"He is," I said. "A really good, busy guy."

"Beats dating a slacker," John said.

"True. Something in the middle would be nice too," I said with a smile.

Mia said over the group, "Amanda, you missed our congratulatory toast to John. Just think, now whenever you write anything political, John will be your editor."

"What has this world come to?" I shouted.

"You'll have to let us know which one of us is better," Mia said.

Terry piped in, "If she can deal with Herr Perry, she can deal with anyone."

Just the mention of Daniel Perry made me grimace. I wasn't acutely afraid of him anymore, but after years of bearing the brunt of his verbal assaults, I doubted if I'd ever be able to hear his name without reacting negatively in some way.

"Amanda," John said after the group resumed their boisterous conversation, "I should apologize again." I looked at him with curiosity. "For my attitude today," he added.

"It's no big deal, John. You were just being protective. That's what friends are for."

"I guess you could look at it that way," he said.

I tried to read John's expression but I got nothing; not because it was devoid of meaning but because my ability to read John had never been honed. He looked at the group, then specifically at Anne, who smiled at him, and then he said to me, "I should explain something to you."

"Okay," I said.

"When you first came to the paper I..."

John's eyes were looking past me. I then noticed the entire group had gone quiet and was staring at the same vantage point as John, just behind my head. I turned and saw Steven standing a few feet from me. If everyone and everything had been sucked into a black hole at that moment, I wouldn't have noticed.

"Hi there," John said. Friendly. Ignorant.

"Hi," Steven said, leaning around me to shake John's hand. He then fixed his eyes on me, and then looked to the group.

Malcolm yelled "Hello!" and gave Steven a big smile and a wave, which was reciprocated.

Steven said, "Anne, Ravenna," and offered them a respectful nod.

"What are you doing here?" I asked.

"I tried calling but you didn't answer," Steven said.

John turned away from us but remained close.

"My phone is inside," I said.

Steven took notice of John's proximity, and then stepped closer to me and lowered his voice. "I wanted to talk to you. I drove by and Mr. DC's matchbox car isn't in the driveway, so I knocked on the door."

"You didn't," I said.

"A guy answered and told me the party's around back," he said with a shrug.

My jaw hung open at the thought that Timothy had just encountered Steven without knowing it.

"Careful, you'll catch flies in there," Steven said.

"Steven, you have to go," I whispered.

"Steven!" Malcolm said with a sudden, hearty smack on Steven's back.

"There he is!" Steven said boisterously, as big men do. "Gentlemen, hide the Scotch and the women."

"You two know each other?" I asked.

"Oh, hell yes," Malcolm said. "And I'm a better man for it!"

"Couldn't get any worse," Steven said. Malcolm laughed with his whole body.

I shot a glance at the terrace and found it clear. I took a sip of sangria and remembered that Timothy didn't know about Steven. *Calm down.* I looked desperately for my friends and saw Ravenna squeezing through the group to make her way toward me.

"Helluva good tip you gave me, Steven. Got my ass out at just the right time," Malcolm said.

"I told ya," Steven said to him.

Ravenna appeared at Malcolm's side and said, "You're talking business?"

"There she is," Malcolm said.

Steven and Ravenna exchanged a knowing stare.

"Amanda, dear girl, tell me how you know this cad!" Malcolm said.

"Not now, darling," Ravenna said, patting Malcolm's belly. "You've had too much to drink, I sink."

I was stunned that Steven and Malcolm knew each other. *How could I get rid of him now*? Ravenna must have read my mind because she tried to steer Malcolm back to the group, which was still gathered near the main table. Thankfully, John had rejoined them.

"Nonsense," Malcolm proclaimed. "She's always looking out for me, this one." He kissed Ravenna on the side of her forehead.

"Malcolm, you've certainly done well for yourself," Steven said, referring to Ravenna.

"The best a man could do," Malcolm responded sincerely.

"You know what they say about French girls," Steven said with a wink.

Malcolm made a gun with his hand and fired it at Steven. "I love this guy. Love this guy!" he said.

Ravenna's eyes were suddenly fixed above me, beyond my head. Her mouth hung slightly open; she wanted to say something but either she couldn't find the words or the right moment.

"I bet you could use a drink," Malcolm said to Steven.

"That I could, sir," Steven said. He looked at me as Malcolm led him to the bar.

As soon as they were sucked into the group, I whispered to Ravenna, "What am I going to do?"

"*Mon amie*," she said, raising her chin to suggest *behind you*. I knew Timothy had to be standing there, so I put on my best smile and turned around.

40

. . .

There stood Paul. He looked at me as though I'd run over his dog. "Hello!" Ravenna said to him, leaning to exchange a double-cheek kiss.

Paul noticed Anne standing nearby and raised his hand in an almost-wave to acknowledge her. She waved back, smiled, and said, "Hi, Paul!" She then looked at me to say *holy shit* with her eyes.

"Paul," I said, forcing myself to smile.

"Thinking? This is what you call thinking?" Paul waved his arms to encompass the scene. Everyone turned at the volume of his voice. Mia, John, Malcolm, Terry. At the edge of my line of sight I saw Steven begin to make his way around the serving table.

"Paul—" I began, unsure of how to proceed.

"I can't believe this! I come here to surprise you and," he took my hand, "you're not even wearing it!"

"Paul, please calm down," I said, embarrassed as I looked at my friends.

"Calm down? I come here to see my fiancée and..." He put his hands on his hips and nodded despondently downward. "All this time," Paul said to the ground, "I'm thinking you're sitting here considering everything and planning how to tell me yes." He looked up at me, then to the group. His expression changed at the same moment I noticed Steven walking toward us. Ravenna turned, noticed Steven's approach, and slinked away.

"You're fucking kidding me," Paul said.

"Mr. California," Steven said.

Mia, Terry, and John whispered among themselves. I looked at Anne and Ravenna, just to be reminded of their presence.

"Oh, I see," Paul said, gesturing toward Steven. "This is why you're not wearing the ring?"

"I'm—" I began.

"Of course she's not wearing it," Steven said flatly. "Can you blame her?"

Oh shit. Oh shit. Oh shit.

"Steven, please," I said.

Paul looked like he was going to explode.

"I knew it!" he yelled. "You're with him."

"I am not with him," I said strongly.

"Yeah right," Paul scoffed. "I knew that night at the benefit there was something going on." Paul avoided Steven's unflinching stare. "This," he waved dismissively toward Steven, "is why you needed 'time to think.'" He air-quoted the words.

"Paul," I said, "you walked in on something here that looks a certain way, but I swear—"

"I bet you haven't worn the ring since I left," he said.

"No, she's worn it," Steven said, casually sipping his drink. "Not exactly what I'd call a fashion statement."

Ohhhh shit. I had never known Paul to strike another person but right then I feared he would punch Steven in the face.

"Oh yeah?" Paul said, taking the bait. Damn Steven, he could always reel someone in. "That happens to be a rare vintage ring," he said.

"Vintage," Steven said. "As in used."

Paul's fists clenched. Steven noticed it.

"Don't go there, pal," Steven said, taking another sip. Paul sensed Steven's warning was real and he backed off ever so slightly.

"This isn't happening," I said aloud to myself, shaking my head in disbelief.

"Amanda, this is between us," Paul said with a huff. "Let's go somewhere else."

"Paul, I have a house full of people here," I said as quietly as possible.

Paul raised his voice to the group and said, "Anyone mind if my fiancée and I take a few minutes?"

My friends didn't respond and I was monumentally grateful.

"Paul, please don't involve them." I rubbed my forehead, stole a glance to the terrace doors, and tried to figure a way out of this disaster.

"Amanda, I just came all the way from New York," he stressed. "You won't even talk to me?"

"Of course I'll talk to you." I kept my voice down as I turned again to check the terrace doors for Timothy. "But we need more than a few minutes. Can I please just call you later?"

"I can't even stay?" Paul looked at Steven. "He can stay, but I can't?"

"He's not staying either," I said.

"He looks pretty fucking comfortable. He's obviously been here more than a few minutes."

"Forget him!" I said, straining to keep my yelling in check. "You can't do this, Paul. You can't just show up here and command me. You did that with the proposal, now you're doing it with my answer. You're making a scene, embarrassing me in front of my friends." I didn't mean to say all that. It just came out.

"This is because of him," Paul said with disgust in Steven's direction. "You're obviously together and you don't even have enough respect for me to tell the truth!"

"Paul, I swear to you, on my car,"—something he knew I'd never gamble on—"Steven is not here with me."

Everyone turned as the screen door swung open and Timothy flew down the steps and arrived at my side.

"He is," I said.

Timothy kissed my cheek, then said rather loudly, "Sorry, all. That took ten times longer than I thought it would." The group collectively smiled at him but nobody moved.

"Who the hell is this?" Paul demanded, registering Timothy by my side.

"Mr. DC," Steven said.

"Excuse me?" Timothy said.

Twenty minutes earlier Steven probably hadn't realized that the guy who answered my door and directed him to the party was Timothy. But it didn't take a genius to recognize that same guy, currently holding me and kissing my cheek, was "Mr. DC."

"Steven Jameson," he said, extending his hand to shake Timothy's.

"Good to meet you. I see you found the party," Timothy said warmly. "Hey there," he said to Paul, extending his hand.

Paul reluctantly shook Timothy's hand but stared at me as he did so, glowering and piercing me with his deep blue eyes.

John leaned in to hand Timothy a beer. "You're going to need this."

"Thanks!" Timothy took a gulp, then squeezed me and said, "So what'd I miss?"

Anne and Ravenna both held up their hands in a helpless gesture and I nodded briefly for them to stay put. I knew I had to face the music alone. Timothy raised and circled his beer toward Steven and Paul and said, "So how do you all know each other?"

Steven pursed his mouth just shy of a grin but said nothing.

Paul stood in a snit and waited.

"Well, um, Paul and I used to date," I said.

"Oh." Timothy gave Paul a quick twice-over.

"She used to date him too," Paul said snidely, referring to Steven. "Though you'll have to ask her if 'used to' is accurate. Right, Amanda?"

"Paul, stop." I begged him with my eyes to turn down the amplitude.

"Okay, well," Timothy said, keeping his arm around me, taking the scene in stride. I was surprised. And impressed.

"Don't pay attention to Mr. California there," Steven said casually.

"What the fuck is your problem?" Paul turned abruptly to face off with Steven.

All noise in the vicinity silenced immediately. No crickets. No squirrels chewing nuts. No bees buzzing. No ice clinking in glasses.

"Eh, shut your pie hole," Steven said. Then he said to Timothy, "You understand that. Pie hole? Pi? Three point one four one five—"

Timothy grinned and held up his hand to quiet Steven. "Hey, man, leave me out of this."

"You're right," Steven said bluntly but sincerely. "My apologies."

Timothy tilted his head to say *no problem*.

"Amanda, want to tell me what's going on here?" Timothy asked.

"Well—" I said.

"Don't," Steven interrupted. "This isn't her fault." He spoke directly to Timothy as Paul stood by and boiled. "I came here to talk to Amanda. She didn't invite me. I know a few people here and she wasn't rude enough to ask me to leave."

"That's cool," Timothy said, tightening his grip on my waist. "No problem."

"This is such bullshit," Paul yelled.

"Paul, please," I said pointedly.

"What's your problem, man?" Timothy said.

"My problem?" Paul laughed. "Your girlfriend is my fiancée, that's my problem."

Oh shit. Oh shit. Oh shit.

"Amanda?" Timothy said.

I looked at my friends, and then at Steven, who stared at me intently and seemed to be waiting to jump in. But it wasn't his responsibility to rescue me. This was my party, in every sense.

"Okay, here it is," I said, turning to face Timothy directly. "Paul and I were together years ago, and I hadn't seen him in *years.* Then last week he came here out of the blue and proposed to me." Timothy's face registered shock; it was the most unsmiling expression I'd ever seen on him. I allowed him time to digest the information.

"Uh, if you're going to marry him," he said, still digesting, "why would you let me come here?"

I opened my mouth to speak but Steven jumped in.

"Because she's not going to marry him," he said.

Paul said nothing; he just stared at Steven, then at me.

"Okay, wait. Are you two together?" Timothy asked me, gesturing toward Paul.

"No," I said gently.

"Well, are you two together?" Timothy asked, referring to Steven.

"No, we're not," Steven answered in his matter-of-fact tone that didn't leave an ounce of doubt. Timothy nodded in acknowledgement.

Steven downed the last of his cocktail in one deft swallow and added, "I didn't presume that simply walking back into Amanda's life was enough to merit a relationship." He turned his eyes to Paul and said, "It's like you don't even know her."

"I know her better than you ever could," Paul said.

"I recall Amanda saying you were smart," Steven said, squinting as if he were deeply pondering the idea. "I don't see it."

I was mortified—for myself, for Timothy, and for Paul.

"This is a nightmare," I said. "Timothy, I'm so sorry. You don't deserve this."

"I'm just trying to get a handle on the situation here," he said, loosening his grip on me.

"Amanda," Paul said, stepping in front of Timothy and taking my hand, "just marry me. It's simple. Just marry me. Forget this asshole," he tilted his head toward Steven. "And whoever you are," he said to Timothy, "you seem like a good guy but she's taken."

I pulled my hand from Paul's.

"This guy is unbelievable," Steven laughed. "At least I admit I'm a selfish asshole."

"What's that supposed to mean?" Paul asked him.

"Your big proposal," Steven said with jazz hands, "you did that for yourself, for everyone to be impressed with you. That way," Steven looked at me, "if you say no, you're crazy, because look at all he did for you."

Paul scoffed but he didn't respond. Something about Steven's assessment must have struck a chord. It did with me too.

"Amanda is with him now," Steven said, lifting his chin toward Timothy. "Deal with it."

Paul laughed dramatically. "You deal with it! Don't act like you know what's between us."

"I'm not acting," Steven said.

"That's it," Paul said, stepping up to Steven until their faces were inches apart.

I escaped Timothy's hold around my waist.

"Steven, I think you should go," I said.

"Yeah," he said, staring at Paul.

Steven would never fight him. It wasn't his way. He could, but he wouldn't. He wouldn't do that to me. Instead he stepped aside to shake Timothy's hand.

"Sorry," Steven said. "Don't let this ruin your trip."

Timothy laughed once with appreciation and shook Steven's hand. "Thanks."

Steven set his glass on one of the rickety wood tables and excused himself. As he started to walk away, he patted Timothy on the shoulder and said, "By the way, BMW, good car. I used to have one."

Timothy smiled at the compliment. "What'd you have?"

"M-three, a long time ago," Steven said.

"What do you have now?"

"An old Porsche," Steven shrugged, glancing toward me, allowing a momentary connection between us.

"Yeah?" Timothy said. "What year?"

I cleared my throat to break up their car love fest.

"We'll catch up and talk cars next time," Steven said.

"Sounds good," Timothy said.

Steven half-waved to the group, gestured *I'll call you* to Malcolm, walked across the yard, unlatched the gate, and disappeared. The air changed the moment I heard the click of the gate behind him.

I turned to Timothy and said, "I'm so sorry. I really need to talk to Paul. Is that okay?"

"Sure," he said.

"We'll just be on the front steps." I hoped he understood my meaning; I wasn't going far and I'd still be within his reach.

Timothy squeezed my hand, then released it. He watched me walk away with Paul, and then he went to join the others.

41

. . .

Paul waited for me on the front steps while I went inside for a minute. When I came out he was seated on the top step, staring out at the street. The pink and yellow early sunset illuminated his face, creating a serene silhouette quite the opposite from the aggression and anger that had consumed him just minutes earlier. I sat down next to him.

"You're not going to marry me," he said as though he'd discovered a major life truth after years of searching. "Tell me the truth," he said calmly. "Is it because of that guy, Steven?"

"No," I said.

Paul sighed.

"Because of that other guy? The short one?"

"No."

Paul turned to look at me. "Then why?"

His eyes looked so beautiful.

"Looking at you like this takes me back to our early days," I said.

"I loved those days," Paul said.

His presence emanated warmth and I wanted to touch it, so I did. I placed my hand against his cheek and thought I could feel the sun between our skin. He placed his hand on mine and I felt the lump in my throat return. I had been able to hold back tears when Anne and I argued in the kitchen before the party. I had been able to hold back tears at other times over the past week. But at that moment, locking eyes with Paul, my first real love, I could not hold back the tears any longer.

"I loved those days too," I said.

"Why are you crying?" Paul said gently.

"Because I'm afraid," I said.

"Of what?" He slid my hand off his face and held it between his hands.

"Of making the biggest mistake of my life," I said.

"You were always the strong one, Amanda. You always held it together. Held me together. When I was just starting out, you were there. You were always there."

I smiled through my soft crying; a reflex, not because I was happy.

"I wasn't really there for you, I know," Paul said. "But I want to be."

"I know," I said sincerely.

"Marry me," he said. "Then you'll never wonder if you made a mistake." Paul was so hopeful and romantic. I looked away from him as tears welled in my eyes.

"Will you?" he said. "We can forget that whole ugly thing back there. Please say you will."

"I can't," I said.

"Why? You just said you're afraid of making a huge mistake."

I held back the floodgates long enough to say what I truly felt. "I'm afraid marrying you would be the mistake."

I looked at his handsome face. His eyes were glossed with wetness. Then I started to really cry. What I had just said could never be unsaid. It could never be taken back. Paul would remember it forever. There was no going back.

I cried for our years together. I cried for our time spent apart when I had wondered what would become of us. I cried from the release of finally speaking the truth. I cried at the thought I would never see Paul again. I cried for myself, not in pity, but in solidarity. And I cried for Paul. Because Paul loved me, but I didn't love him back. Not anymore.

I brought my other hand across my lap and opened my fist, revealing the ring in my hand.

"This is why you went inside," he said.

I nodded.

Paul lifted the ring from my hand.

"I really thought this is what you wanted," he said.

"I thought so too. For a long time."

"I don't know if you love me anymore, but I love you, Amanda."

I was overwhelmed with the desire to kiss him, so I did. It was soft and wet with tears.

"I can't promise that I'll give up on you," Paul said.

I smiled at him and together we stood. He wiped the tears gently from my face and I did the same to him. Our crying had calmed with our affection.

"Would it have made any difference if I hadn't come today?" he asked. "If I'd waited until the weekend like we planned?"

I shook my head.

"You're with that other guy now," he said.

I nodded.

"I'm such an idiot," Paul said sadly. "It didn't even occur to me that you were seeing someone. Didn't even enter my mind."

"I could have told you," I said. "I should have told you."

"Is he good to you?"

"Yes, he's kind and a gentleman," I said.

"How long have you been together?"

"A few months," I said. "We're not serious yet but it's heading there. Of course, who knows after all this." I laughed sadly.

"I'll apologize to him," Paul said.

"It's okay," I said.

"The other guy, the asshole," Paul said, lowering his gaze, "he loves you, you know."

It was the last thing on earth I expected Paul to say.

"I don't know your story with him," he said, "but he would have fought me back there."

"That doesn't mean he loves me," I said.

"He does."

"It's not important," I said.

"Because you're with...?"

"Timothy? No. It's just not important." And it wasn't, not at that moment, not to my reason for refusing Paul.

Paul kissed my cheek and held my hand as he began to walk down the front steps. My arm extended further with each step he took until our fingers were barely touching.

"I'd leave the ring with you," he said as the sunset cast a warm glow on his face, "but I might ask you again someday."

I watched Paul walk down the street and he looked back at me many times. Each time I felt a fleeting urge to run after him. Eventually he turned the corner and disappeared.

I stood on my front steps and stared at the corner, but Paul didn't come back. After a few minutes I heard laughter and conversation streaming from my backyard. It had been there all along, but I noticed it only after Paul was gone. I went inside to splash cold water on my face and freshen up. After all, I still had a party to host.

42

...

Ice-cold water proved a miracle worker. By the time I walked through my terrace doors to rejoin the party, I felt almost normal again. I hoped the evening wasn't completely ruined by the drama of my big three. When Timothy saw me he hopped up the steps from the yard.

"Are you okay?" he said.

"I should be asking you that," I said. "I feel awful, Timothy. I'm so sorry."

"Look," he said, "I'm still not clear on what, exactly, went down tonight. But I am clear about one thing." He stepped as close to me as he could get without our noses touching. "I have been falling for you since our first date and that hasn't changed for me. Has it changed for you?"

"No," I said. He noticed the surprise in my eyes.

"You seem shocked to hear that," he said sweetly.

"Most guys would have taken off already," I said.

"I'm too smart for that," he said, raising an eyebrow.

"Yes, I've heard you MIT guys are pretty smart."

"Amanda, I can't get angry with you that other men have wanted you. We both have pasts. Your friends filled me in a little bit on the history there."

I was relieved; I was tired of history. Ravenna and Anne would know what not to share, and my friends from the paper didn't know enough to relay anything dangerous.

"That guy, Paul, I can't blame him for freaking out. He didn't know about me. Why didn't you tell him?"

I wasn't sure how honest I should be, but in the spirit of the evening I opted for complete truth. "Because I don't know exactly where we are, Timothy. That's okay, but—"

"What? Talk to me," Timothy said softly.

"I barely heard from you for a couple weeks," I said. "An e-mail here or a text there, but I wondered if we were over."

Timothy looked at me curiously.

I continued, "You know, one of those breakups that never really happens, where people just stop communicating. And then Paul showed up out of nowhere and wanted to give things another shot, and then he proposed, and I didn't want to hurt him."

"I understand," Timothy said.

"And this was all before I even knew you were coming to visit. He lives in Manhattan, you're in DC. I never thought your paths would cross."

"It's not your fault," Timothy said. His maturity and lack of drama was like a warm blanket. "But I have to ask, Amanda, did you consider marrying him?"

"Yes," I said.

Timothy's face skewed downward.

"I'm just being honest," I added.

"I appreciate it," Timothy said sincerely.

"And since I'm being so honest, I'll tell you why." Timothy looked directly at me. "Paul and I were together for a long time, but that was a long time ago. He's always kept in touch with me. He'd call every few months, or sometimes longer intervals would go by. And even though I've had other serious relationships—"

"Like Porsche guy," Timothy interjected.

I rolled my eyes. "Yes, Steven is one. But despite having other relationships, Paul always had a keen habit of calling me right when things would go south with someone. After enough time you start to think that's a sign of something. So there I was, thinking your career, or maybe a lack of liking me enough, was about to end us, and then Paul showed up."

"Makes sense," Timothy said.

"Does it?" I laughed. "Good, because I feel nuts explaining it."

"Well, love is nuts sometimes," he said. "I mean, how nuts does a guy have to be to stay away from you for weeks at a time?"

Timothy smiled at me as I registered the implication of his statement. *Did he just say he loves me*?

"But," Timothy added, "I'm still fuzzy about Porsche guy."

"Okay," I exhaled strongly, resigned to lay it all out. "Ask me anything."

"How did he know I have a BMW?"

Shit. I had to come clean, not only because I couldn't come up with a decent lie, but because Timothy deserved the truth.

"I told him," I said.

"About my car?"

"Yes. Well, kind of." Timothy waited for me to elaborate. "Steven showed up when Paul was in town last week. At that benefit, actually. I hadn't seen him or talked him in over a year," I stressed.

Timothy nodded, swallowed hard, and then said, "But you've obviously talked to him since I got to town. Before tonight, I mean."

"Yes," I sighed. "I met him for coffee. You were at the university working."

There, the truth was out.

Timothy leaned his head back and looked at the sky.

"Wow," he said.

"Nothing happened," I said. Okay, so the whole truth wasn't out, but a woman has to keep some secrets. "I can't begin to explain what the past week has been like for me, Timothy. I'm not asking for sympathy, I'm just telling you what you walked into. But it's all over now. Paul's gone. Steven's gone. And I'm here with you. Only you."

"You look like you want to say something else," he said.

"Can I say that I'm with only you?" I asked Timothy as much as myself.

"Do you want to be with anyone else?" he asked.

I pushed Steven from my mind.

"I'm afraid your work is your only priority," I said. "I really want to see where this goes with us, but we never seem to get enough time."

Timothy wrapped his arms around my waist.

"I've always believed we make time for what's important to us," he said.

"So what's a girl to do when a guy has to pencil her in his schedule?"

"She has to remember that if he didn't want to see her, he wouldn't." Timothy kissed me gently. "And the guy has to remember that she's just as important as his other pursuits. And that she's obviously in demand! So he better not take her for granted."

"We're good, then?" I asked.

"We're good." Timothy and I kissed quite deeply, as though nothing unusual had transpired since he left for work that morning. I felt his eight-o'clock shadow grate against my skin. It felt good.

"Are you going to join the party or what?" Malcolm yelled from the far end of the yard.

"Yes!" Timothy called out to him. "Staking my claim here, give me a minute." His comment elicited a communal laugh.

Timothy and I rejoined the party and he was immediately sucked into a drunken game of charades led by Terry. Anne and Ravenna each hugged me, and then resumed their conversations with John and Malcolm, respectively.

"I hope there's some sangria left," I said to Mia, who'd been standing by the bar table, quietly texting someone. She leaned under the table and brought up the pitcher.

"I saved it for you," she said, pulling the plastic wrap off the top.

"This is why you're such a great editor," I said. "You anticipate."

"Are you all right?" she asked.

"Who knows," I said with a small laugh.

"You said no to the proposal."

I nodded.

"And what about the other guy?"

I didn't know how to reply to her inquiry about Steven, so I drank some sangria.

"He certainly came to your defense," she said.

"Yes, he certainly did," I said.

The way Steven took on Paul left me filled with questions. Unfortunately, they were questions only Steven could answer.

"He's got a vibe, that one," Mia said.

"Yes, he certainly does," I said.

"Seems like he'd make a good writer," she said. "He's got a biting way."

I imagined Steven's teeth working their way down my neck.

"Yes, he does," I said.

"And Timothy's okay with everything?" Mia asked with a skeptical look.

"Apparently," I said.

Mia and I said more with our eyes than with words, as women instinctively do when certain things shouldn't be said aloud. She finished her text messages and we watched the group make asses of themselves until Terry fell down.

Mia called down to him, "You realize it's Wednesday night. You have to work tomorrow."

"It's all good," Terry said, clumsily brushing pollen and dirt off of his clothes.

Mia and John helped him up as Anne and Ravenna started to carry things inside.

John stepped aside as Mia attempted to keep Terry vertical.

"We actually work with these people," John said to me, loud enough so they'd hear it.

"Which makes you damn lucky, and don't you forget it!" Terry said.

"How much has he had to drink?" I asked.

"Barely anything," John said, mocking him. "He's like you. A few drinks and he's done."

"Where'd that guy go?" Terry said, positioning his sunglasses on his head.

"What guy?" Mia said.

"The tall drink of water," Terry said. "Mama, deliver me."

"He's talking about Paul," I said quietly to Mia and John. Paul looked enough like a model that Terry would definitely be into him.

"No," Terry said. "Though he can make me breakfast anytime. Lordy, that guy's got some beautiful eyes. Beau-tee-ful."

I smiled uncomfortably. Terry was right about Paul's eyes. Luckily Timothy didn't hear the exchange; he was too wrapped up in work talk with Malcolm. Not that I could blame him. He was leaving the next day and probably worried about a million details.

I waved Terry off but he couldn't be easily silenced.

"No, the tall drink of water," he insisted. "You know, 'shut your pi hole'." Terry cracked up.

I glanced at Timothy, who must have heard this last outburst. He smiled at me. He was either pretending not to hear or care, or he truly wasn't paying attention.

"That man! Good Lord, Amanda." Terry planted a hand on my shoulder. "Girl, you gotta be outta your mind to let him walk off."

"Okay," Mia said. "Someone's had enough for tonight. I'm taking this sorry sot home." She led Terry into the house.

"Well, this turned out to be quite an evening," John said.

"Sorry about everything," I said.

"Sorry about what?" John asked rhetorically. "Life gets messy sometimes. I believe I read that somewhere." He was referring to one of my columns.

"How are things with you?" I tilted my head in Anne's direction.

"Good. Fine," he said with a smile. "Let me help you clean up."

I accepted John's help and wished fervently that he could help me clean *everything* up.

"Hey, you were going to tell me something," I said as we began to gather glasses and plates. "Something about when I first started at the paper?"

"Oh, right. It's nothing," John said, placing plastic cups one by one inside each other.

"You sure?"

"Yeah," he said.

John stared down at the stack of cups in his hand.

"Just be careful of Daniel Perry," he said, and then looked at me.

I sighed. Being a protective friend is one thing. Acting like a parent is another.

"John, I appreciate the concern, but—"

"I've known him a long time. He does nothing, I mean nothing, without a selfish motive."

"I can handle Daniel Perry," I said.

John laughed, "After what I saw tonight, I think you can handle anything."

I didn't agree with John about my handling abilities, but I thanked him. As we carried the party supplies inside, I decided that the next time I wanted to host a spontaneous party, I'd think twice.

43

$\bullet\ \bullet\ \bullet$

I helped Timothy put the last of his belongings into his tiny car. We had already made two trips around the corner to where he was parked.

"Jeez, you accumulated a lot of stuff in just a few days," I said.

"As soon as I get back to DC I'll be swamped with other work. If I don't take all this with me, I'll lose track of it." He kissed me on the cheek. "Wouldn't want me to come back here, would you?"

"I don't want you to leave," I said.

"I don't either," he said.

"Liar," I joked. "You can't wait to get into your office."

"I do miss my actual office," he said, "but that's it."

We stood, embracing on the sidewalk, resting our foreheads against one another.

"So I've been thinking about your guest room," Timothy said, lifting his head and taking my hands in his. "I would never ask to share your office, but maybe I could put a desk in the other room?" He tilted his head. "Maybe a little file cabinet. A bookshelf?"

I felt a strange current run through me.

"You can keep anything you'd like here," I said.

"I'll be back in a couple weeks. We can run to Ikea and get a few things. You know, nothing permanent," he added with a cute grin. He must have sensed my nervousness.

"I do need to look at coffee tables," I said.

"Perfect. In the meantime, you want to head to DC next weekend? There's a function I have to attend and I'd love you to come
with me."

I smiled and kissed him to say *yes*.

"What time are you leaving?" I asked.

"I have to run over to the university, and then I'm off."

"You remember how to get to the highway?"

"I'll find my way," he said. "I need to learn, right? I plan on
spending a lot of time here."

Timothy and I kissed again. After he was settled in his car, and
the top was down, I leaned over his door and asked a question that
had been bugging me.

"Why didn't you park in the driveway last night?"

"I would have, but by the time I got here someone was already
parked there. I think it was Mia."

"Ah," I said. I knew Steven wouldn't have stopped by if he had
seen Timothy's car in the driveway. "Call me when you get home.
I like to know you made it safe and sound."

"I'll call you before then," he said.

I smiled, but I knew we wouldn't talk again until after he
returned home. Timothy stretched upward and gently pulled my
head down for a final kiss. A minute later I watched him drive off.

• • •

Timothy was gone. My world was calm. I didn't go downtown
to the paper. I stayed in my home office and worked all day. I only
took a break when Ravenna stopped over to say goodbye. She promised she'd be back soon, probably in a few days if Malcolm had his
way. We took a long, leisurely walk. It was a bright, hot, humid
day. I wore a chambray button-down with the sleeves rolled up,

white linen shorts, and flip-flops. Ravenna was styled as usual, in an ankle-length black jersey dress with spaghetti straps, and platform espadrille sandals.

"Malcolm sinks I should move here," she said.

"That makes two of us," I said.

"How are sings wis Timothy?"

"Good. Surprising, isn't it?"

"He's all smiles, zat one."

"He does have an amazing ability to not freak out. I guess that's maturity," I laughed.

"I sink is just his personality. It's good for you. For now."

I wondered how Ravenna truly felt about Timothy. She didn't know him well, mostly from my talking, but considering all that had happened in recent days, I felt comfortable enough to finally ask her.

"You're not crazy about Timothy, are you?"

"What do you mean?" She fished a cigarette from her purse and lit it.

"You can tell me, you won't hurt my feelings."

"I sink he is a great guy," Ravenna said. "I do!"

"Okay." I smiled and didn't push the subject further.

Ravenna and I walked along, enjoying the singing birds and warm sun.

"Have you heard from him?" she eventually asked.

I knew she wasn't referring to Paul. I leaned my head back to bathe it in sunlight.

"No," I said.

"You will."

"I don't think so. When he told Paul that I'm with Timothy now, that closed the book on it."

"He had to say zat," Ravenna said. "You were standing zer wis a man's arms around you."

I hadn't considered that picture; what the scene had looked like from Steven's perspective.

"Zat is maturity," Ravenna said.

I hadn't considered that either.

"He did make that pi comment to Timothy," I said.

"Eh, nobody is perfect," Ravenna said.

Another good point.

"Did you tell Timothy about zee kiss?"

"No," I said.

"Good." She exhaled a smooth stream of smoke that trailed behind us like a jet stream.

Ravenna's certainty comforted me. I had always considered myself to be a person of rules, but recent events had taught me that many rules were meant to be broken because they were groundless.

"Something just occurred to me," I said, and then stopped walking.

Ravenna stopped, took a puff, and looked at me.

"I don't have to choose," I said.

"Choose?"

"A guy. A love. I don't have to choose one."

Ravenna thought about that. After a few moments she said with mild surprise, "No, you don't."

The realization made me feel lighter and almost giddy.

"I hate that you're leaving." I put my arm through hers.

"Maybe you come to zee city zis weekend."

"That's an idea," I said.

"If you don't have plans," she added.

"Ravenna, I'm not going to see him. Probably ever again."

She laughed to herself and patted my hand. "*Mon amie, tu es trop mignonne.*"

I leaned my head against her shoulder. "Did you just call me a tramp?"

"*Oui.*"

Weeks later, as I was trying for the umpteenth time to learn French on my computer and failing miserably, I discovered that Ravenna hadn't called me a tramp. She had merely said in French what anyone would say to a friend who had just said something naïve or downright silly. The phrase translates literally as, "you're too nice," but in casual speech it means, "you're too funny." Of course from then on I called Ravenna *trop mignonne* every chance I got.

44
• • •

I woke up Friday morning to a late-night e-mail from Timothy. It said he was still smiling about our time together and he couldn't wait to see me again next weekend. After he left the previous morning, he drove straight to his office and cranked work for hours, catching up on all he had missed while he was away. Just as I'd suspected, he didn't call when he reached DC to let me know he'd made it safely; he called many hours later. But he did call, and that was worth something.

Friday passed as Fridays do, with a feeling of completion. I stopped at the paper and had pleasant, normal, everyday conversations with Terry, John, and Mia as though they hadn't witnessed the implosion of my romantic life.

Mia briefly discussed my upcoming column, alerted me to a few minor edits, and bade me a nice weekend. She was going on a day trip with whichever friend she'd been texting at my party, and I told her I wanted to hear all about it come Monday morning.

Daniel Perry walked past my desk and asked me to come talk in his office. No summons this time. A few minutes later people noticed me walk in there with my requisite pen and notepad, but because of our current lack of hostility, my trip to the glass cage didn't raise antennae as it used to. I entered the office, closed the door behind me, and Daniel gestured for me to sit.

"So you're not getting married," he said, tilting his chin toward my ringless hand.

"Uh, no, I'm not," I said.

John Mayes walked past the glass cage and gave me a brief smile, then glared at Daniel, then smiled at me again.

"Good. Then you're free for a few assignments?" Daniel said.

"Assignments?"

"John's going to Washington for a couple days to cover the DNC scandal. Guys in the DC bureau are swamped and John's been pressing to go anyway."

I nodded and pretended to take the minutes of this meeting. I wrote *do laundry.*

"We need someone to cover him in Editorial until he gets back," Daniel said.

"Okay," I said, pretending to make a note of it.

Daniel stared at me.

"You mean me?"

"Why not," Daniel said.

"Can I do that as a freelancer?" The paper had very strict rules about such things.

"If I say so, yes. But don't think you'll be paid by the word. We'll go by the hour and it won't be much. Editorial's got enough in their budget for a few days' worth."

I was dumbfounded that Daniel hadn't asked his bitchy liege, Leona Vargas. She was a fairly new addition to the paper but Daniel had worked with her back in his *Wall Street Journal* days. I forgot her a moment later.

"That sounds great. Thank you, Daniel." It felt weird to be pleasant with Daniel Perry.

"This is not going to lead to a staff position," he said firmly. "We're about to cut more people as it is."

"I understand. I don't want that anyway," I said nicely.

"You like being free," he said as though he knew me well.

"With my work, yes."

Daniel played with his fancy pen and looked at it as he did so.

"I'll want another piece from you next week," he said.

"Any subject in particular?"

"Surprise me," he said flatly.

45

• • •

On Saturday morning I woke up to another late-night e-mail from Timothy. It was sweet and short, sent from his work email shortly before dawn. I knew I'd see Anne later in the day and hear about her date with Charlie the night before. Or maybe it was with John Mayes. I'd been in a haze since Timothy left town, which was compounded by Daniel Perry's unlikely work offer. Writing wasn't in the cards for me that day; I'd been at it almost constantly since Thursday morning. Now that my life had returned to normal, my usual antsy-ness had returned along with it.

I went into the backyard in the hope that gardening would sate me. The humidity was thick and there was no breeze. For an hour I weeded and pruned on hands and knees. I happened upon vestiges of Wednesday night's party. A few errant cigarette butts, no doubt dropped by Terry who smoked only when he drank and always flicked the butts theatrically. There were fruit rinds dropped from sangria, martinis, or gin and tonics. Ants were enjoying them so I let them be. I saw Malcolm's business card, perhaps offered to Mia or John in case they wanted to contact him about the museum. Cocktail napkins. Three plastic cups. Stirring straws. I collected the debris and placed it on the nearest little wooden table. There was a car key sitting on it.

I changed my position to give my knees a break and turned the key to look at it from every angle. Such an intense inspection isn't necessary when you see the Porsche logo but anything involving Steven grabbed my attention. I laughed to myself, thinking he must have dropped his extra key and not even noticed. "Idiot," I said, then put the key in my jean shorts pocket. I would never admit that I felt relieved and excited because I would probably hear from him again; Steven would be frantic about losing the key and that would give him an excuse to call me.

"I hope you don't plan on keeping that." The voice came from behind me. I didn't need to turn to see who it was.

"That depends," I said, already feeling flushed.

"On?"

"On what it's a key to," I said.

"Come take a look," Steven said.

I turned to see Steven sitting on the ground a few feet away from me. I felt frozen and hot at the same time.

"There's all manner of grossness on this yard," I said. "God only knows what'll be stuck to your shorts when you get up."

Steven's expression turned pensive, and then he said, "I'll let that one go."

He sipped from a huge plastic cup with a fat green straw. He looked good. I suddenly remembered that I looked like hell, with dirt and sweat on my face and in my hair.

"I was just about to go in and get something to drink," I said.

Steven reached behind his back and presented a large cup of lemonade. I recognized the white cup and bright pink straw from a tiny drinks-only shop in his neighborhood. The place was a hole in the wall but long lines formed every day for their unique con-coctions. Steven and I used to go there often.

"Thank you." I drew a long sip. "They still make the best lem-onade in the world."

"I drove around the block this time. Didn't see Mr. DC's car anywhere," Steven said.

I nodded slightly. Timothy definitely was not here.

"Doesn't mean he won't be back any minute," I said.

"True, the absence of his car does not mean that," Steven said. "But I know he won't."

I bristled at the implication that Timothy was never to return, and Steven read it on my face. "I talked to Malcolm," he said. Ah, that explained it. Malcolm was such a talker and networker, he would have gladly offered Timothy's project schedule.

I nodded and picked at blades of grass to busy my hands.

"He said the university museum project's on hold as of yesterday," Steven said and then watched my reaction to the news that Timothy would no longer have work as a reason to visit.

This was the first I'd heard of the project's moratorium but I didn't want Steven to know that. I was bothered that Timothy hadn't relayed the news to me, at least in an e-mail if not in a phone call.

"You know how those big projects go," I said casually. "Sometimes it takes years to complete them."

I felt the old lump in my throat return, but this time it wasn't guilt. It was the lump of disappointment that Timothy had regressed into workaholic mode; it happens when people return to their own worlds. It was safe to assume our big relationship-making trip to Ikea for his desk and bookshelf wouldn't happen, at least not the following weekend. I felt sad and foolish sitting there discussing Timothy's work with Steven.

Just then my cell phone pinged. I reached for it from a nearby wood table. It was from Timothy: Hi! Those a-holes pulled the plug on the museum, won't get rolling again until fall. Hope you're having a good day. Can't wait for next weekend☺.

I smiled. Steven noticed.

"DC?" he asked.

"Anne," I lied.

I laughed at myself, at how quickly I'd presumed Timothy would go back to his usual ways. It wasn't fair to him. He had handled all my romantic drama like a champ. And even though we hadn't definitively established a serious relationship—or had we?—he was still very much in my life and I shouldn't be so quick to think the worst. But, then, I wouldn't be me. It did bother me that Steven knew about Timothy's schedule before I did. But Timothy would not end our relationship abruptly, coldly, and without explanation like Steven had done a year ago—or would he?—and I could be happy knowing we were okay.

All those thoughts flitted away when I looked directly at Steven. I tried to bring them back but they were gone. Steven's rich brown eyes were earthy and real. His voice was strong, and it filled the space around him when he spoke. His mind was solid and focused. His personality was high-octane, but he had control over it. He wasn't whimsical and his tastes didn't jump around. Steven wasn't searching for himself, he already knew who he was. Above all, he was present. In every way.

"Mind if I smoke?" he asked.

"Go ahead. I thought you quit."

"I did," he said, lighting a cigarette. He offered me one but I declined.

"Steven."

"Yeah," he said, biting the cigarette between his teeth. Jesus, he looked sexy.

"Thank you for the other night."

He squinted at the sun.

"You could have gone a bit easier on Paul," I said, "but thank you for defending me."

"That guy doesn't deserve easy," Steven said, still not looking at me.

"You don't even know him. Why do you hate him?"

"I don't hate him," he said. Finally, his eyes met mine.

I smirked at him.

"He's a baby," he said.

I should have mounted a defense of Paul but I couldn't muster the effort. I was still disheartened by his behavior—snubbing John Mayes and his date at the benefit, the instances of snippy attitude thrown my way, and his tantrum at my party.

"I read that guy the second I met him at the benefit," Steven said.

"You did, huh."

"I knew you wouldn't say yes, even if you still love him," he said.

"Was it Malcolm who told you about the proposal?" I had been curious how Steven had learned about Paul's big proposal at the newspaper.

"Yeah," Steven said. "But it was all over the local blogosphere anyway."

"Another mystery solved," I said, and then began playing with the grass again, tugging at the tips and running my palm along the soft tops of the blades.

"So, do you?" Steven asked, looking off to the distance and taking a last drag of his cigarette before putting it out under his hiking shoe.

I pulled the car key from my pocket, nodded toward the street, and said, "So what's out there?"

"Learn at your own peril," he said.

"Everything I do with you is at my peril," I said, getting up and brushing dirt from my legs.

Steven followed me across the yard. We reached the gate that led to the front walk but I couldn't undo the latch.

"What'd you do to this thing?" I asked.

"Here," he said, reaching around me and placing his hand over mine. He didn't jiggle the latch; he stood still, and rested his hand on mine. I could feel him standing behind me, though our bodies weren't touching. Energy emanated from Steven like a magnetic field. His arm lay atop mine and his thumb grazed mine, back and forth.

"Do you?" he asked softly. I hadn't realized his head had moved so close. I could feel the power behind his voice despite his gentle tone.

"Do I what?" I managed to say.

"Still love him."

"No," I said, almost inaudibly.

Steven's cheek touched mine and it sent a tickle across my face. He stepped closer to me until his chest was flush with my back. My messy ponytail had caused tendrils to dangle against my face and he gently moved them aside with his mouth. He lifted my hand from the latch and held it as we stood, not facing each other.

"That wasn't Anne," he said into my ear as his lips traveled around it. I was so consumed by his touch that I didn't understand him. I was about to inquire when he said, "That text message. It wasn't Anne."

Steven moved closer and wrapped himself around me completely. His fingers slid slowly up my arms. Despite the summer heat, I was covered in goose bumps. Upon feeling them under his touch, Steven smiled against my face.

"Do you love him?" he inquired about Timothy.

The question snapped me back to my senses for a fleeting moment.

"I don't know," I said.

"If anyone knows when she loves someone, it's you."

To hear Steven speak softly was like a drug, one I obviously hadn't detoxed from.

"You can tell me," he said.

"What do you want?" I managed to ask.

Steven moved his head around mine and spoke into my other ear.

"This," he said. "Every day."

I should have felt guilt. I should have felt something, anything other than the overwhelming desire to consume Steven, and be consumed by him. I wanted him to pick me up, carry me inside, throw me on my bed, on the kitchen counter, on the couch, on the floor, or against the wall and let me have my way with him. I wanted to bite him and dig my nails into him and see his eyes fix on mine as we went near the edge, again and again, until finally going over it.

But I couldn't do it. The tiny part of my brain that retained lucidity amidst the torrent of chemistry told me to refrain. It told me that would be going too far. It told me *it's too soon*. It told me I shouldn't confuse the Steven I fell in love with more than a year ago with the Steven who dumped me without warning and broke my heart. It told me Timothy was a good man, and despite his distance and workaholic tendencies, he was a nice guy who deserved my word to be worth something. And even if he didn't end up deserving it, I did.

I could feel Steven's pulse racing through his skin. I could feel his entire body, hard and tense, pressed against me. I knew he was holding back. I knew he wanted to say things and do things. But he let his lips and fingers travel softly over me rather than ravage me.

"Could you ever trust me again?" he asked. His words floated over my cheek, my eyes, my nose, my forehead. He was like a tornado. The smallest movement from him nearly blew me over.

"I don't know," I said.

Steven lifted his head and gently removed my ponytail holder.

My hair fell down my back and around my face as he rested his forehead against the back of my head.

"I don't deserve it," he said.

I knew I could fall in love with Steven again. It might have happened already. But I didn't know if I would ever trust him again. Ironically, Steven's words about Paul rang true for him as well; even if I loved him, I might not choose to be with him.

"What should I do?" he asked as his hands slowly came to a stop in their travels. "If I take you inside, it's all over." I knew he meant that in a good way.

"Then take me out there." I nudged my head forward. "Show me what's in the driveway."

Again I felt Steven smile. I was that attuned to him.

He exhaled forcefully, and then undid the stubborn latch on the gate and pushed it open.

"We left our drinks on the ground," I said. "Ice is probably melted by now."

"Let's get fresh ones," he said.

• • •

Steven let me drive. The moment I heard the growl of the engine come to life, the antsy-ness I'd felt while gardening disappeared. He had the car only for the weekend so we couldn't beat it up. But we could drive it to the ends of the earth as long as he had it back first thing Monday morning. We stopped at our favorite lemonade and iced tea joint. I pulled up in front and Steven hopped out to pick up the drinks. Five minutes later I headed for the highway. Steven asked no questions about our destination and made no suggestions. Those hours were a gorgeous slice of life that, just a few years earlier, my own set of rules, or a sense of guilt, would have kept me from experiencing.

Wind whipped through the open windows and I was relieved we hadn't slept together. In the end, we didn't need to. Real sex, great sex, connected sex happened not only in the body, but also the mind. That afternoon, in a fit of passion, Steven and I *had* slept together—on my bed, on the kitchen counter, on the couch, on the floor, and against the wall.

Maybe what I'd already done standing at the gate was as good as cheating. Maybe the test drive and lemonade outing left no further doubt about it. But I knew I felt as much passion for the man seated next to me as Timothy did for his work. And the excitement and liberation and release I felt behind that wheel were three big things I could say, without any doubt, I loved with all my heart.

46

. . .

Aside from seeing Anne and watching a decent romantic comedy together, I spent the rest of the weekend writing. I heard from Timothy and Steven, but Steven was the only one to call. Timothy texted about twenty times. It was still dangerous for me to hear Steven's voice because it made me stupid and turned-on and anxious, but I redirected all of it into my writing, including a new piece for Daniel Perry.

He had asked to be surprised and I had every intention of doing just that. Daniel Perry knew I had secrets. Somehow he knew. I still despised him, but my hatred had dulled. I didn't know how things would play out with my status at the newspaper, including the fate of my column. I would have to see over time, like everything else in my life.

On Monday I popped into the newsroom to pick up mail. I stopped briefly at my desk to make sure Daniel Perry hadn't left chicken-scratched notes taped to my monitor. Mia noticed me and walked over. She'd already read the book excerpt I e-mailed to her the night before. She loved it, she said. It would make a great series, she added. I declined because it was not meant to be whittled down for a newspaper. Mia stood at my desk and read part of it aloud.

"What if you never find three? What if you marry your first love and stay together forever? What if you are facing three loves and think: *what if it's not these three?* These are just some of the questions poking holes in a beautiful idea."

Mia flipped to the next page and continued reading. "I wish someone had told me you can't make yourself love someone, and you can't make yourself stop loving someone. I might have saved myself a ton of grief and frustration had I learned those facts years earlier. Why didn't all those women's magazines ever mention anything about that? For every time they tell you how to firm your butt, style your hair, treat your skin, increase your chances of orgasm, or touch your man 'just there,' they never tell you how to navigate the part of the body that's most important—the heart."

Mia flipped the top page down, and with a bewildered look she asked, "How long have you been working on this?"

"A while," I said.

"Amanda, I love it."

"Thanks, Mia. That means a lot."

"I won't ask how everything turned out," she said.

"We never really know how things will turn out, do we?"

"I guess not," she said.

"The not knowing is part of the fun," I said.

"That it is."

"I'm heading home." I pulled my purse over my shoulder.

"I'm having a little party this weekend," Mia said. "There'll be great food and plenty of sangria. You can bring your friends."

"Sounds great," I said. "If I'm in town, count me in."

I didn't know what that weekend would bring. For the first time in a long time, I liked not knowing what was to come.